DINERS, DRIVE-INS, AND LIES

---

a Sunny Side UP mystery

MISTY SIMON

DINERS, DRIVE-INS, AND LIES
Copyright © 2024 by Misty Simon
Cover design by Daniela Colleo
of www.StunningBookCovers.com

Published by Gemma Halliday Publishing Inc
All Rights Reserved. Except for use in any review, the reproduction or utilization of this work in whole or in part in any form by any electronic, mechanical, or other means, now known or hereafter invented, including xerography, photocopying and recording, or in any information storage and retrieval system is forbidden without the written permission of the publisher, Gemma Halliday.

This is a work of fiction. Names, characters, places, and incidents are either the product of the author's imagination or are used fictitiously, and any resemblance to actual persons, living or dead, business establishments, or events or locales is entirely coincidental.

This book is for all the wonderful servers I've known over the years. May we know them, may we love them, may we tip them well.

Also, to my Boot Squad, who make all things possible! Another one in the can, my lovelies!

CHAPTER ONE

The bell dinged on the silver counter above the griddle, barely noticeable over the din of conversation in the Sunny Side Up Diner. "Number seven up!"

I hid my smile when Terri, our cook, rolled her eyes as she put the next plate up on the passthrough for the table of two. We had asked her to shout out the orders to keep in character with the atmosphere we were aiming for in the eating establishment my best friend and I had purchased six months ago. The decor was on point, the food was awesome, and the atmosphere just needed that little bit of retro that went with a busy eatery tinged lightly with nostalgia.

"Eight up!" The clatter of the porcelain dish hitting the counter rang under the yell but didn't hide the sigh Terri gusted out as she closed her eyes.

"Do you think she'll quit if we make her keep doing that?" I asked.

"Nah." Danielle Brighton, my partner in this venture, nudged me out of the way at the register to deliver another set of wrapped cutlery to the bin next to the folder of menus. Then she nudged me from the other direction, so she could put more register tape on the shelving unit attached to the counter.

"A little personal space goes a long way." I stepped back, and she almost collided with the counter before righting herself and giving me the stink eye.

"Jax Tapman, we are in the middle of setting up our dream from when we were kids working here over the summers. There was never personal space back then. You have to know, without a shadow of a doubt, that we're about to be that much more in each other's lives when this place gets back to what it was before the last owner ruined it."

Yes, the last owner had run it into the ground by trying to take what had always been a diner, the quintessential place for coffee, greasy spoon food, chatter about the world and our small town in general, and turn it into a smoothie cafe whose primary drinks had kale, wheat grass, and tofu.

We'd put the small diner to rights by installing new grills, repainting the interior to its original red, black, and white glory, and restoring the shine to the seats at the counter back to their original awesomeness. The cherry on top, of course, was finding the old jukeboxes for every table in the storage in the back room. We had an awning constructed with *Sunny Side Up Diner* in bold script situated over the front door and potted plants to welcome all the old and new customers.

Not everyone who used to sit and mingle here in the red leather booths and chrome-edged tables had come back after we reopened, but more and more were showing up every morning. And for that we were incredibly thankful. So grateful, in fact, that we were taking ourselves out to a fancy dinner tonight at my aunt's four-star restaurant down the road to celebrate.

We could have made ourselves something here, of course, but Dani had nixed that idea because she didn't want to cook. According to my co-owner and rabble-rouser, we wouldn't be able to enjoy it as much if someone else wasn't doing all the work.

"You set up the reservation, right?" Dani asked, stacking the silverware in a careful pyramid like the waitresses weren't just going to reach in and grab what they needed when seating people. I'd told her a hundred times in the last six months that it didn't need to be perfect, but she didn't listen. Not that I'd expected her to. It just would have been nice for a change.

"Yes, we're all set, and Aunt Hildy is pulling out all the stops." I had no idea how I was going to pay for that, due to some recent complications with my bank account, but I'd figure it out or have my aunt put it on a tab. I certainly didn't want to tell her I was nearly penniless. She didn't have to know, and neither did anyone else. I'd come up with something if she asked or redirect her to her favorite subject of why I hadn't just come to work for her.

"What time?" Dani asked, pushing a button on the smartwatch thing on her wrist. She was probably going to ensure she had it correct in her calendar, as well as set a reminder to wash her hair, do her nails, spiff up her wardrobe, and make sure her shoes were the right tone to set the evening off with glitz and glamor after we closed at two.

I, however, still had a paper calendar and was happy if my short, light brown hair stayed slightly tame instead of wild and free as it liked to do. My shoes were those made for tennis, my nails were short, my wardrobe was mainly jeans and T-shirts with fun sayings, and tone didn't matter to me as long as it wasn't angry.

"Number nine is up! Come and get it!"

I shot a look through the serving window and caught Terri with her shoulders near her ears and her mouth shaped into a grin you'd find on a three-year-old who'd just figured out how to climb on a counter and grab cookies they weren't supposed to have.

"She might not quit, but it's possible we could totally rue the day we ever came up with this idea." Closing my eyes for a quick second, I visualized my paper calendar, though I knew exactly what time dinner was. "Six tonight, so five hours. And it's almost time to close here today."

That set her scurrying off, and I got my personal space back.

I loved her, I truly did, but with this re-opening, and my own personal stuff, I had things to sort out, and I didn't need to be caged in to do that.

"Table nine! It's divine!"

There was a distinct snicker from behind me when I stopped in my tracks. Two could play this game, and Terri, a petite redhead with some serious attitude, knew it.

But that would have to wait as I had a dinner to attend and maybe some dishes to wash in the kitchen of a fancy restaurant if my aunt wasn't willing to float me the tab.

Poplarsville Inn sat back from the road in the country, about a mile out of town, but it felt like thirty. Small-town Pennsylvania tended to be like that. I'd loved the inn from the first time my parents had brought me here and loved it still, but it was too fancy for my tastes on the daily. I much preferred the diner. The restaurant had stood in this same spot for the last sixty years and had been passed down from generation to generation with little fanfare and definitely no changes.

The landscape around the one-story, sprawling inn offered trees and bushes, some flowers depending on the time of year, and always tiny strings of twinkling lights that glowed along the ground, lighting your way in. No glaring streetlights fought for purchase in the gathering darkness as Hildy had placed gas lamps along the outer edges of the macadam. The only sounds were the lowing of cows off in the distance and the swaying of corn stalks in the extensive field to the left.

And it had been like that when my aunt's great-grandfather had first opened the fancy eatery with its haute cuisine mixed in with forty-dollar steaks and fresh seafood that was driven in every single day.

I won't lie. It had been tempting when I'd graduated from college to come work here. My aunt, though not related to me by blood, had been in my life since I was born and was my godmother. She had expectations I would come help her run this monstrosity, even though we'd never really talked about it. But when my diner had gone up for sale, I couldn't resist calling up Dani in Jersey to float the idea of going for the thing we had talked about for hours when we'd served tables during high school at what was formerly called Jeb's Diner.

To be honest, some people still called it that, but I tried not to listen. They'd come around to calling it Sunny Side Up Diner eventually. Especially when we started handing out the merch I'd picked up from the local printer on my way over here.

After I parked my compact car in the lot on the side of the inn, I debated going in the back to say hi to everyone before being seated, maybe grab a nibble of something or other on my way. But I nixed that idea because I wanted to experience this from the front door. Tonight, we were celebrating. And I was not on the clock, nor was I going to get roped in.

Closing and then locking my door, I pocketed my keys and headed for the stone archway with its two sconces embedded in the wall. The whole thing was modeled like a one-story castle, and you couldn't fault the architecture. The turret that hung off the right side was only for show from what I'd ever seen, and the huge oak doors weighed a ton, but there was history here and ambience. I wanted that for the Sunny Side Up Diner, even if it was more skewed toward lazy Sunday mornings instead of mythic knights and gentle steeds.

After I opened one of the enormous doors, I glanced around for Dani. In my mind, the door had always needed to have an ominous creak to accompany its swing outward, but Aunt Hildy and her staff were too handy with the WD-40 to ever let that happen.

The lights were dimmed in the entryway and gave off a glow that immediately brought you and the hustle of life to a crawl. Many partnerships and background handshakes had happened here, plenty of lucrative business deals and future speculations, but it remained a low-key place with high prices.

Waiting in line behind four other sets of patrons to see the hostess, I checked out the floral arrangements Hildy commissioned from a woman who did all her crafts out of her garage and had for over fifty years. Tasteful and understated were two good words for them, but also magnificent and eye-catching. And fresh. They were never stored and reused, just enjoyed until they wilted and needed to be replaced.

Someone cleared their throat in front of me. I guess I'd been staring at the brightly colored leaves and fall colors used in the arrangements for too long and missed that the line to be seated had dwindled down to nothing in front of me.

The waitstaff still wore light pink dress shirts, black bow ties, and black cummerbunds. I wasn't the only one who liked to throw back in time, though I was about the 50s, and Hildy remained a lover of the 80s.

The hostess tonight, Marcella, smiled at me when I finally looked up.

"I have you all set up in the back, just in case the celebration gets out of hand," she said, a cheeky smile on her face.

I laughed because whoever knew with the two of us? Dani and I had been problem children when we were teenagers, like a more rambunctious set of the Three Musketeers but with just two of us—all for one and one for all the fun things and shenanigans we could get into. People had often stepped out of our way when we'd come streaming into any business in town, knowing we would be full of chatter and enthusiasm and verve. We were a little older now but not much had changed.

When I'd called Dani about the diner nine months ago, she hadn't hesitated at all to drop her job, her life, and her responsibilities to come back to our hometown and make this diner work in ways we'd dreamed of when we were younger. Yes, it had been ten years, which didn't seem like a long time, but we'd dreamed of owning this diner and making it ours since way before we'd worked there. Dani used to set up a breakfast counter in my playroom when we were in preschool, and she could often be found taking one of my mom's old ordering pads to play away the entire afternoon cooking and ordering and being the hostess. And as soon as we'd been old enough, we'd applied for and been hired as waitresses. The job itself had been a little different than we'd expected, and it wasn't all having fun with customers and dropping off eggs. But it was our life now, and we loved it.

With a sigh of contentment, I let the worries about money and making this venture work slide off my back like snow from a heated roof and followed along as Marcella headed for an alcove in the back of the restaurant close to the kitchen.

Maybe I'd get to say hi to Dean, who I'd grown up with, or Taylor, who was a master baker, though he liked to remind everyone that he really was only a cake maker. He even refused to have anything to do with pies, just cake. I planned on eating a piece of the most decadent chocolate cake they might have available. Although that had been before I realized I had nothing in the bank, and it wasn't because I'd spent it all.

Tearing my brain away from things I couldn't change at the moment, I waved to Dani as I came around the corner. I wasn't surprised at all that she'd beat me here, even though I was on time. Well, sort of on time, but definitely close to time. Within ten minutes at least.

"I've been sitting here for thirty minutes," Dani said with a frown on her face that pulled her dark eyebrows down and almost made them become one line. She wouldn't be happy to hear that, so I kept it to myself. She glanced up at me over her menu with her green eyes narrowed. "I won't complain, though. At least it's still within the same hour."

Oh man. Whoops. I grinned sheepishly, knowing I was not always the best at gauging how long things took. It had been one of the hardest lessons when we'd taken over the diner and were working to reopen it. I would have sworn at the beginning that two weeks was enough to get up and rolling. Actually, I did swear it to the local newspaper. But then I had to print an update when my two weeks turned into four, and we were turning people away due to construction.

I took the chair across from her at the two-top and opened my own menu. I already knew what I was having, but this way I could hide my mouth as I snarked at my best friend under my breath.

"Ladies!" Aunt Hildy came streaming into the alcove like a heat-seeking missile. Her hair was bundled on top of her head in a complicated bun that was streaked with gray. Her dimples had always popped out at the best times and had made me giggle when I was little. Now I just smiled back.

"I'm delighted to see you tonight!" she continued. "What a wonderful occasion and so much to celebrate! Let's start with an appetizer, and then we can move to the special dinner I've had Eliot working on all day. You're going to absolutely love it!"

Wait, who was Eliot?

"I'm sure we will since it's coming from your kitchen, Hildy." Dani was such a suck-up sometimes, so I wasn't surprised when she commented first. "Where's Dean?"

That had been my question, but I was thankful Dani had asked it so I didn't have to.

"Oh, he's out in the hydro-house working on some kind of herb thing that he's desperate to bring in to enhance one of his soups. He's got Tobias out there with him, which means I don't have to deal with the spills and thrills he seems to bring every time I put him on the schedule." Her face had fallen into a frown, but she kicked the smile back up almost immediately. "We're not slammed tonight, so I figured it wouldn't hurt to let Dean do what he loves and take the kid with him while we break in Eliot, the new chef. He just moved here from Idaho, but he came highly recommended." With that, she whisked off to the front hostess podium after briefly stopping to talk with the bartender.

"Does she already know you'll want a Manhattan?" I asked Dani.

"No, I told her to just bring us both a soda."

I was shocked, but my wallet definitely gave a sigh of relief. "We're not drinking tonight?" I could have sworn Dani would have at least ordered a bottle of bubbly or something to commemorate this momentous occasion. We'd finally made our dream come true, and it was going so well.

"Nah." Dani placed her menu to the side of the table and then folded her hands in front of her. "I want an earlier night since I'm doing the first shift in the morning, and I need to place our orders if we want to be able to have all the food we need for our breakfast rushes."

Those things were epic. Not on day one since no one had been sure we would actually open. But ever since then, customers had been rolling in with orders for eggs and bacon and pancakes and waffles and creamed chipped beef. Not to mention the sausage gravy and biscuits the diner had been known for before the last owner had tried to vegetable people to death.

"We're doing well, though, right?" I drummed my fingers on

the wood table. "This is what we wanted. I just want to make sure now that we're eyeballs deep in it that we're still all on board."

My words were met with a scoff and a frown.

"Of course we are." Dani rested her hands on the table, as if she were going to spring across the expanse at me. "You?"

"Of course, I am." I swallowed down the words that wanted to break out about my financial situation. Instead, I smiled as Hildy came back to the table with a pitcher of soda and three wine glasses. So we would look like we were drinking, even though we weren't? I could do that and so could my wallet.

"Then why are you asking?" Dani tapped her fingernails on the menu in a drum-like beat. She tilted her head to the side in the way she used to when she was about to challenge me and my world views, which she had done often when we were teenagers. I'd grown up in a pretty conservative household while Dani had pretty much been able to do whatever she wanted, whenever she wanted, as long as CPS was never called to the house. She'd pushed my boundaries, and while I had thought it was cool when we were young, I felt a little like she was putting a spotlight on me now, and I didn't need it.

"I just… well, I mean I was the one who asked you to drop everything and come running back home when you had your own life and things going on. I just want to make sure you're not regretting it or feeling like I pressured you into doing this just because we talked about it endlessly when we were younger. It could have still been my dream but not something you wanted after high school."

"Sometimes," Dani said, shaking her head and groaning the word. "Look, I love you, bestie. I have since we were preschoolers running around trying to see who could get more Valentines in that paper bag Mrs. Detweiler made us craft to hold them all."

"She used to make her own for herself so she'd have more," Hildy called out as she walked by our table with a laden tray of delicacies, outing me after all these years.

"You did not!"

I shrugged. "I did. That's why I always won. No one asked me to prove it, and we just did the counting. So, I would pick someone and say they gave me two because they really liked me, but really, it was me giving myself one."

Dani laughed so loud the people at the table across the room peeked their heads around the stone barrier. Aunt Hildy shooed them back to their own table and smiled at me.

"Well, this changes my entire life," my best friend said. "I've lived a lie for nigh on twenty-two years. How have I never heard this before? I might want to change my mind about being in business with you if that's what you consider winning."

I rolled my eyes, but inside I did have just a small jolt of panic. If only they knew what I was lying about now. "You've known. I've told you, and maybe you just didn't actually listen. That seems to happen a lot, like when I asked you to get two different colored buckets to hold the salt and sugar, but somehow, we have two white buckets. How are we going to distinguish them? You both know I got busted down to chief toast butterer when I was young for mixing them up. The whole diner was spitting out salty coffee."

And that was a story I knew they knew about, no question. I told it enough and still answered for it even this many years later. It was also a memory that I had held on to for years—wanting this diner, falling in love with it, then being a waitress with my best friend through tenth, eleventh, and twelfth grades in the evenings and weekends and all week during the summer. Dani was my chosen family, and I was hers, but if she was here because of feeling guilted into a promise she had made when we were fifteen, then I didn't want that for us. It might just be better to sell now before anyone found out I had nothing more to give.

Dani hopped her chair around the corner of the table to sandwich me in between her and the wall. Then she leaned over my bread plate with her glass in hand. "Jax, are you saying you think I am here against my will, to do something I know would make you happy but is my worst nightmare ever in the whole wide world, just because I didn't want to disappoint the girl who would give herself her own valentine to come out ahead of everyone else?"

Hildy snickered, put her straight face on, and frowned. "I don't know, Dani. Are you also up to your neck in debt for a business that means absolutely nothing to you, and you haven't dreamed of the day when you and Jax could work together and do all these amazing things like the Two Musketeers you always were and want to be again?" She raised her eyebrow, and they both turned to me.

I wasn't quick enough to catch the water that seemed to be mysteriously dripping out of my eyes.

"There's no crying in restaurant owning." They both said it at the same time, and we all laughed because there had already been a lot of crying over things in a restaurant, and there would probably be more but not between us.

I needed to figure out how to tell Dani about my financial status. Hildy would probably want to know also and would most likely float me any money I might need, but I just couldn't do that.

And definitely not tonight.

I picked up my empty glass to clink with Dani's, and then we each filled them with soda and raised them for a toast.

"To us," I said.

"To us," Dani repeated.

"To you," Hildy added.

And then all hell broke loose as someone drowned Hildy out by screaming, "Where is he?"

CHAPTER TWO

Complete silence ruled the entire restaurant as Delilah Westerbrook charged into the dining room from the foyer. Her teased, frosted hair was styled within an inch of being a helmet, and her make-up was straight out of a cosmetic counter saleswoman's dream. At sixty, I would have expected her to have a little more decorum, but this was Delilah, and everyone knew she was like a steam train shooting down a mountain with no brakes when she was crossed. The rage was nearly spurting out of her ears, and her eyes were a single degree away from glowing like the coal in the engine of said steam train.

This time, instead of screaming, she growled. I wasn't aware that was physically possible, but she owned it. "Where. Is. He?"

Whoever he was—and it could have been a number of different men—I did not envy him when she found him.

Dani shot me a glance and tucked her lips in. She was trying not to laugh. I could tell by the way her shoulders were shaking slightly. I had a feeling Hildy would probably look exactly the same, but I wasn't going to glance over at her. We were the people who you did not want to sit next to at a solemn function. One misstep, and we'd have broken out into gales of laughter, followed by a few very inelegant snorts, and probably a knee slap or two.

It wasn't that Delilah's plight itself would have been funny. In the years I'd lived here, it was hard to keep up with who she was currently seeing because they changed so quickly and got younger and younger. With that being the case, I had to assume she was in the middle of one more break-up or issue-laden relationship. And it wasn't that I begrudged her desire to always be on the lookout for happiness. It was that she treated them like her personal little toys. But at least that was better than how she treated anyone else she thought was beneath her, which was pretty much everyone.

I did steal a second glance at what she was wearing since she could usually be counted on to rock that early 90s wardrobe like it hadn't gone out of style. Sure enough, the shoulder pads were very much on display, looking more like she'd left the hanger in her dress by accident when she put it on. The shocking pink get-up screamed to be seen and was covered by a double-breasted short jacket with fringe that should have been labeled neon.

She'd been around town for a number of years—no one would ever have the guts to ask how many—and she always seemed to be able to make it through life with the most any one person could ever want. Yet per my mom's local grapevine, Delilah had no money of her own and had never worked a day of her life. For years, people had tried to figure out how that was possible, but no one had ever been able to tell. And no one would ask because that would have been worse than trying to guess how old she really was. I assumed sixty, but I could be completely wrong.

Our diner was somewhere she wouldn't have been seen in. Even dead, she would probably have gotten up and made her way out to the sidewalk before dying again. I hadn't seen her in some time, and I found myself wishing that streak had gone on for several more years.

She struck a pose at the far side of the restaurant, probably to call even more attention to herself, but after that last glance, I kept my head down and my mouth shut.

"Someone had better speak up and speak up soon," she said into the quiet. No one was even trying to eat, and there was no clink of silverware on the heavy plates.

"Delilah, darling, why don't you have a seat, and we'll get you a refreshment? Let Eliot get you a chair." Aunt Hildy strode toward the woman with purpose and absolute resolution. I'd seen that glint in her eye before, and it was right before she'd taken my uncle to task for something she was not going to stand for, no matter how many excuses and reasons he had.

Part of me hoped Delilah would read the mood and not fight back, but another part of me was ready to break out the popcorn and see a good old-fashioned showdown. Is that why this Eliot, who was obviously a chef here, had abandoned his station to see what was going on?

I got the former when Delilah took the seat that was pulled out for her by a very tall man in a chef's hat. Eliot. Hmmm. He wasn't someone I had seen before, and I would have remembered because he was extremely handsome, with his chiseled features and stunningly green eyes. I should have looked away altogether when I got that unexpected flutter in my stomach. Instead, I let my eyes drift down to take in the white coat paired with checkered pants that could have made optical illusions if I stared long enough.

But even though I didn't see the optical illusion, I still stared too long. When I looked up, his gaze was right on me, and there was a quirk to his mouth that I didn't particularly care for.

"Uh oh," Dani said, putting her napkin on the table. "I know that look, and it often spells trouble for us." She took a long pull on the straw in her soda.

I closed my eyes and waited for the rest of the story because I knew it wouldn't end there.

"I remember when you got that look in the summer between tenth and eleventh grade. His name was Watson, wasn't it? Or Flotsam? Something with that kind of construction." She patted my hand this time, and I opened my eyes. "We couldn't even get you to fold the silverware into the napkins right, and you kept dropping them on the floor when he went around a corner because you were craning your neck so hard. We got in trouble with the dishwashers that time, didn't we?"

I kept silent because it never helped to egg her on.

Dani nodded vigorously. Her head was going to fall off if she didn't stop that sooner rather than later. "Yes, that was the dishwasher riot, but the real issue was later that summer when Carson came in for a milkshake every afternoon. No matter who was at the machine, or what they were doing with it, you'd hip check us out of the way to zoom right on through preparing his special drink."

I closed my eyes again to gather myself because she wasn't wrong, and I actually remembered being far harder in the fall than she was giving me a pass for.

Glancing at her for just a second, I plucked at my own napkin. "There's no look in my eyes. I just didn't know who he was, and he's so… big." I cleared my throat. "He's so big I couldn't see around him. Do you think he heard the commotion Delilah was making, so he came out of the kitchen? I would think a chef would want to man his grill."

Because there was still activity at Delilah's table, Dani kept the volume down on her laughter, but I knew she would have been guffawing if we'd been in our own establishment. Now she completely disregarded my question and my attempt to divert the conversation.

Grabbing up my own soda, I ignored the way the straw nearly stabbed me in the eye in my haste to keep myself from saying anything else. I drank hard and fast, hoping I wouldn't choke in my haste. I had been boy crazy during high school, and I wasn't afraid to admit it. The problem was I still hadn't seemed to learn that not all guys were good, and some could crash your bank account without batting an eye.

I yanked myself out of that train of thought. I could not afford to even think about that at the moment, or Dani might sniff out my weakness. Instead, I gave her the evil eye and tuned back in.

Delilah was ordering the most expensive thing on the menu along with a glass of top-shelf liquor. She'd asked them to bring the bottle so she could deal with this new wrinkle in her life, but I caught Aunt Hildy's scowl before she rounded the corner. Delilah would be lucky if her drink wasn't three-quarters water.

"What do you think that was about?" I finally asked after I knew I'd calmed myself to the point where I wouldn't blurt anything out.

"I heard she might be dating Roderick Benningfield over at the golf club." Dani moved her napkin across the table and then bunched it in her hand.

"Oh, that guy. I swear he's on every billboard and advertisement around here. I can't get through two streets without seeing his smarmy face telling me to come 'Putt my stuff' with that cheeky elbow in the ribs look." Roderick was also commonly known to be a ladies' man, so it wouldn't have surprised me if the two hadn't gotten together with Delilah thinking he'd change for her.

"He's a jerk, and he had been nosing around my mom, but my dad shut him down. He deserves whatever he gets."

"No doubt. Do you think he's actually here?" I asked.

"He is." Hildy said the words low, quietly, and very close to my ear. Dani leaned in as Hildy delivered more drinks to our table. Since we'd both been drinking them like we were in a desert, it at least made sense and would look natural. "I'm going to ask you a favor, Jacklynn." My aunt had refused to call me Jax since forever, so I didn't mind it from her.

"Whatever you need."

"You might want to hear it before you agree," she said back.

"Nope, whatever you need, I've got it. Let me know and it's

yours."

"I need you to go outside around back and give Roderick your keys. He's going to want to take your car since he was dropped off earlier by his son and doesn't have transportation, so please let him have your keys. Dinner is on the house tonight if you will do this."

I couldn't help but stare at her for longer than I probably should have. Why did I have to let him take my car? Why had his son dropped him off? Why did he have to be snuck out like a spy across enemy lines? She nudged me. I had definitely stared without an answer for longer than I should have. "Sure, I'll do that for you. When can I get my car back?"

"I'll handle that tonight. First, I just need you to get him out of here before she blows her lid."

The secrecy and desire to ask what on earth was going on was killing me, but this was my aunt and my godmother. If she asked, she got. Especially if dinner was on the house since that meant I didn't have to worry about just eating a side salad. I could maybe afford to get an actual entrée without my credit card screaming foul.

She waved me out with a flap of her hand behind her back. Was she trying to make a diversion? Delilah wasn't even looking our way anymore, so she must have been nose deep in that appetizer the big guy had brought out for her. Someone wasn't getting their expensive pre-dinner snack on time since it was currently being devoured by the woman in neon instead of being delivered to their table. He couldn't have made it that fast unless it was already made.

Hildy waved to another table as she left, and I figured their appetizer at least would probably be on the house.

Slipping out of my chair, I grabbed my car keys and headed for the restrooms in the back, knowing there was a door to the outside I could access and not be in Delilah's line of sight at all. I ducked along the corridor, hoping not to actually meet anyone on my way to the restroom. I didn't want to have to explain what I was doing, and I didn't want Hildy's quick plan to run aground with me being waylaid.

As I approached the door, though, the big guy stood in the hallway opposite me, leaning on the frame of the entry to the kitchen.

"She's got you doing the dirty work, I see." His voice fit him, a big but low sound that seemed to rattle my bones a little and not in an unpleasant way. I had always been a sucker for bass, and this one was no exception.

"It's not dirty. I'm just helping out." I flipped the key ring around my finger a few times, wanting so badly to just get this done and get back to my friend at our table, so I could actually celebrate tonight. Free food and drinks, great time with Dani as we celebrated our success and planned for more. That was what I was here for, right after this little detour.

"Yeah, well, I hope no one gets hurt this time." He turned, and I had to admit I watched him walk away for as long as possible. Those broad shoulders were almost as wide as the door. His short brown hair stuck out just beneath the edge of his chef's hat. He had a cleft chin I could no longer see, and his green eyes might haunt me in my sleep tonight, but I was definitely going to enjoy keeping the snapshot of him walking away in mind.

And then what he said registered in my brain. This time? Had someone gotten hurt before? Come to think of it, Hildy had sounded like this wasn't the first time she'd had to save Roderick from Delilah. I gulped and got my head back in the game that was afoot. I had to leave through the back door of the kitchen, find Roderick, give him my keys, and then come back in.

At the last second, I remembered the door would automatically lock behind me as soon I let it close and would make it hard for reentry, so I used my phone as a doorstop to make sure I could come back in after I accomplished my task. It certainly wouldn't be good for me to have appeared to go to the bathroom only to have to come back around to the front door.

I had expected Roderick to be right outside the back door when I exited but he wasn't. Where was he then?

Briefly, I considered going back in to ask Hildy what she wanted me to do or where he might have gone off to, but that would only prolong my time away from my dinner. So, I crept along the back of the building in the shadows, looking for Roderick. I couldn't exactly yell for him. I had no idea why I was creeping since no one was out here. It was pitch dark at this point, except for the three spotlights Hildy had, two at the corners of the building and the light over the door I'd just exited. The main parking lot with its gas lamps and twinkling lights was out front and to the right of the building.

This area back here was where the trucks came to deliver food, the employees emptied the trash into a fenced-in enclosure down to the right, which housed a dumpster to keep the aesthetic of the upscale restaurant pretty. I really should have left my wallet in the door and brought my phone so I could have used the flashlight. But I hadn't brought anything but the keys and my phone, thinking this would be a quick run. I hated to go back when I'd almost reached the next spotlight at the end of the building.

Except the light flickered, and then it went out.

Uh-oh, why did I suddenly have a horrible feeling in the pit of my stomach? Maybe it was all the true crime murder podcasts I'd been listening to lately. I kept telling myself to lay off them, maybe do some meditation ones or even those on how to be a better person or a better businessperson. But I still kept coming back to the murder podcasts, which then made me suspect everything and everyone.

And this whole thing was very suspect.

I heard a thud to my left a second before I was hit in the back of the legs. I tripped, stumbled a few feet, and then fell into the enclosed area where Hildy kept the dumpster.

And came face-to-face with a very dead Roderick.

CHAPTER THREE

Part of me hoped, at least for a second, that maybe Roderick was actually just taking a nap on the concrete. It could have been possible, right?

Maybe he had been so tired from his extracurricular activities that he had needed to take a brief siesta. But the angle of his head, with something wrapped around his neck, and the way his mouth hung half open, along with how his entire body was still, made me have to face the reality pretty quickly.

I scrambled again, even though I'd never been much of a scrambler. But then I stopped before completely leaving the scene. I should have been freaking out that there was a dead body at my feet, especially because I was in the back parking lot where no one could hear me, all by myself.

But I had been raised by a nurse and a cop, and you didn't make it through that kind of upbringing without some insider knowledge that the average kid didn't exactly discuss over dinner.

I'd even considered, just briefly, moving into nursing like my mom instead of business management. In the end, I couldn't commit to that, knowing someday I would want to own the diner of my dreams.

So, while I wasn't exactly horrified at being near a dead body, I was still scared. I patted my pockets and then remembered I had left my phone in the door jamb to keep it open. ACK! Why had I done that? I should have put my jacket in there or a freaking shoe. Anything other than the one thing I'd needed three times since I'd done it.

But I didn't want to leave the body and run out to get it. Not to mention someone had pushed me. They might still be out there, waiting. And what if something happened while I was gone? Not like he would be more dead if I left him, but what if…

My thought was interrupted by a clanging outside the

enclosure. Was the murderer still here? Wow, that probably should have been my first question. Especially when I'd been shoved into the enclosure and had no idea who'd done the shoving or why.

Yikes. Looking up from my crouch, though, I realized I couldn't see anything outside where I was unless I peeked my head out. I did not want to do that. A second later, I nearly peed myself when a raccoon shot past the metal door and banged into it. It was the same sound.

I was going to have to keep my cool. Because Hildy hadn't wanted Roderick to be found here in the first place, and I had a feeling that him being dead was not going to be something she wanted either.

Decisions, decisions.

Then again, I really only had two choices. I could either go out and get my phone, hoping no one would stumble across poor Roderick. Or I could try to grab the attention of someone in the kitchen, someone I knew and could trust to bring me Hildy without asking any questions I couldn't or didn't want to answer. Neither felt like a good idea.

Walking backward out of the trash enclosure toward the door to the kitchen, I kept an eye on Roderick and hoped I wasn't about to run into anyone who wouldn't want to be found or stumble over something else I didn't want to find.

Plus, there was Hildy's reputation to think of and how a dead body could make or break her.

That might have sounded bad to anyone who didn't own a business, but reputation was paramount in these instances. And while I would never think Hildy would want to hide the body or not tell anyone about a death at the restaurant, I had a feeling she'd rather not have a ton of people fleeing in the middle of their crab-stuffed lobster tail, fresh-caught from Maryland or Maine, to see what had happened out here.

More backing away then, but this time toward the trash area again. But I didn't really want to go there. I stopped myself about ten feet from the enclosure and took a deep breath.

A wave of some very pungent cologne hit my nose, and I froze. Was that from the garbage? Had that scent been on Roderick because of his ladies' man vibes, and I just hadn't noticed it because I had been too taken aback by the dead body?

I was very aware that curiosity killed the cat. I had a Siamese who toed that line almost every day, but in this instance, I was going to have to risk it. Not that I wanted to come face-to-face with a killer, but if whoever had taken Roderick's life was in the fenced garbage area with him now, I could possibly keep them locked in with the garbage and Roderick and then just call the police.

As quickly as I could, I ran over to the back door of the restaurant and grabbed my cell phone, letting the door close without shoving anything else in it. I had to have it. Fourth time was a must. I crept back over to the enclosure and was about to open the door when it slammed open almost in my face. It barely missed my nose, but it still hit me in the shoulder and knocked me off-balance.

Windmilling my arms did not help at all.

Maybe I should have creeped some more.

It was inevitable that I was going to fall, so I was more concerned with not landing flat on my face than trying to stay upright. I twisted to land on my back instead of my front. It kind of worked in that my face didn't come in contact with the dirty pavement. However, the back of my head did a little bounce, and I saw stars sitting on top of the stars that were already in the night sky. All my plans were foiled, and my nicest outfit was covered in dirt no matter how I landed.

I closed my eyes for a moment to just breathe, but then I heard rushing footsteps and popped my eyes open again.

From this angle, I only saw a dark figure with some kind of flowing clothes heading into the cornfield behind the restaurant.

So much for a celebration dinner for new beginnings.

And I still had a dead body to deal with since I hadn't seen the fleeing person carrying Roderick over their shoulder.

If my head hadn't hurt so much, I probably would have given it another little bounce, but as it was, I was still waiting for those extra stars to go away.

What was I going to do, and how was I going to do it? These were the questions running through my mind as I mentally checked for any breaks. Everything felt okay for the most part, other than the back of my head. I reached a hand up and came away with a bit of wetness. Telling myself to calm the heck down before assuming the back of my head was bleeding profusely, I turned on my phone's flashlight, that I wished I'd had several times over the last little while, and saw my fingers were glittering, not red.

The glitter could be from anything. I was in a parking lot, on the ground, outside the garbage area. Could have been the remains of a celebration, maybe from inside a card, perhaps some decorations from a wonderful occasion. You know, like something I should have been celebrating myself. Instead, I was out here and starting to get cold.

Finally, I felt ready to at least try to sit up.

"Owwwwww..." Places hurt that I didn't even realize could hurt. And now I was going to have to figure out how to get back into the restaurant, talk to Hildy while also calling the police, and getting a message to Dani that I'd somehow embroiled myself in yet one more situation in which I should not have had any part. This wasn't my first rodeo of being at the wrong place at the wrong time, though it was my first time finding a dead body.

And that reminded me that not only could my phone be used as a flashlight, but it could also be used to get help out here. *Duh.*

Fortunately, I'd talked to Hildy recently, so I pulled her up on the call list and hit the screen to dial. I waited through the ringing, and then when voicemail came on, I hung up. I was not going to leave her a message about this.

She was probably still trying to keep Delilah occupied until I came back in and gave the all-clear sign, which was never coming now. Man, this was bad.

Next, I tried Dani because she, more than anyone, always had her phone on her, and she should be wondering where I was by now.

She also didn't pick up, and I wasn't going to leave her a message. She'd freak out and start running through the restaurant screaming my name.

At this point, I knew I should just be calling the police. But since my dad was still a cop, I really did not want to have to talk with any of his cronies before I talked to Hildy.

This should not have been so hard, and yet here I was, trying to think my way through what the best of the worst-case scenarios might be for this situation.

I finally sat up all the way because I just couldn't take being prone on the ground anymore. I highly doubted the fleeing figure was going to come back this way now that they were free, but I was going to have to call the police. And I really, really, really did not want to do that.

Instead, I went to the back door of the kitchen where the staff would normally enter. Right now, it was my best bet.

It was also opened by the one person I had hoped not to see.

"What happened to you?" Eliot asked with his arms crossed over that impressive chest and pretty much barring me from entering the kitchen. I didn't fault him since I wouldn't have wanted someone who was covered in whatever I was covered in at the moment into my pristine kitchen either, but he could have been a little nicer about it.

"Get Hildy for me." I tried not to sound as pathetic as I felt, but the way he raised an eyebrow at me made me think that most likely I hadn't hit the mark very well.

"Please get Hildy for me?" A little more pathetic, perhaps a smidge of begging thrown in there. I should've been golden.

But he remained in the doorway.

I was about to resort to shouting and demanding when Hildy moved him out of the way and took my free hand in hers. She stepped outside with me, clucking under her tongue.

"Did something happen, darling? He didn't hurt you, did he? Or did she? I was trying to warn you that she'd left, and I was afraid she might have followed you, but her car's gone, and you never answered."

Because let's make it my fault that I left my phone in the door instead of taking it with me. Although on second thought, that was my fault and not a smart move at all, so we'd just keep that under wraps for the moment.

"I didn't see her." At least I didn't think so, but I highly doubted she would have been able to flee like that person who'd gone into the cornfield. Not in the heels she'd been wearing, anyway.

"What happened then?"

And that's when I started to feel like I was going to cry. My lips trembled, and I folded them in on each other to get the movement to stop. But then I also had to squint my eyes to keep the tears from dropping and clench my hands to keep them from shaking.

Eliot sidestepped both Hildy and me and went out into the parking lot. I wanted to warn him to be careful, but I couldn't get the words to come out.

Why was this hitting so hard right now? Did it matter? There was a dead guy outside. I'd admit to not having known him well, but he was still dead, and that was sad whether or not I'd grown up hearing ER stories mixed with solving murders and hauling in perps. That didn't change the fact that I'd just seen a dead body and didn't know what to do next.

Hildy opened her arms to hug me, but then seemed to see the state of my hair and my outfit, and settled on patting my shoulder while murmuring that it was going to be okay.

Eliot came back to the door with his cell phone to his ear and a thunderous expression on his way too handsome face even with the scowl.

"Yes, if you could send an officer down this way, it seems someone found something near the dumpster out back at the restaurant. I can give you any details you need. Please don't come in with the lights and sirens blazing. You don't need to do that in this case. He's already dead." And he hung up.

Hildy gasped, and something crashed behind her, but I couldn't take my eyes out of the locked-gaze contest I seemed to be having with Eliot, the man with the big chef hat and the illusion-inspiring pants.

"You're going to have a lot of explaining to do. I hope you've got some good reasons thought up before the whole police department gets here and wants to know why a lanyard with your restaurant name is cinched around his neck," Eliot said.

No way. No one had any of those. I'd just picked them up from the printer today and they were currently in the front seat of my locked car...

Oh no.

CHAPTER FOUR

Growing up in a town where your dad was on the police force was not always a wonderful check mark in the plus column of your virtues as a friend. Some people had thought they could get a free pass if they used his name when I was younger or talk their way out of things because they were in my circle.

The truth was it weighed heavily against you when it came to doing bad things and getting caught. My dad expected more from me and from my friends than he would from other people. Those other people were allowed to make some mistakes and live them down. Me? Not so much. I still heard about how I wanted a pencil with a bear on the top, and when my parents said no, I went back into the store and stuffed it in my jacket pocket, stealing it because I had no money at nine years old.

My dad marched me back into the store after he saw me using it for my homework. Since I couldn't return it because it had been sharpened, I had to sweep the floor until he felt I had worked off the two dollars it would have cost. I didn't see that pencil again until I was thirteen and rooting through my parents' closet for a Halloween costume. I took it to him, and he laughed, saying I could keep it now. I still had it in a cup on my desk with other writing implements I'd collected throughout the years. Ones I'd paid for.

So, with that kind of history, and his desire not only to see me do well but also do better, I was not looking forward to his talk about how I managed to find a corpse and what I did after I found it. Especially if Eliot the Giant Pain was going to tattle on me for handling things all wrong. Who was he anyway that he thought he knew better than a cop's daughter?

Hildy asked for everything to go back to normal until the cops came, so I was shooed back to my table with Dani. I didn't know how much I was allowed to tell her, so I wasn't going to tell her anything.

"Nice hair and what's with the glitter? I hope you didn't buy that to look festive because I don't think the sparkly orange highlights are doing your hazel eyes or brown hair any real favors. You'd need to be blonde and blue-eyed to pull that off." She looked me over from tip to toe, and I knew I had to be a mess.

I thought she was done, but I was wrong.

"I know you, and I know something just happened, so spill or I'm taking your soda," Dani said with her hand already outstretched.

I snatched up my wine glass and held it out to where she couldn't possibly reach it. That of course put it right in Hildy's range, and I found myself drinkless in less than three seconds.

Didn't that woman have anything else to do in a busy restaurant with the cops on their way?

My shoulders slumped, and I blew out a breath. "It's nothing I'm allowed to talk about right now, but I promise I'll share as I get more information."

Dani frowned and Hildy gave me my drink back then walked away.

"That sounds a lot like you know exactly what's going on but won't tell me, like you used to do when we'd bring you a rumor from home, and you could neither confirm nor deny that Joe Frietag had been caught dancing in the fountain in the center of town in his birthday suit."

"I still can't confirm or deny that." Maybe if I could keep her off the topic of what had happened here it would be easier to not tell her anything I shouldn't. Yet, since apparently Roderick had been taken out of the scene altogether, and I was the one who found him, I had a feeling people were going to know that sooner than I wanted them to anyway. And she might not trust me if I kept it from her. Then again, maybe she shouldn't be trusting me at the moment anyway since we were potentially one broken appliance away from having to throw in the towel if I couldn't help with expenses.

Stuff was piling up in my brain, and that was never a good thing when it came to talking out of turn.

"I found Roderick out at the dumpster. You know, the one out back that has the six-foot-tall fencing around it? I don't know how he got there, but I'm sure Hildy is taking care of things now." I grabbed my menu again, as if I didn't know what I wanted to eat, as if I wanted to eat at all after seeing my first ever dead body in the wild. I hid behind the sides and desserts portion until Dani scooted her chair back to its original position and took the hint that I was calling the conversation over.

Like I really thought that was going to last…

Dani pulled down one side of my menu.

"You do realize this does not allow you off the hook. I want to enjoy this dinner, so let's go ahead and do that now. But tomorrow, when we get to work to do prep, you'd better be ready to spill all the beans about everything, or I am not going to be a happy camper. And you know how much you hate me as the unhappy camper."

"I can live with that." I'd have to, but it always went better if I appeared to truly mean I'd do it.

I could figure out ways to escape her later if my father did end up running the lead on this case, which would leave me in a spot where I really couldn't talk about certain things.

Hildy glanced my way. I dipped my head to let her know we needed a server over here. She was wringing her hands but stopped immediately and hustled over with the biggest smile on her face.

"What can I get you ladies?" she asked. "Are you ready to order yet? I heard Eliot is making a mean lobster bisque this evening if you're interested."

That sounded divine and just the thing to concentrate on instead of a dead guy out in front of the dumpster. She had mentioned a special dinner earlier, but I couldn't remember what it was with everything that had just happened. A mean lobster bisque could be just what I needed.

I closed my heavy menu and placed it on the table. "I'll take that, some of your delicious garlic parmesan bread, and then an order of scallops."

"Going big, huh?" she said, smiling.

"Well, you shouldn't have told me that you're comping us before I ordered." I smiled and she laughed, and it felt normal just for a second, even though we both knew it was anything but right now.

Dani followed suit and got surf and turf as well as the soup. I would not have wanted to see the bill even if I could afford it. I was happy to sit back for a minute and enjoy my soda as I let Dani talk about the new spatulas she'd picked up from the kitchen store in the next town over.

I knew it wouldn't be able to last, but I had at least hoped I could eat my food before my father came storming into the dining area. He paused at the door, all six feet two of him with his silver hair and slightly portly belly. His uniform fit him as it had for years, and even though he didn't technically have to wear it as a detective, he'd never even considered changing it out for a blazer and dress pants.

During the pause it was obvious, at least to me, that he was calming himself down and putting on a face that wouldn't scare anyone into asking a ton of questions before he had any answers.

I made my excuses to Dani before he had to come get me. "I'll be right back. My dad is here, so I should probably go see what he wants." I stopped short of blaming it on some family thing or a personal issue. There was hiding the truth, and then there was flat out lying. I didn't want to do either, but I very much didn't want to do the second one more than the first.

Dani sputtered, opened her mouth, then abruptly closed it when she glanced in my dad's direction.

Chuck Tapman cut an intimidating figure even if he wasn't trying to. Of course, Dani knew he was actually a big teddy bear most times. But I was intimidated by the stoic look on his face, and I had grown up with him and been around him for years. I was sure my friend was wary of that look, and if she was wary, then other diners would be on guard. Neither of those reactions were wanted, so I picked up my step and was trotting before I got halfway to him.

For his part, he turned to reenter the kitchen when he saw me start moving, so I hoped any kind of damage would be minimal. Well, until everyone found out through the grapevine that one of their own was dead.

My dad would want to nip that like a weed before it even got a chance to poke out of the ground.

As soon as I hit the two-way kitchen door, my dad planted his hand around my bicep and steered me over to the office where Hildy spent most of her time when she wasn't glad-handing her patrons. Opening the door, I saw that Eliot and Hildy were seated in the only two chairs and resigned myself to standing against a wall while I got taken down a notch for messing this up from the very beginning.

But then Eliot stood, moving around behind the chair, and placing his hands on the top of the back to hold it for me. Was that a good or bad thing? Was he being a gentleman, or were they about to tie me to the chair and interrogate me while my scallops got cold?

"What the heck happened out there?" This from Hildy when I'd really expected my father to speak first and ask his question with a little more force and probably some swear words.

I shrugged, looking around at all of them because I wasn't sure what to say. I didn't have a big story, but I had a feeling they were all looking for one, and I wasn't going to be able to provide it.

"Just tell us what happened," Eliot said, leaning against the wall next to the big desk Hildy sat behind.

I cleared my throat. "Well..." I felt like there was a frog in there, so I tried again while also trying to think my way through how to be helpful but not get in trouble for yet again being at the wrong place at the wrong time.

"Take a couple of breaths, honey." Aunt Hildy jumped in to save the day like she had for years. "We just need to know what happened. No one's blaming you necessarily, but it's important that we know as much as your dad needs and I need before we tell anyone anything."

That sounded like a really tall order and also a lot of pressure, but at least they weren't angry.

"I went out the back door like Hildy told me to because Roderick was supposed to be out there waiting for my car keys, so he could get away from Delilah, who had just stormed in wanting to know where he was, and he didn't want to be found." I took another breath, and this one was easier but would probably be the easiest one I took for the next little while. "I stuck my cell phone in the door jamb, so I wouldn't get locked out of the restaurant and have to come back around to the front when supposedly I was going to the bathroom." I turned to Hildy. "Your big guy here said he didn't agree that I should go out at all and hoped that no one got hurt this time. What's happened here before?"

My dad cut Hildy off before she could answer or tell me it was nothing. Or at least I hoped that was what she had been ready to say.

"That's not what I need to know at the moment, though I'm sure it will come up in the near future," he said. "Right now, I just need to know what you did and how you did it, so I can let the tech guys know what to process and what might have your fingerprints all over it."

Yep, that last breath had been the easy one. For someone who watched endless hours of true crime, I had not thought my way through this to the end yet, or even the next step. There was every possibility people might say I did this, or I made this happen since I was the last one to see him. Not like I had anything against him, and certainly nothing big enough to make me a true prime suspect, but if they had no one else, then I could be at the top of the list simply by default.

Things just got a lot worse, and I started shaking a little.

"Stop," Dad said. "Don't get yourself worked up and don't go spinning those stories in your head for how this *could* go. I only need to know how it went. I'll work with the rest of the team on what actually happened."

Well, that was better than I thought it was going to be, so I took a second to clear my head. Then I started from the beginning again, laying out how I had propped the door open with my phone, not seen Roderick anywhere, gotten shoved, stumbled, and fell into the garbage enclosure where I came face-to-face with the very deceased Roderick.

"How did you know he was dead and not just knocked out?" Dad asked.

That gave me pause. I had to go back over the scene in my head and figure it out to give a correct answer. "Because he wasn't moving and his eyes were open. And he wasn't breathing." Thinking about it definitely brought it into clear focus and also reminded me to tell them about the raccoon that made me jump before getting shoved and then seeing the person fleeing.

"Was it a tall person? Short person? Were you able to determine if the person was a male or female?"

I sighed. "No, only that they didn't appear to be carrying anything. I don't know why that was important at the time, but it was. I'm sorry that I don't have more, Dad."

"It's okay, honey. This isn't your job. It's mine. I don't expect you to be able to do it all, especially since you were probably taken aback with seeing your first dead person outside of a coffin."

"Well, I did take that one anatomy class where they had us stand in during an autopsy."

"Right and some people have watched a whole lot of crime TV and follow NCIS religiously, so they're sure if they were to come across a dead body, they'd be able to tell time of death and method with a single glance. I get it all the time. I just need the facts not speculation, honey. No pressure."

"Except that he was strangled with a lanyard with my diner's name on it, and I just picked those up this afternoon from the printer, and they were in my locked car. How did that happen?"

I watched as my dad got his trusty notepad out and licked his finger to turn to the next page. I'd made fun of him over the years for not being able to move into the twenty-first century with iPads and other techno tools, but he'd held fast to wanting it written down on paper, and he'd never changed that. He was only a couple years away from retiring, so I highly doubted he was going to change before he decided that his time as a detective was up.

I had to admit I wished I could see what he was writing this time. I used to draw him pictures in those notebooks when I snuck into my parents' room while he was sleeping on the couch and my mom was making dinner. Once I could read, though, he'd put them in places I couldn't find. It frustrated me until I did find it one time and read through a statement that chilled me to my bones about a man killing his wife and how he did it.

So, I never looked again, and I wouldn't be looking now. I would just trust that he was taking down all the info and would ask me follow up questions as needed. In the meantime, I was hoping we were almost done with things, so I could go back to my friend, give her the barest of details, forget the whole thing, and leave it in my father's capable hands.

"So, here's the thing, and this stays in this room. There's far more going on here than meets the eye, and this is not an isolated incident," my dad said.

My head snapped up as Eliot hummed under his breath, and Hildy groaned.

"There's something particularly wrong about this one, though, and I'm going to have to comb through the evidence to see if I need anything else from you. I know where to find you, Jax. But I won't involve you if I don't have to."

"They used one of my lanyards. They must have broken into my car to get it. I'm going to say I'm pretty involved if they're trying to pin the murder on me." Now why had I said that? My dad had been ready to let me off the hook and just do his thing but only bother me if he needed me, and here I was trying to make a case for helping more.

"There is that, and we'll look over your car to see if there's any evidence," he said, tapping his notepad on his thigh. "And there could be problems down the line if it takes too long to connect the dots to who actually did this."

"Eliot could help," Hildy said.

The man in question grunted and shot his gaze over to his boss, who was doing her darndest to look innocent but not pulling it off by a longshot.

"No, Eliot cannot help." His voice was deep and big like I said before, but this time, it had a note of steel in it that felt like it could slice through the most determined of people.

"Why would Eliot help?" I asked.

"Eliot is not helping, and I'm done talking about myself in third person. If you need me, I'll be in the kitchen preparing scallops for someone in this room." He stalked out, and I would have sworn he would slam the door closed behind him, but he actually closed it very gently with barely a sound as the latch engaged.

"Why would Eliot help?" I asked again, and my dad smiled at me.

"Eliot is a former cop, and he'd help because he would want to do the right thing, but you might have to convince him that you need that help."

Why me?

CHAPTER FIVE

"Why do I have to be the one to convince him?" was what I actually asked since "why me?" sounded like whining in my head.

"Because something very bad happened five years ago that made him quit the force in Monroeville, which is about forty miles away. He's cooking because he doesn't want to be involved in bringing another person harm." Hildy swung her desk chair back and forth slightly as she tapped a ballpoint pen on the blotter covering her desk. "He could definitely help. In fact, I bet he'd be able to make all kinds of moves under the radar if you need that, Chuck. He could help get info that won't tip people off to this being a bigger picture than just a dead Lothario next to a dumpster."

"That's precisely what I was thinking, but how do we get him to do it?" Dad paced around the small room, and I couldn't swivel enough in my chair to keep him in my line of sight.

"We use Jacklynn."

"I think Jax has been through enough tonight," I said, also referring to myself in the third person, which made me feel itchy. "Look, I'm traumatized over finding a dead body, and I have a diner to run and other things going on. I can't help with a murder investigation…" No matter how much I admired those amateur sleuths in the books I loved to read. But that was not relevant to the current situation.

"I'm not looking for *your* help so much as *his*."

Well, that put me in my place, now, didn't it? I tried to not be sensitive about that, but I wasn't sure if it was going to work.

I was actually closer to offended not sensitive, but that wasn't going to be productive either. So, I sat there and waited for whatever was going to come next.

"Now, Chuck, let's not discount how much gossip there is to be had at the diner Jacklynn is running and the way she could put feelers out while she's serving up those eggs and bacon."

That at least was a little better.

"Just as long as she doesn't chase everyone out with salty coffee." Dad chuckled, and now it was my turn to groan.

Never. Live. It. Down.

"Yes, well I wasn't the one who bought the two white buckets this time for the salt and sugar, so if your coffee is salty then blame it on Dani. I specifically told her to get two different colors when she bought them, and she didn't listen to me."

"Poor baby," Dad said with a smirk.

That surprised a laugh out of me. "All right, so I really am whining this time." I quickly turned serious. "But what are we going to do? I know most people won't believe that I would actually hurt someone, much less kill them, let alone be stupid enough to do it with my own business swag. But I can't know for certain that no one is going to believe it, or even maybe boycott the diner right when we're celebrating being open six months, and things are finally starting to turn around."

"Don't worry. I'll talk to Eliot," Hildy said. "We'll get things sorted out. You might have to show him around town a little bit, but I have a feeling that won't be bothersome to you, will it, Jacklynn?"

I would not blush. As in, Would. Not.

But just in case I did, I turned away for a moment and pretended to be looking for something on the wall. When I knew I had myself under control, I turned back toward my father and my godmother, and they were both smiling knowingly at me. Crud!

"Whatever it takes, let's get this done." Dad put his notepad away into the breast pocket of his uniform. "I'm not going to be able to share much with you, and I'm not going to want to give you things to look for. I don't want to skew the information toward a specific person if we can't prove it and shut ourselves off to other options. Just know there are a lot of things going on around here, and it's possible Roderick's death could be just the next step in some plan we don't understand."

"Got it," Hildy said, answering for both of us, though I didn't get it at all.

My dad left through the door, closing it harder than Eliot had but not in anger. Hilda and I sat and stared at each other for a few seconds before she started tapping that pen on the blotter again.

"You didn't see anything you aren't telling your dad, are you?"

"No, not that I'm aware of. The raccoon, the fleeing shadow, and a dead guy, not necessarily in that order, but that was about all I had to share. There was a loud noise right after I found the body, but I'm pretty sure it was the raccoon coming to investigate who was in his territory."

"They have crime scene techs out there looking around, so they'll hopefully catch any clues, and that's all good information."

"But?" Because the way she said that inferred there was a *but* in there somewhere.

"Well, we might need to do some quick and hard convincing to get Eliot to agree to help at all."

"What's his story?" Not that it was any of my business. Really, I didn't need to know, but I was intrigued by him in a way I hadn't been intrigued in a while, even before my last boyfriend, and I wasn't sure why.

"His story isn't mine to tell, but the basics are that he was a cop for a number of years, and then he helped put someone in jail for a crime they didn't actually commit. By the time the guy proved his innocence, he'd been in prison for years and lost out on time with his young child and then his wife left him."

"Oh." Yeah, that had to have hurt, not only to be wrong but then also to ruin someone else's life. I had a hard time imagining how horrible that would be for the innocent man and also for the guy who thought he was doing his job but did it wrong and affected so many lives.

"But this is too important, and if there's something going on in our area, then we should know and use all our tools to find out what it is and stop it."

"I have a feeling Eliot would not want to be called a tool."

"And you'd be right," the man in question said from behind me. I hadn't even heard the door open, so I jumped at the sound of his voice.

"My ears were burning," he said. "So, I figured you must be talking about me because I doubt it is anyone who is enjoying their perfectly prepared meals."

Man, my perfectly prepared scallops, and I wasn't going to be able to eat them until after Hildy released me, which I had a feeling hinged on convincing Eliot he did in fact want to help me infiltrate our small town and look for gossip and possible suspects without involving the police force. Easy as pie, right? I was pretty sure that was the opposite of easy.

"If I leave you a stellar review of my much-anticipated scallops, will you help me out?" He opened his mouth, so I rushed on. "Just a little question here and there, things that maybe the cops can't ask. You'd know what can't be asked without warrants and subpoenas and stuff, but as a citizen, there's nothing holding us back from looking into whatever comes up, supported with facts or not. Just asking questions, getting some gossip, looking for answers?" I smiled harder as his frown intensified. "I could show you how to make the most perfect fried eggs to add to the burgers Hildy fought hard against adding to her posh menu here. I know all the tricks."

He sighed, but he didn't say no, so I steamrolled on.

"You don't really have to do anything, just help me figure out who to push on and what to do with any information I can find on my own. Maybe help me make a chart or something like a diagram, where we map out who fits where and how. Then we can eliminate this person or that person to give my dad a jump start on what might really be going on. This is your town too, and you'd be doing a heap of community service with little effort."

He turned to Hildy with his eyes wide. "She's worse than you are."

"Sometimes the pupil becomes the master, my dear Mr. Myers. And that is a shining moment in any mentor's life."

"So, you'll do it?" I asked, wanting to get a commitment before I made any more promises to keep him under the radar that I couldn't keep and didn't know what they entailed.

"On one condition."

Hildy snorted, and I braced myself.

"You have to show me how you used to make the hasselback potatoes that I hear about all the time. Apparently, mine are good, but we had a review the other day that specifically said they weren't yours, and they were just okay but not divine like Jax's."

That I could do.

About five minutes later, I was able to return to the table but was met with a very disgruntled friend and co-owner, who was not happy that she still hadn't been served.

"I'm so sorry. I told them to go ahead and bring your food out." I sat in my chair and pulled my napkin onto my lap.

"And I told them to take it back or put it in someone else's order because this is our celebration. Both of us. Not just me, while you traipse off being the great Jax detective." Dani sat back in her chair with her arms crossed and a frown on her face. I'd never been frowned at so much in my life, even when I'd tried to talk my parents into letting me get a baby cow that I could keep in my room.

Needless to say, my powers of persuasion did not work in that scenario, but at least they'd worked this time with Eliot.

I snorted out a laugh. I couldn't help it. Dani still looked disgruntled, but in a few seconds, she'd joined me in laughter, probably because she wouldn't want to be the only one making a fuss.

"Would it help to hear that I was very firmly ensconced in a meeting with the very cute and yummy Eliot? And he's going to be my sidekick for the next little while as we help my dad figure out what happened?"

She narrowed her eyes. "A little," Dani grudgingly said.

"What about if my dad is also concerned that people thinking I killed Roderick, even though I had absolutely no motive, could hurt our fledgling business?"

Now that got her attention right as our piping hot dinners were served with a soup tureen of lobster bisque and tiny plates of the most decadent-looking dessert in the world. It had curves and curls of chocolate strewn over a peanut butter pie that I knew for absolute certain was an amazing creamy peanut butter silk filling that would be laced with slivers of chocolate. My uncle had made it years ago, and they'd just recently brought it back to the restaurant. Everything all at once was initially overwhelming, but once we started digging in and got back on track to our original celebration, it was everything I could have hoped for.

Roderick was still at the back of my mind, but I let it go into hiding while I sat with the one woman who had dropped everything to make our long-ago dreams come true.

I hoped she wanted this as much as I did. I almost asked again but didn't want to ruin the vibe we had going on at the table— jovial, joking, hopeful. I'd get back to the nitty gritty of what my father was asking and what I'd have to do and be on the lookout for tomorrow.

"So, is it really going to be that big of a deal to have two white buckets for the sugar and salt?" Dani was mellow after polishing off most of her dinner and tucking into the pie. "Oh, my heavens, don't answer that yet. I need to just be in the moment with this divine pie. Do you think they'd make them for us too? It could be like an advertisement to have lunch with us and dinner here if you think about it properly."

I laughed.

"I'm not quite sure that's how things work," I said. "But we can ask."

Hildy came hustling out of the kitchen like she was on a mission. I almost got up to follow her, but when we made eye contact, she shook her head at me.

"What *is* going on, Jax?" Dani asked. "I know we're avoiding talking about it because you seem to shy away anytime we step near it. This was supposed to be our celebration of a chunk of good work, but I feel like maybe I should know what you've gotten yourself into, not only as your friend but also as co-owner of the diner. Should I be on the lookout for anything? Are you in trouble?"

I shook my head, wishing we could have held off for another twelve hours or so but did understand why she would ask and why I should answer now. "I don't know all the facts, and my dad said he couldn't tell me everything, but Roderick's death might not be the first bad thing to have happened. I'm mainly supposed to keep my ear to the ground for any gossip that might come out in the diner and share it with my dad."

I waffled on mentioning Eliot again but figured it might actually distract her from what more could happen or had already happened.

"And I'll be working with Eliot, so it could be good. Maybe I could get a few recipes. Either way, they think he could help with gathering info, so we're going to be sharing what we hear or find and making sure we corroborate anything we find if possible. My dad knows I can do it and thinks for whatever reason Eliot can too. I think Hildy wants him in on things just because it happened at her restaurant."

That wasn't exactly true, but it wasn't a lie either, and I was so very tired of making excuses for myself.

"Here's the thing. We want to make sure the right person is caught and that we hand over anything we hear. So, I'm going to ask you to keep your ear to the ground also. Let me know if you're hearing gossip or if anyone says something that seems out of line. I'll keep track of it and make sure it gets to the right people. Roderick might not have been the most scrupulous of men, but no one deserves to be strangled and left at the foot of a dumpster."

"Truth." Dani twirled some more of the fettuccine Alfredo on her fork. I couldn't eat things randomly like that. I always had to eat all of one thing before moving on to the next. But good for her. "Okay, I know there's more you aren't telling me. Will you be able to at some point?"

There were things I had promised not to tell anyone, and normally, I would totally throw that aside because this was my best friend, but this time, I just couldn't do it. "I'm not going to lie to you, Dad and Aunt Hildy think there's a lot more going on here than meets the eye, but I'm only going to do my part."

Hildy came back in just as I finished talking and stopped by our table. "Everything good, ladies?"

Nods around the table and smiles. "For the most part, this was awesome. I do think I'm going to want that recipe for the pie, though."

"Ha! You'll have to pry it out of my dead, cold hands," Hildy said, but then her face dropped, and she looked horrified that she'd said it.

"Aunt Hildy!" I shot out from my seat and put an arm around her then guided her to my open chair. "Sit for a minute and just breathe."

"It's just that this could be absolutely horrendous for everything around here. And I don't even know where Delilah got off to when she left."

"Is she your business?" I asked, moving some of my scallops onto a small bread plate and gently pushing them in front of her. She shook her head but picked up my salad fork and popped one in her mouth.

"These really are delicious. I should have them more often. Eliot does something to them that I just haven't been able to duplicate, and he won't share." She chuckled, then closed her eyes, and let her head fall back for a moment.

Dani and I shared a look before she also forked a few bites of her meal onto the small bread plate.

"I couldn't," Hildy said, but we disagreed with her.

"You're not getting up until you eat something and take a breather. The world will not come to an end if you rest for a minute."

We wouldn't go into how I should take my own advice because this wasn't about me.

"Do you know why Delilah was looking for Roderick? Was it really because she thought he was cheating?" I asked. So much for the breather, I told myself.

"He was." A new voice joined the table, and I was not surprised to see Jasper Longrave gesture to the occupants of the table next to us that he wanted to take their extra chair. Of course, it involved him putting the poor woman's purse on the floor and shifting her roses up onto the small round table, crowding out her dinner and almost tipping over her drink.

CHAPTER SIX

Now you had to know Jasper to understand how his world worked. Well, that wasn't exactly true. All you had to know was anyone whose whole world revolved around themselves, but they were so nice about it that you didn't realize you'd been railroaded until it was too late to turn back because the lines had been cut. That was Jasper in a nutshell.

The woman at the next table smiled and hooked her purse onto the back of her chair then moved the flowers to the floor, where I desperately hoped she wouldn't accidentally kick them over. To make sure that didn't happen, I picked them up and put them on the stone ledge behind her dinner companion's head, where she'd be able to see them, but they wouldn't be in the way of anyone's feet or elbows or any other stray body part.

"Sorry," I said quietly, and she just laughed.

"He's my cousin, no harm, no foul. You should see him at Christmas. It's like the whole holiday was created just for him."

"I heard that, Beatrice. No one needs your negativity, love." He turned in his chair and zeroed in on her. When they were seated facing each other like that, the familial line was very easy to see.

"And no one needs your interference, Jasper. I'm pretty sure these lovely women were having an intimate conversation and didn't need you to put a third chair at a two-top, but what do I know?" She raised an eyebrow at him, and he huffed, but he did turn around. She smiled then winked at me.

"How do you know Roderick was cheating?" Hildy asked the question, and since this was her establishment, I let her run the show.

"Funny you should ask," he said.

Although it really wasn't funny since he was the one who'd introduced the topic. But it wasn't worth getting into it with him if it got us some answers and maybe a jumping off point to start figuring out what happened, why it happened, and ultimately who did it. I would have been fine with it being Delilah herself since it meant she'd stop being a menace around town.

That was me, always trying to find the silver lining and drawing it myself if I had to.

"Yes, hysterical," Dani deadpanned. "Now answer it."

"Touchy. Maybe your pie wasn't quite up to the happy ending standards?" He made a grab for her plate, and she came within an inch of stabbing him with her fork before he yanked his hand back and pouted.

"Let's just get your information you feel the need to share, and then you can move along. This is actually a private party. I'm sure my niece and her friend would like to get back to celebrating." Hildy looked tired and about done in, and the restaurant would still be open for another five hours. Then there'd be closing. It was going to be a long night for her.

"Fine." He tugged on his chin whiskers that he probably thought made a wonderful goatee and then smacked his hand on the table. I would have sworn that he was going to say eureka or something else completely inane, but instead, he drew in a breath before he unloaded.

"I saw Roderick and a lady friend over at the grocery store this morning, and then I saw him an hour later with another lady friend. Fifteen minutes after that, he was with a third woman. This one he was kissing, and then forty minutes later, he was with a woman I've never seen before around town, so she might have flown in, or that was what I might have inferred from the suitcase she had rolling toward his car."

"And how did you see him all those times, that close together, but at all different places?" Dani asked. It was a good question.

"I don't reveal my sources, but they're very reliable."

"And why do you have sources?" Another valid question, this one from Hildy.

"That's not important at the moment. The important thing is that he was with six different women today, and they each offered a different kind of attitude and personality, so why were they all with him? He's not old necessarily, but he's not exactly a young spring chicken either."

No, he definitely wasn't. He'd looked old and sad out there

next to the dumpster, and it had broken my heart to find him like that, even as it had made me very scared that the killer might still be around.

"So, what are you saying? He was with several women today, only one you saw him have physical contact with, and that tells us what?" I asked.

"That you very much should be looking at cheated-on husbands if something happened to Roderick. And I have a list."

"A what?" Did he mean what I thought he meant? Did he actually have a list of every woman Roderick had ever been near as well as all their husbands?

"A list." And he handed it over with a flourish. Of course, Jasper did everything with a flourish, but after he'd left our table, not putting the chair back where he'd taken it from, I ran my gaze over it and knew just about every name on it. Hildy removed it from my hands and stuffed it in her pocket.

"Later," she said. "Right now, you have celebrating to do. Whatever this means, it can wait until tomorrow."

"Do you want me to hang around and help?" I asked Hildy. I had to get up early in the morning, but I hated to not offer.

"Absolutely not. I have an entire staff who can manage but thank you."

Right about then, Dani realized what time it was. She needed to leave because she had to work at four-thirty in the morning to prep for and be ready to meet the breakfast rush. We plowed through the rest of our food at that point and laughed as much as we talked. I grabbed Jasper's list from a reluctant Hildy before we left. All in all, it was good to finally make this a celebration.

We said goodbye at our cars with hugs and one more "woohoo" about how far we'd come in our business and how much further we'd like to go over the years. I drove home to my townhouse on the edge of town and then pretty much fell into bed. Thankfully, my dad had cleared my car as any part of the crime scene. It had not appeared to be broken into, so there was another mystery.

Today had been a long one, and tomorrow was soon enough to start trying to help my dad. One thing I should do would be to count those lanyards to see how many were missing, but that would have to wait. It didn't hurt that I might get a chance to see more of Eliot.

I wasn't going to lie. He intrigued me, even though I should have been worrying about my last boyfriend and where he'd gone off to with some of my stuff, including the bulk of my checking and saving accounts due to me thinking that we should share money and information. I was the only one who actually did any sharing, and I was paying for that. Literally.

I hadn't told anyone yet. I had no intention of changing that, but things were tight. I was so thankful for the free dinner tonight, even if it had come garnished with a dead body and the directive to help the police and Eliot uncover any information that could help with finding the killer.

The tables were hopping and so were the lunch counter seats when I entered the Sunny Side Up Diner the next morning. I waved to Dani and headed through the crowd to make my way to the back. I considered going the back way when I parked my car out in our employee spaces, but I wanted to see what I was walking into. Knowing the size of the crowd and the buzz going on while I had a specific mission made it easier. This way I could make decisions while I stored my things in a cubby and formulated a plan on who to talk to and how to make things happen before heading back out into the fray.

Of course, on the surface that made sense, but in actuality, my plan went out the door as soon as I swung through the pass-through and knocked Jennifer, one of our favorite servers, in the elbow, causing her to almost lose her tray of pancakes, eggs, and scrapple.

"Oh, Jennifer, I'm so sorry!" I reached out a hand to help her rebalance then snatched it back when she righted the load by herself.

"No worries, just trying to keep up with the flow. You just missed the first tidal wave, and our next one is due in about fifteen minutes if they stick to their normal routine. You might want to make sure you're ready for battle."

She quickly stepped past me and replaced her frown with a big smile for table twelve.

I'd sailed right past everyone, with my eye on getting back to the storeroom, and had missed the way certain people were grouped together. I peeked out the door and saw we had the daytimers, the ladies' group, the bowlers, the veterans, and the warehouse guys all in separate corners. All the usual suspects. I spotted a few who were on the list Jasper had given us and wondered how I could get close enough to find out what they were talking about—if anything. This town had a grapevine that would make any gossip jealous of how fast news traveled. Only twelve hours after Roderick's death, and it seemed everyone knew. I was only too happy that they chose to discuss it here as it meant more customers and, hopefully, new information for the investigation I was supposed to be doing with Eliot.

Were they relieved Roderick was gone because that meant their wives would stay away from him? Were they even aware they would be on Jasper's list? I had forgotten to ask Jasper if he'd spoken with any of the men, or if he'd just taken a tally and figured that once he had enough ammo, he'd hit them with questions and maybe accusations all at once.

He'd left before we could say much about the list at all, and then Hildy had been pulled away for an issue in the kitchen, and Dani had realized the time—all simultaneously pretty much. And since we'd all gone our separate ways, I hadn't had a chance to talk with anyone to see if there were any new developments.

I'd try to corner my friend as I could throughout the day, but I had a shift to work, and those sugar containers weren't going to fill themselves.

Reaching under the silver counter, I pulled out the first white bucket and snickered when I saw that Dani had not only written sugar in huge letters, but she'd also drawn a picture of a sugar shaker that looked a lot like the one from *Blue's Clues* and had taped a picture of the Morton Salt girl with her big umbrella and bright yellow dress to the side of the other container.

"Did you see this?" I asked Jennifer when she flew past me with a stack of menus and an exasperated sigh. She stuck a hand on her curvy hip and brushed her blonde hair back over her shoulder.

"I did. She showed it to me this morning and told me that if you didn't notice she was going to make a doctor's appointment to get you checked out."

I snickered, and Jennifer blew out another breath.

And then I saw Dani make a beeline for me and braced myself for what that stern look on her face might mean for me.

"Hey, what's up? You look like you're bordering on a snit."

"It's nothing to discuss out here," Dani said as she grabbed my arm and dragged me around the corner into a separate dining room. We were still working on it to get up to snuff for a banquet room to rent out. It was filled with all manner of things from the refurbishing of the diner when we'd first bought it, including a huge painting of avocados that we still hadn't found a buyer for.

"What is going on?" I asked as soon as she slammed the door behind us. It rattled in its frame. Another thing we might have to replace but not just yet. "People are going to think something is wrong with how you just pulled me into a dark room and threw the door closed."

"Something is wrong." She wrung her hands over and over as I waited for her to continue that thought.

When she didn't, I stared for a few more seconds before I cleared my throat and narrowed my eyes at her.

"So, what is wrong? Are we running out of eggs? Did Benny decide that he doesn't like to make mouse head-shaped pancakes for kids? Did we run out of napkins again?" That last one had been an almost total disaster last month. One that required us to really learn the inventory game and how to play it without tanking ourselves.

"We're really busy, and everyone is running around like mice in a maze."

"Okay, so let's see if anyone else can come in. How does it help for us to be shut in this room when we could be out taking orders or delivering them at least?"

"I looked over the list last night, and Herbert is on there."

Whoa. I had not expected that. How did she get the list? I had taken it home with me after making a reluctant Hildy hand it over. "Herbert, your stepdad? And how did you get the list?"

"I took it out of your pocket when we hugged. But that's not important when the answer to your other question is yes, Herbert, my stepdad, is on that list. Do you think Roderick was cheating with my mom?"

Dani's mom was a touchy subject almost any day of the week, but this would be a whole new level of issues if that were true.

"Um."

"Yeah, and half the guys Jasper wrote out have already been in this morning. I can barely look them in the eyes. What if their wives were cheating, and now we know? But they might not know. And if they don't know, we can't exactly ask, now can we? Because that could make their lives horrible, and we'd ruin things we have absolutely no business putting our noses into." More hand-wringing. I expected her to start gnashing her teeth at any moment, so I grabbed her hands and held them in mine, forcing her to break her panic.

"First of all, we are not confronting anyone. Jasper may think he's got some kind of master list of suspects, and they might all have ample reason to have wanted Roderick dead. Some of the couples are divorced, so why would the man want to go after Roderick now if he's a former husband? And there are probably a million other possibilities, and we can't put all our eggs into this basket, thinking that it has to be the angry-husband motive. It could be anything. Not to mention that Herbert has been married six times, and any of those women could have placed him on the list. We have no idea when Jasper started creating the list, or why he decided to do it unless maybe his dad is on there too? Why else would he need to track Roderick like that?"

She shook her head. "His dad wasn't on there. I checked once I saw Herbert. But there are quite a few men around town, and I don't think any of them are going to be happy to be called out for being cuckolded." She rested back against an oil on canvas of a giant fruit salad with those strange little chia seeds that seemed to grow green gooey nimbus when introduced to water.

"No one wants to be told they've been cheated on, and I'm pretty sure we could ask about things without actually coming out and saying that, but I do get what you mean. Let's talk this afternoon after we close, and we'll come up with a game plan. In the meantime, just keep your ears open to whatever's being said. No need to ask questions, just listen."

She blew out a third breath, but this one sounded more like relief instead of concern or irritation, so I'd take it.

"I'm so sorry you were worried about that all morning. You could have called me earlier before I got here."

"Ha, I didn't have any time. We had a mad rush first thing this morning, and I don't think anyone was listening too much because we were slammed at the grill. I'll try to write down anything I remember though and will start keeping track of things from now on."

How were we going to keep track of it though? And then an idea hit me. I patted my apron and came up with my order pad, and then I grabbed one of the extra receipt spikes we had on a shelf and popped it onto the counter. I wrote out the words Who Done It and then smashed it down on the spindle like we did when a check was paid.

"Voila. And then we can take them off at the end of the day and see if we can't piece some things together with the information."

"That's actually pretty smart," Dani said.

"Why do you sound so surprised? I think I might be offended by that."

She nudged me with her elbow. "I just mean that's something I would have never thought of, so good for you for thinking it. And then you'll have a big old pile of receipts with holes to share with that hunk of a cook Eliot, so that could really work for you and for him."

"Don't even start. I haven't been single for long enough to miss having to deal with someone else and their wants and needs. I'm still trying to figure out my own."

"I can tell you one need." She gestured to the small window out to the dining room on the other side of the door. "You're going to need another order pad, and I think the willingness to play waitress until the nine o'clock girls get here. If I'm seeing this right, that line is all the way out the door and maybe around the corner. We'd better get to it."

She wasn't kidding, and she wasn't far off. As soon as we emerged from the banquet room, I had two waitresses trying to flag me over and then a line at the door that went outside and to the right. I could see through the plate glass front window that it went all the way down to the corner. I did some quick math and glanced at the booths as well as the lunch counter, and it would be a tight squeeze, but we could make it work. So, I put on my best hostess face and went to greet the masses. Hopefully, they were here not only to open their wallets for a delicious breakfast, but also their mouths to deal out the gossip, so I could write it on a check and browse through it after the day was done.

CHAPTER SEVEN

With a tall glass of chocolate milk in front of me and a chocolate muffin that I'd snagged out of the case right before someone else bought the last one, I sat at the lunch counter with Dani, who'd stayed way after the shift we'd originally agreed on. It was three o'clock, and we were closed for the day. Finally. I had never been so thankful to sit on a chrome barstool with shiny red vinyl and just sip chocolate milk through a straw.

Dani dropped a quarter into the small jukebox on the counter beside the condiments basket and then clicked two buttons to choose what song she wanted to play. We all pretty much knew the selections and their corresponding letter and number by heart, so I wasn't surprised when she didn't flip the menu inside the plastic dome on the front to see what was available and how to access it.

"I cannot believe the last owner almost threw these away. The man was an idiot for thinking our town would survive only on things that grew in the ground and on trees, but even he had to have known how valuable these little babies are." The track started, and we both paused to enjoy the first strains of "Unchained Melody" as it started spinning.

Yeah, these babies were worth a pretty penny, and I couldn't lie and say that it hadn't occurred to me that selling even one of them could go a long way toward recouping my savings. But I also knew how much people loved playing them or even just looking at them. And they were a big part of our ambience, so instead, I focused on what we were here to do not what I'd like to be doing, like tackling my ex-boyfriend and making him confess.

"So how do you want to organize these?" she asked, thankfully breaking into my vengeful thoughts.

"I have no idea. Since we had five different people writing down anything they heard that might be gossip and I couldn't give them specifics, I'm thinking we might want to start out by separating those that have absolutely nothing to do with Roderick. We won't throw them away since they might be useful at another time, but we'll put them aside." I picked up the first spike and started removing the papers, turning them so the words were all going the same direction.

"Might be useful later." She hummed and then laughed. "Maybe there's something in here that we could blackmail someone with in order to fix the dishwasher."

My stomach sank into the bottom of my sneakers. "What is wrong with the dishwasher?" I had no money to offer, and I was tapped out on credit cards and possibly any more credit through loans. We could not afford to replace anything or even fix it for that matter.

"Wow, you went from eager amateur sleuth to old, constantly worrying crone in a matter of two breaths. Are you okay?"

Shaking my head, I drew in a soft breath. "I am. Sorry. There's just a lot going on right now, and we're finally in a good place with the diner. I'd really like some time without anything new happening that requires more money."

She patted me on the back and then returned to organizing her own papers to all face the same way. "I get that. Our business account isn't exactly flourishing, but it will get there. We put a ton of time and effort into bringing this place back to Jeb's standards and then bypassing that. We just have to get every day to be like today. And the dishwasher is fine for the moment. I was just thinking ahead since it's been making some noises I don't particularly like."

We'd had a ton of customers, and while there had been a lull between tidal wave one and two, there had never been an end to that second tidal wave. Not until we flipped the sign out front to *Closed* and waited for those who were eating to finish up and usher them out the door before locking it behind them.

"So, we need to have a murder every week or so in order for us to be the gossip hub that supplies the coffee and syrup?" I was joking, but everything about that would be okay—except the murder part, of course.

She nudged me as the music flipped to "The Lion Sleeps Tonight." "It wouldn't have to be a murder. It could just be something big going on. Something that requires you to be seen in the right place at the right time. I know you really want that banquet room opened. I think that will be a good idea too, but right now we might want to focus more on getting customers to come in on a daily basis, so we can pay for the new space outright instead of having to rely on more loans."

She wasn't wrong at all, but that didn't mean I had to like it. "I still think we should do a yard sale of all the things in that room and see if that won't work toward also paying things off. I mean, who doesn't want an enormous painting of an avocado to hang on their wall? Maybe we should see if we have two just in case we have a bidding war over the first one."

"Hey, it could happen." Her frown was fierce but only for a second or two.

"Dani, ever the optimist." I smiled and felt the glow of what we had set out to do being accomplished, and that was a good thing. "But let's get back to these bits of gossip. We can be optimistic about finding some kernel in here that could set the whole chase off. Get the perpetrator long before those true crime shows say you have to before it becomes a cold case."

"I'm pretty sure your dad would not let this move into cold case territory, especially since you have Eliot by your side now."

She nudged me again, and I knew what was coming. She didn't disappoint.

"So, Eliot, what's his story? Why is he single?"

"I don't know, and I don't know." Which was technically true but not all the way true. I was very uncomfortable with how the lies or at least omissions seemed to be piling up in an almost hourly fashion.

"You were back with your aunt and Eliot and your dad long enough for me to have to hear everything about this new guy that Samantha at the next table is considering going out with but will not consider having an actual relationship with because she doesn't want that burden. The least you can do is share the good stuff with me since I took one for the team there so you didn't have to."

"As if she's not going to make me sit through the whole thing when I see her next." Samantha was another friend from our high school days and Hildy's assistant manager, or I would have stolen her for our diner.

Dani conceded that with a laugh. "Seriously though, why is he involved? Did he know Roderick?"

That I could answer honestly. "No, not that I was told. I guess Eliot has a background that my dad thinks can help with getting information without tipping people off to what he's doing.

Hildy asked him to help so the reputation of her restaurant and our diner isn't ruined by something that has nothing to do with us."

That was close enough to be true and yet not reveal too much.

I saw her open her mouth and cut her off. "Don't ask me anything else. I don't have all the deets, and the ones I do have my dad asked me not to talk about. I'm trying to ride a line here, but I swear if it in any way could hurt you or us, I wouldn't let my dad keep me from sharing it with you. You have to know that."

"Of course I do. I'm just not used to us having secrets," she said, looking down at the receipts she was still sorting while mine remained in a stack in front of me. "I know when we lived far away from each other that we didn't talk every day or anything, but if something big happened, we checked in with one another. It just feels like it should be more like high school, I guess, now that we're in each other's vicinity, and that means holding nothing back."

I sighed because she was right, and I hated keeping the low funds thing from her, and this was not worth adding to that pile of crap.

Three more songs had started and moved on to the next since we'd sat down, and Dani's quarter had run out. Shifting in my seat, I put my forearm on the counter and nudged her seat so she faced me.

"I will tell you this, but you have to keep it to yourself under any and all circumstances. Do not ask questions that would lead people to think you know more than you should, and do not give out any of this information no matter who asks or what they ask for."

She vigorously shook her head and folded her hands under her chin like she was praying or maybe just in anticipation of whatever juicy morsel she thought I was about to serve up.

"He's an ex-cop. I guess he quit the force because someone he helped put away in prison wasn't actually guilty, and it made him doubt whether he knew how to do the job." Succinct, full disclosure, and no real room for questions. Perfect.

Draping herself over the counter, she rested the back of her hand on her forehead and sighed dramatically. "So, he's a lost, former superhero who made a mistake and needs to make amends by helping a strong woman figure out who is trying to frame her for his redemption? I'm halfway in love already."

"I knew you were going to say that!"

"And why wouldn't I? He's very cute, a really big guy, which you should like since they give the best hugs. And he's obviously a good cook, as well as being intelligent, capable of thinking through things, and taking on responsibility that isn't his because his integrity means something to him. That doesn't light your candle on fire at all? Not even a flicker of flame? Like a dancing little spark?"

There was no good way to answer that question. If I said yes, then she'd crow in delight, and if I said no, she'd crow in anger and keep pushing. Instead, I was thankful when I looked down and saw a note in Jennifer's handwriting.

"Oh, look at this!"

"You are not changing the subject."

"I'm shifting it, not changing it, since this could help lead to all that redemption arc stuff you're so jazzed about." I smoothed the green and white rectangle on the counter and let my eyes scan over the message again.

"*Land he owned is not going to who they think it will. Someone's going to be very angry if they killed him for no reason and now can't get him to change will,*" I read out.

"What's that word?" Dani pointed to where the spindle had pierced the paper, creating a hole that blanked out the word entirely.

"I have no idea." And looking at the words before and after showed me that it could be incredibly important. "*Jay believes will* then blank then *property.*"

"Of course it's the one word that's the most important."

"Of course it is."

"But it's Jennifer's writing, so she should be able to remember what she wrote."

"Let's hope so." I texted her while we went through the rest of the order pages and came up with little else. There were people who thought Roderick deserved what he got for being a womanizer and a user of pretty much anyone who got anywhere close to him. People who thought it was a shame because his family had been in the area for generations, and he was one of the few remaining Benningfields. Someone was sure the land he owned would now go to his son who didn't see any use in keeping it. And a few others speculated that he'd finally messed financially with the wrong person. All tidbits but nothing concrete and no real names other than the son to forward to my dad. Dang it.

"Should we do this again tomorrow?" Dani asked as she lined the edges up on the ones that involved gossip outside Roderick's death, including what Farrah Lewis was up to and why she seemed to go through money like water, and another set that involved the barber and how he might be running a slot machine ring in his back room. That one I was thinking about passing on to my dad anyway, but since that had nothing to do with Roderick's death, I decided to keep it aside.

"I guess so. Maybe not as hardcore. But we need to figure out how to get people to stay on topic and give names that might give us some actual clues. In the meantime, I'm going to head home and spend some time with my cat if she'll have me and then probably watch a movie or read a book."

"You're not going to meet with Eliot, so you can go over what might be needed in order to save him and start his redemption arc? Don't you think that's a dereliction of your duties to this community?"

Yet another question that I really didn't think I wanted to answer since there was no way to do so without throwing myself under a bus or two.

"I will touch base with him, but he's probably working."

Her smile turned coy as she focused over my shoulder. "Or he could be here to see how you're doing and if you figured it all out to put him back in the winner's circle." Jutting her chin out slightly to gesture behind me, her smile widened.

I had to turn around, even if I didn't really want to.

And there he was, standing at my front door, pointing at the *Closed* sign, then shrugging.

If it were anyone else, I'd nod and shoo them on, but I couldn't do that to him. Then I realized I didn't have the decision to make anyway because Dani had her keys in hand and was already walking to the door to let him in.

"Hey! Eliot, right? We kind of met last night, and you made the most divine surf and turf. If we could steal you, I bet you'd make a mean eggs Benedict."

He chuckled, and the notes reverberated in my chest, making my stomach feel tingly. Not exactly the reaction I had hoped for, but I could put that aside to focus on what he was actually here to do. Most likely that was to come up with a plan on how to get information my dad couldn't get while not showing our hand. Dani could help.

"Okay, I'm out. Errands to do, things to see, places to visit, people to chat up. See you tomorrow, Jax, and see you around, Eliot.

Dines, Drive-Ins, and Lies | 59

Take good care of our girl, or there will be no place you can hide." She chuckled, but it sounded far more sinister than it should have if she was just joking.

"Kind of feel like I've just been threatened within an inch of my life." He took his jacket off and laid it over the counter to the left of where Dani, the traitor, had been sitting moments ago.

"She may be scrappy, but she's not a scrapper. She's all bark and no bite." Why was I falling back so hard on stock phrases with no imagination or originality? Surely, I could come up with some more intelligent conversation than that.

"Nicely done on the cliches. My brother loved those when we were growing up."

"He doesn't anymore?"

"He passed a few years ago."

Could I have stepped into a more horrible way to start any conversation? I was hard pressed to think how. "I'm so sorry for your loss."

"I appreciate it, but it wasn't unexpected. I'm sure you don't want to take the time to go through all of that, though, so let's get down to business. What did you find out today?" He glanced down at the stack of papers in front of him and squinted at it. "Delilah was seen at the hairdresser getting fake lashes." He flipped to the next paper. "Barbie Malone had a boob job? Was she someone Roderick was seeing? Did he pay for it?"

"Um, no I don't think so. Dani and I were going through all the notes that were taken today to see what was relevant and what was just everyday gossip. That probably goes in the *not involved* pile." I tried to snatch it out of his hand, but he whisked it out of the way too quickly for me to be successful.

"Well, now we're not sure about that because he could have been involved with her as he seems to be with a bunch of the women in town. Hildy said you had some kind of list from Jasper?"

"Yep, I'll be right back." I jumped off the stool without waiting for him to answer and trotted back to the locker where my purse was stashed. Dani had given it to me earlier, and I'd put it there so I didn't misplace it. I probably should have had the list out when Dani and I sat down. What if Barbie's husband was on Jasper's list, and that full body sculpt was more significant than just creating a need for a bigger bra?

While I was out of his visual field, I went ahead and checked myself in the mirror to make sure I wasn't a horrible mess. I found that while not horrible, I definitely would not have called myself that put together either. I took a quick second to smooth down my unruly hair and clean up my smudgy eyeliner under my eyes. I put on some lip gloss and stopped short of reapplying mascara. Seriously, once I got home, I'd probably take a shower to wash off the grease from the day and then just veg for the rest of the night. New mascara would just make the circles under my eyes more pronounced anyway.

I grabbed the list from my purse, turned to head back to the front counter, and came face to chest with Eliot.

"Someone who I haven't seen before has walked in front of your building four times trying to look like he's not actually scoping the place out, even though he very much is. I'd feel better if you stay back here while I go around the building and see if I can confront him and find out what he wants."

"How about if we just call the cops?"

He shot me an annoyed look just as we heard the front door rattling like someone was desperate to get in.

CHAPTER EIGHT

"Stay here."

He had to be kidding. There was no way I was staying in the back while he decided to do some kind of knight in tarnished armor thing. As if. I could handle myself, and while I was certain I would appreciate his help, I wasn't going to depend on it for more than Aunt Hildy had talked him into.

I couldn't beat him out to the front, so I trailed along in his wake, grumbling under my breath about his long strides and being left behind.

When I rounded the corner and came out to the dining room, it was to see Dani smooshed against the glass front door.

Why was Dani plastered against the glass door like one of those stuffed cats people liked to suction cup to their car windows with their fur wild and their eyes wide in fright? I had no idea, but she started talking, and I was not a lipreader.

Eliot yanked the door open before I could, and she fell in, stumbling until Eliot stepped forward to catch her. She landed in his arms with a grunt but then smiled up at him, like he'd just saved her from certain death.

Why did I want to knock her into the booth?

A question for later.

Right now, I needed to figure out what my friend was doing. And why had she looked like she was frightened, yet after landing in Eliot's arms, she looked very pleased with herself?

"Dani, what on earth are you doing? You just left here ten minutes ago." But as soon as I said it, I remembered Eliot had mentioned a strange man walking by the windows over and over, as if checking things out without being noticed. "You didn't get accosted, did you? Tell Eliot exactly what he looked like, and then we'll go to the police because Eliot saw him walking around, and it's probably the same guy. No one messes with my restaurant and my friend and gets away with it without some serious consequences."

I was all heated up and ready to take down anyone and everyone.

Or at least, that's how I felt until I looked over and found both Eliot and Dani staring at me as if I'd stapled an order pad to my head.

"What?" I asked, forcing my hands to stay by my side and not raise them toward my head to see if something was amiss.

"You, uh, went from zero to a thousand right there before our very eyes in about two point three seconds, my friend. What the heck happened?"

"Eliot, tell her." Because I didn't want to go on a ramble again and was trying to catch my breath from the last one.

"Did you see a man with reddish hair, dressed in a plaid shirt and tan pants walking around the block? He's come by the windows a few times, and I've never seen him before. That doesn't really mean anything, of course, since I don't get out much, and I haven't lived here my whole life. But I was worried he was trying to break in."

Reddish hair? Plaid shirt? Tan pants? I groaned. "That's not a stranger. That's Timothy Dailey. He always walks the same route every day at this exact time. It's his lunch break from the train station maintenance shed, and he likes the hill out front. Gah, I wish I had asked what he looked like before I got scared! Did he have Tobias with him? I heard he was trying to get an apprenticeship, with things falling through on his other dream career."

Note to self for the future—ask before freaking out.

Although speaking of freaking out, if Dani wasn't accosted, then why had she looked like she was in danger?

"Which brings us back to you, Dani. What the heck were you doing stuck against the door?"

"I was just messing with you. I saw you come storming into the front behind Eliot here and thought that I'd ham it up. Tobias egged me on before he left, so it's not all my fault. He thought it would be fun to give you a little mystery for your new career as an amateur sleuth. See what the Big Man would do if I was in danger." She turned to that big man. "Good catch by the way and much appreciated. I hadn't expected you to yank the door so hard."

"Sorry about that. I really thought you were in trouble. Not knowing you have a regular walker who looks more like a stalker, I was more concerned with getting you in the door than I was making sure to open it gently." He didn't look very sorry with his arms crossed over his broad chest and his wide-legged stance, but I wasn't going to be the one to tell him that.

Moving on.

"I am not starting any kind of amateur sleuth thing, either. Did you tell Tobias that? I'm just doing this because my dad might need some help that we can give, and they used one of our lanyards to kill him. If that information gets out, then it could affect our reputation. I'd like to get in front of that by finding out who the real killer is and delivering him or her to my dad with a nice big red bow."

"Now, Jax." Eliot turned to me. "I don't know if we'll actually be the ones delivering him. I'd rather get together as much information as possible and then hand it all over to the police, so they can pick the person up through the right channels without making mistakes on our part."

Now where was the adventure in that? I kept that to myself too. I might run on inappropriate thoughts and sarcasm, but that didn't mean I had to share them with someone I had just met and thought I might be interested in.

He was still staring at me like he'd asked a question, so I went over what he'd said in my mind and realized he was probably looking for me to agree with him. I could do that. "Of course, yes, of course. Hand the info to my dad and not do anything more. No big red bow. No bow at all. Got it."

But even though I was agreeing with him, I had a feeling I'd want to do a whole lot more if we started finding clues, and I wasn't going to let something go until I followed it to its full conclusion. I didn't want to hand my dad a bunch of order pad tickets about Barbie getting new boobs on the off chance it might be a clue. I wanted to be sure of what I was handing over before I did so.

However, from the stormy expression on Eliot's face, I thought it might be better to just let that lie for the moment and go along with the program until I didn't want to anymore.

"You can stop scowling now. I don't do well with scowling. Ask my dad."

He didn't even try to smooth out his face or the lines formed between his dark eyebrows. Fine with me, that was up to him if he wanted to prematurely get more wrinkles.

I turned to Dani. "So besides wanting to be a joker and scaring me, did you have anything else you needed to tell me, or are you really just that much of a menace?"

"Well, I was at the post office, and I heard Matt at the counter tell a woman with silver hair that Roderick had closed his post office box down a month ago, and that's why the key no longer worked."

"Could you tell who it was?" The person could be added to our list from Jasper, or the one we were trying to cobble together from the spindle of meal tickets. Either way it could be something.

"No, I couldn't." She shrugged. "I asked Matt, and he said he hadn't seen her before so he couldn't help either."

Eliot pinched the bridge of his nose and then glanced at his watch. "I have to go. I'm supposed to be at work in an hour, but I wanted to see if there was anything I could tell Hildy to keep her from harassing me all night when all I want to do is cook. I should never have agreed to this."

I wasn't sure if he was talking to himself or not, but I couldn't let that slide. "You're more than welcome to let Aunt Hildy know that you're out, Eliot. No one can make you do something you don't want to do, and I'm capable of listening to gossip all on my own." Dani snorted. I nodded to let her know I hadn't been done. "Or with the help of my very capable friends and people I know in town. We can't go running off after every person who decides to take a walk around the block because you're suspicious so just go let Hildy know you're tapping out. We'll do the rest." It would probably be easier that way anyway. What did I need with another guy hanging around? Why would I want to put myself in that kind of position when I was still dealing with the fallout from the last one?

I was so struck with my own presentation of an out that I totally missed the expression on his face until I glanced back over at him.

Frown was a mild word for the way his mouth was turned down. The dimple I'd seen earlier was nowhere to be seen. If thunder was an expression, he'd have it nailed down to a science.

Even though I wanted to reach out and smooth the furrows in his brow, I kept my hands to myself and my mouth shut. I'd given him the out. If he wanted it, he'd take it, and if he didn't, then we'd have to set some ground rules. I didn't do very well with being bossed around on a normal day, especially after my relationship with the man who stole all my money. When I was trying to find out who killed someone and wanted to link it to me, somehow even the normal day level would have been out of range.

Dani nudged me when he continued to stare, but I wasn't breaking eye contact with him and his beautiful green eyes. They were dark, but with the early afternoon sun glinting off the chrome on the chairs and jukeboxes, they took on a glow that was almost mesmerizing.

Almost.

I was not going to be the one who talked first. I'd said my piece, now it was time for him to put up or shut up.

He chose to scoff instead. And then he shook his head but didn't look away from me, so I couldn't look away yet either.

He grunted and threw his hands in the air, finally breaking eye contact. I slowly released the breath I'd been holding so as not to give myself away.

Jeez, that had not been easy, and intense was too mild of a word to describe it.

"I am just trying to help you stay out of trouble. Your dad said we could help, but he also specifically said for you not to get into trouble. That's a line you don't want to cross. I promise you."

"I'm not planning on crossing any lines at all, just my t's, before I hand any information to my dad. I won't waste his time if it's something I can make sure is a valid lead, and you can help me with that as long as you can unbend enough not to be suspicious of every person out there."

"I reserve the right to pull things back to ground level if they get out of hand."

I bristled inside, but there was a part of me that knew he was the professional, even if he no longer did the job. It would behoove me to stay on his good side and follow his lead on some things. Not that I had to tell him that.

"Should we shake on it?" I asked.

Eliot stuck out his hand without hesitating, and I met him in the middle.

Dani, freakishly weird person that she was, brought the shake machine to life with a quick whirl, breaking the tension and the moment.

"I'll try to be vague with Hildy," Eliot said. "She's going to want to know everything I'm doing and what we've found. At this point, I'd keep everything from her like you're doing with your dad. She can be flighty if she wants to be, and we don't need anyone flittering about asking a thousand questions at the wrong time and in front of the wrong people."

I laughed because if anyone was going to do that it would be Hildy. "Don't forget that if we even showed her the Jasper list, she'd probably accost any customer who came in to eat to see if they were the one. She tends not to be able to leave things alone if she thinks she can fix it."

Which was just one of the many reasons I had not told her about the ex and the money. There wasn't a way to fix it, and I wasn't going to have her on the run after someone who was as horrible as Steven Jameson, aka Smitty.

"Deal then. You let me know if you find anything or if there's anyone in particular you want to approach. We can either do that together, or I can maybe give you some pointers on how to get information if you need them."

I was so glad he tacked that on to the end because I knew how to get information out of people. Heck, most people just talked to me at random about all manner of things. I often joked I must have had a sign on my forehead inviting people to tell me their life stories and deepest secrets, but it wasn't a sign I'd ever seen.

"Deal, and if you can share with me anything that you find so we can add it to the pile of info, I'd appreciate it. That way we're not doing double work and narrowing down the suspects with everything pooled in one spot. I think that will work best."

"Agreed." But he said it roughly and kind of squinted at me. Why did I have a feeling we hadn't really agreed to anything?

CHAPTER NINE

Dani and I sat for a little while, taking turns playing different trios of music on the jukebox as we talked about any menu changes for the weekend, and if there was anything else we'd like to implement now that we'd passed the six-month mark and were still standing. She'd decided to stay since Eliot had left for work. Apparently, she didn't have anyone to talk to or chat up or see. Go figure.

I glanced at the big vintage Cadillac clock above her head and realized that I had to get moving. My cat was waiting for me at home.

"I'd better go. You want to grab something for dinner? You know I'm always up for take-out."

Dani flapped her hands at me. "Go, go, and no I don't want to get dinner. I have a feeling I'm going to want something like ramen tonight, all by myself. My mom called earlier, and I just need to decompress and have a movie and chill night alone."

"I'll have my phone if you need me."

"Of course you will." She smiled and gave me a hug. "Go do dinner and don't let this overwhelm you. I was totally kidding earlier about the amateur sleuth gig, but we have a lot going on here. I can't give you a pass to skip out for the next week or so while you hunt down a killer with Mr. Dreamy making eyes at you."

"He was not making eyes at me!"

"Oh, my dear, Jax, he most certainly was." And with that, she picked up her things and headed back out the front door just as Timothy made one more pass by the front window.

He looked at her and then looked in at me. I waved and smiled, but he did not return the gesture. Maybe things weren't going well at the train depot.

I didn't have time to think more about that since my phone rang. With an unidentified number. I wasn't usually worried about answering that kind of call since it was almost always a robocall, and I could just hang up, but this one felt different for some reason. Maybe just because so many things were going on, and I felt unsettled.

I answered anyway. "Hello?"

"Don't dismiss anyone in this whole thing. There's more going on than you will want to believe, but you're going to have to believe it anyway. You've got this, Super Sleuther. I told people to come to the diner if they have any information. Just make sure you don't mistake the salt for the sugar." And then the person hung up without another word.

I sat in the booth for a full minute while "Nothing but a Hound Dog" played out of the jukebox. What did it mean and who had that been? I hadn't been able to get a feel for anything such as an accent or a region or even an age before they'd hung up. Not that I was an expert on that kind of stuff, but with how many people I talked to on a daily basis, I'd gotten pretty good at recognizing differences in voices and dialects. I'd heard nothing out of place. The voice itself had also sounded neutral, as far as if it was a man or woman. It hadn't been a threat but had sounded like a kind warning and help, even though I hadn't asked for it and had no idea who was trying to be the helper.

So now what? There was a lot to unpack in that brief call. I couldn't call it an exchange—I hadn't been able to get a word in except a greeting. And since the number was unavailable, I had no idea how to trace the call.

Talk about frustrating.

But also, and this time I was not lying at all, very intriguing. Very intriguing.

Glancing at the clock again, I realized Eliot had probably already clocked in at work, and I didn't want to irritate Hildy by calling his cell while he was creating some hundred-dollar delicacy.

I would save it for later, maybe even tomorrow since he was working tonight and wouldn't probably get home until sometime after midnight. I had to be up at five because I was opening, and I wasn't invested enough to want to stay up way past my bedtime.

Grabbing my keys and making sure the jukebox had run out of quarters, I locked the front door and then headed out the back to my car.

I'd go home, have a few minutes to myself with my cat,

Stella Luna, and then decide what to do for dinner by myself. I wished that Dani would have been willing to come along as I would have appreciated a distraction this evening. I had a feeling my mother was going to be calling now that I was helping my dad, and I wanted a reason not to take her call.

I still hadn't told them about the true damage from the break-up, and I wasn't talking about my heart. That hadn't been nearly as bad as I thought it would be. But they would definitely want to know that I had no money, and I was definitely not telling them. Call it pride, call it embarrassment, but I was going to guard that secret until my dying day if possible.

I sighed as I locked the back door of my dream and headed toward my car. Our trash bin was not hidden in any kind of enclosure like Hildy's. We were far more basic than that. But I still averted my eyes, just in case, because I couldn't seem to look at a green oversized bin without immediately remembering seeing Roderick with his eyes staring but no life in them.

What had happened to him? I, of course, knew that it appeared he'd been strangled, but had he been lured out to the garbage enclosure? Hildy had sent him out there to wait for me, but there was no way he would have thought he should wait next to the huge trash receptacle, where I wouldn't be able to see him. So how did he get in there? Had he been running from Delilah, and she sent a goon after him to catch him before he got away?

I couldn't imagine she'd wanted him dead no matter what though. Unless looking for him and shouting it out in the restaurant had been a ruse and a way of solidifying an alibi when he was found dead.

I had to remember to put it on my chart that I was going to start making as soon as I got home.

Hopping in my car, I sped home now that I had a purpose, and with that phone call, a reason to make sure that I did not dismiss a single thing. Any and all of it could be important when put together correctly.

The drive home was a short one. I'd purposely chosen the townhouse to be close to the restaurant two years before the diner was even up for sale. I'd believed with all my heart that it would be mine someday, and I had so much stuff that I never wanted to move again so I'd bought right where I wanted to be for the rest of my life. Or at least for the next forty years or so.

I'd never invited Steven to move in because I hadn't been

sure that we were really going anywhere with the relationship.

But that didn't mean I had been able to completely get rid of all the things he'd left here over the months we'd been a couple. And Stella Luna was a huge fan of dragging them out as presents when I came home from work to show me she loved me.

I opened the front door of the duplex to find one of his socks at the bottom of the stairs, and Stella wrapped up in the other. Somehow, she'd managed to get her leg in the opening and was gnawing on her paw through the small sloths that adorned the thing.

"Silly girl. I need to get rid of all this." I leaned down to grab the sock because I had to be fast and committed when dealing with Stella Luna, but she was still faster and took off with the sock into the kitchen. I heard a crash and figured she'd probably slid across the linoleum floor and into her water bowl as she typically did.

Sure enough, she looked offended and baffled at the same time when I entered the room behind her. The mask on her Siamese face was crinkled up on the sides, and her eyes were slitted. She hissed at the water bowl as if telling it off, then picked up the sock, and sauntered away to rest under the small dinette table where she knew I would not try to get her.

Let her keep the sloth sock. I'd get rid of it later and all the other things Steven had left behind I hadn't had the *oomph* to get rid of. I only wished that he'd left anything worth selling. I'd probably get more for that avocado picture than any of the stupid things he'd left behind, like a sloth sock.

Instead, I sat at the table and grabbed a notepad from the small bookshelf I'd installed in the window seat that made up the seating for the fourth side of the table. The case also held many of my favorite books and a few trinkets that Dani used to send me when she was out traveling the world, and I was here trying to get my life into some semblance of order.

I hadn't quite reached that pinnacle yet, but I was working on it. Or I would work on it more once I replenished my bank account.

I sighed and flipped open the notepad then grabbed a pen from a mason jar on the table. I didn't ever eat here, so it was more like a catch-all than an actual dining table.

I took out Jasper's list and raided the bottom of the jar for a paperclip to attach it to the inside of the cover. Reaching into my jacket pocket, I also removed the stack of tickets that had information on them from gossip around the diner today. I hadn't seen anything that would lead to any kind of real clue, but they deserved a second look. Or maybe a third or fourth as I fanned them out over the surface of the oak table and then just sank my head into my upturned hands.

"What do I think I'm doing?"

Stella Luna meowed to show she was listening, but she didn't have any answers either.

My phone rang again. It almost never rang because so few people actually called me, and I wasn't a fan of talking on the phone anyway. Text was always easier as long as I remembered to check and actually answer it instead of thinking of the answer in my head, truly believing I had typed it in, and then coming to realize a few days later that I didn't really do that last part.

Another unavailable number. At this point, I might as well just open up a phone bank and call it the tip line.

"Look, this time I'm asking for a name before I listen to whatever information you think you have that I need to know but won't actually tell, just be cryptic, so I have no idea what to do with it."

"Hello to you too." And there was that deep bass that felt like it reverberated through my soul. No, no, no. That was not allowed. He was just helping me with something he was good at and only because Hildy had insisted, and most people did not take Hildy's insistence lightly.

I sighed because of course it was Eliot. When would I not make a fool of myself in front of him? I wasn't going to hold my breath waiting for that faraway moment.

"Sorry about that. I got a call earlier about sugar and salt and everything not so nice, and I didn't get a name or anything else. I was going to call you, but I thought you'd be elbow deep in marinara sauce."

He laughed, thankfully, and I could get over my faux pas of answering the phone like a jerk.

"Technically I should be, but I'm training someone new tonight, and we're taking a break so she can get her bearings."

Another new hire? Was Hildy losing people or gaining business? I'd have to ask her when I had a moment to think about anything but the crises I seemed to be wrapped up in at the moment.

"So, you're just calling to say hi on your break?"

"Well, yes, but no."

"Okay."

"There was a man in here this afternoon that Hildy said was nosing around, asking how big her restaurant is, and whether it's for sale."

I heard the din of kitchen work in the background and people yelling back and forth over something or other.

"You know what? I'm going to go out back. Give me a second to get there because I can't talk with all this racket."

I waited about five seconds, and suddenly it was quiet. "Are you out back, as in near where Roderick was found?"

"Yes, they took the crime scene tape down, and I see that the garbage has been removed. I wonder if they took it all. It doesn't usually get picked up until tomorrow." I heard a clang and assumed he was opening the door to the enclosure.

I would probably never forget that sound, as it had been followed closely by me tripping and finding Roderick then being shoved and scared out of my wits by a raccoon. Or had it been the raccoon? I might never know…

"So, this guy, did Hildy know him? She couldn't have, or he would have never asked." I answered my own question.

"Yeah, that was the impression I got too. She was not happy at all and pretty much kicked the guy out without answering any of his questions. He looked pissed when she slammed the front door in his face."

See, there was a good reason then that the doors didn't creak. A creaking door shut in someone's face would be far less satisfying.

"So, some guy comes in randomly and wants to know if she just happens to be selling the restaurant that's been in her family for years? That seems strange. Do you think he was banking on her being ruined by a guy being killed at her establishment?" I didn't really think that would be a thing, but then again, you never knew. Stella Luna jumped into my lap with the sloth sock. I gently pried it out of her mouth while still trying to keep the phone up to my ear and balance on the chair with my cat trying to fight me hard for the sock. I let her have it, and she tumbled off my lap, landing on her feet and howling at me.

"What is that noise? Do you need to go outside too?" Eliot said.

"No, it's my cat, and she can be heard across half the town. Hold please." I put the phone down and stalked after the feline until I caught her—or rather she let me catch her, because Stella Luna never went to anyone unless she was willing, ready, and so inclined.

I gently swept her off the floor, kissed her on the nose, and tickled her under the chin. She started purring and dropped the sock, so I took it and sat on it while stroking her back. She continued to purr and show affection even when I picked up the phone and checked to see if Eliot was still there.

"How long do you have for your break?" I asked.

"Well, I almost never take one, so I'm not entirely sure, but I do have to get back in there and teach kitchen skills to someone who I am having some doubts even knows how to boil water. Why, what do you need?"

In all honesty, what I really needed was for him to keep talking. I'd listen to him recite a grocery list if I could right now.

Stella Luna started clawing at my leg like she was kneading bread, and I squeaked.

"Everything okay over there?"

"Yep, just fine and dandy. Trying to get my cat to retract her claws from my leg, that's all. Nothing to see here."

"No, but it definitely sounds painful. Have you tried grabbing her tail to distract her?"

"That's not going to work. You must be a dog owner."

"Well, I do have Sullivan at home, and she thinks it's a game when I do that. Just trying to help."

"No problem. I'll tell you what, though. Let's reconvene in the morning after I see what the diners have to say. I'm tired as anything, and I'm sure you need to go show the new hire the difference between a measuring spoon and a measuring cup. I'll leave you to it."

"Okay, have a good night."

"Yeah, you too, and try not to find any more dead bodies out there."

"It's not me, it's you that we have to worry about. I'm just the innocent bystander who apparently has to help figure things out."

Well, if he was willing to do that, I wondered if he was any good at finding missing money.

CHAPTER TEN

The next morning dawned way too early. I had to roll out of bed and make sure Stella Luna had her food before I headed out the door to open the diner, so people could come in for all their favorites.

I met Terri at the back door with her coat on and gloves.

"Are we expecting a cold snap today?" I asked, looking at the sky that didn't appear to have a cloud in sight.

"No, but my heater's broken at home. We've been trying to keep warm as best we can until I can get someone to help me figure out what's going on."

Oh, I did not like that. No one should be without heat. I wanted so badly to offer to pay for it. Tell her she could just pay me back. But I'd be in the same boat right now if something went wrong at my house.

"I'm so sorry. Maybe you can take it out on the bell today when you're letting people know their orders are up. If you want to ding it with wild abandon, I'll turn a deaf ear and just smile at anyone who is giving you the side eye."

That got a little chuckle, and I smiled. "If you want any extra hours I can clear it with Dani, no problem. If we had the extra money, we'd just loan it to you, but we don't. I'm sorry."

"No, that's okay. I wasn't going to say anything about it, and I certainly wasn't expecting you to pay for anything. We have savings, so it's more about getting an appointment than anything. The guy who usually helps is doing all these home inspections. He gets paid far more for that, which means I'm low on the list. Plus, he's my brother, so I kind of expect to be moved down for people who aren't paying him in pancakes and home fries."

If only I could pay people in home fries and pancakes.

"As long as you're sure…" Terri had no kids at home, and she lived with her boyfriend, so they were probably fine, just snuggled up under the covers and using that as a really good excuse to not get out of bed. But I wanted to put it out there just in case.

"Seriously, it's fine. I wouldn't have mentioned it if you hadn't asked. And this isn't exactly a cold snap. It's really not that bad, but Bob wouldn't let me out of the house without my coat on and my gloves. I should have taken them off in the car, but I didn't take the time."

"It is a little chilly, so it's not that you look weird or anything. I'm just used to you sweating behind the grill."

Another chuckle and that seemed to break her worry.

"I'm probably going to take you up on that offer to ring the bell with abandon, though. If you're going to make me do it, then I'm going all out." Her cheeky smile made my heart feel better about what we were doing here. She'd been a cook here when I'd been a teenager, and I'd been so happy to find that she was willing to leave her job at a different greasy spoon to come work for us. I didn't think it would have been the same without her.

"We're good, then? You'll ring the bell, and I'll keep Dani from taking it away?"

"Is that a possibility? Because I'll ring that thing all day long if you'll take it away eventually. Don't test me…"

"Is it really that bad?" I didn't want to ask because I was afraid she'd give me an honest answer I couldn't ignore, but I had to.

She blew out a breath as she removed the hat and gloves, a scarf that was tucked under her jacket, the jacket, and a hoodie under that.

"Wow."

"Yeah, Bob has lived here for twenty years now, and he still doesn't have thick blood. He thinks fifty degrees is cold enough for fleece-lined mittens."

I snickered.

"And to answer your question, no. The bell is not that bad, but everything else is perfect, so I have to be able to complain about something, right?"

I would not cry. I refused to.

"Of course, you may also complain with abandon, though I might not be able to save you from getting the side eye."

"I don't expect you to save me from everything, Jax, though I do appreciate you saving me from my last job."

With that she hung her coat up and got down to the business of prepping for what I hoped would be hordes of people coming in for their coffee fix and breakfast needs.

Others started filtering in. Jennifer came bustling through the back door then Wren and Marty. They got their things tucked away in the lockers in the back room, put on their aprons, and set the tables as the first customers started lining up out front.

We had five minutes until we officially opened. And as much as I wanted to unlock the door and let them all in, Dani and I had agreed we would never do that because once it started there was no way to undo it. I'd rather be timely than open early and have people be angry when we did just open on time.

I avoided looking at the front door but kept my eye on the Cadillac clock while I made sure the sugar canisters were full on each table, which brought up the call from last night. Was I reading my own meaning into it when the person said to not mistake the sugar for the salt? I automatically assumed it would be in reference to my mistake all those years ago, but was it really just a dig about my past transgressions, or did it have a different meaning? Was it someone who had been around for the actual mistake, or had they only heard about it around town? Or were they being more general and saying that both sugar and salt were the same color but had very different tastes, so I shouldn't think someone was being sugary to me when, in fact, they were most definitely being salty?

The clock flipped to six, and someone knocked on the glass out front. My bet was on Curtis from the train station where Timothy worked. The man liked his coffee first thing in the morning. Glancing over at the coffee station, I made sure the orange-rimmed carafes and the red ones were brewed to full capacity and nodded at Becca, who already had his cup out and waiting at the counter.

I smiled as I wiped my hands on the front of my apron, even though they weren't wet or dirty. It was another day here at Sunny Side Up Diner, and we would make a killing if the crowd outside was anything to go by. Metaphorically speaking, of course, as we most certainly did not need another dead body in town until long after this murder was solved.

Five hours later, I was as done as the toast I'd managed to burn an hour ago. I hadn't been paying attention and had put it down a second time not realizing that it had just popped up. Man, sometimes I wondered why I even tried. I'd gotten ribbed of course by the three men sitting at the counter, enjoying their eggs and grits and toast that they said was done to perfection because Becca had made it and thankfully not me.

Dani came strolling out of the back, tying her apron on. We'd gone with aprons that just sat on the hips and had two pockets on the front, one emblazoned with our logo, and one with the name of the diner on a black background. It provided an eye-popping contrast with the yellow and red and teal that we'd chosen to use for a sun and the wording.

"Save me." I mouthed the words, and she nodded before standing in front of the men who were still heckling me, and asking if they needed anything else, before she took their plates since they were jabbering instead of eating.

Casey Fontaine actually crossed his hands over his plate like Dani would actually take it. Derek and Edgar laughed at him, transferring their ribbing from me to him. Thank goodness for that.

I took the opportunity to duck out of the way, leaving Becca at the toast maker and taking my apron off as I swept through the door to the breakroom. I hadn't had a chance to sit since we'd opened this morning. I'd asked for a crowd, and I'd gotten one, along with a bunch of tickets with snippets of conversations and possible leads. I wasn't sure that any of them would actually go anywhere, but I appreciated all our employees for keeping up with information. And also, for taking me seriously when I asked that they not put it on the spindle with the spike through a word that might be important. I'd deal with it all later. I just needed a breather for a second. And maybe a moment to think about the delicious Eliot who was helping me—or would help me more eventually.

Speak of the devil and he might just appear. Unfortunately not in the flesh, but in the way of texting me a reminder to count the lanyards. I had forgotten in all the hullabaloo that had happened. I texted back that I'd do it this afternoon.

Opening the back door, I let the breeze of this September late morning brush across my face. There wasn't much to see out the back door except the few parking spaces up against the building and the alleyway. I liked it like that. I didn't want to interact with anyone at the moment, just breathe before heading back in to help out anywhere but buttering toast.

My car looked comfy when I glanced over at it as I took in the scenery. I could recline the front seat and rest my eyes just for a moment.

Something fluttered on the windshield, and my heart

Dines, Drive-Ins, and Lies | 79

stopped. It could be a flyer for someone's kitchenware party. It could be a coupon for ice cream as our one ice cream parlor was trying out staying open all year this year. It could be anything, but I didn't see any flyers on anyone else's car. And very few people would waste advertising or time walking along the back alley of a diner, a thrift store, a smoke shop, and a hair salon. They'd have better luck walking the sidewalk out front and placing things on the windshields of people who were in those establishments already buying stuff.

I found myself afraid to approach my car but also very interested in whatever it might be.

Perhaps a clue, maybe a ticket, though I hadn't gotten one of those in years. There were a few benefits to having your dad on the police force.

I didn't want to look, and yet I really, really did. I had about two seconds to make up my mind before Dani would come out to see why I wasn't helping when the place was so busy.

I darted off the stoop, grabbed the paper, then quickly ran back into the restaurant, and slammed the door behind me.

I wasn't sure why I rushed unless I thought someone would be waiting out there for me to get the paper and use the opportunity to clobber me in the head or something equally nefarious. But since nothing had happened, I told myself to calm the heck down.

Grabbing it was over, and I'd made it through alive. I could either shove it in my pocket and deal with it later, or I could look at it now knowing I couldn't do anything about it for the next three hours. My choice.

Yeah, I opened it right then.

It was a phone number and the name Karen. A joke? Or her name was Karen for real? Who could it be? I didn't recognize the number, but that didn't really mean anything because I didn't always recognize my own number. I relied on my cell phone to tell me who I was calling, by name not number.

"I need you out here, Jax. Break is over."

I shoved the paper in my pocket, hoping Dani hadn't seen it. I knew she had been joking yesterday about me already having a job, but sometimes when Dani joked there was almost always a kernel of truth in there. I didn't want her to feel like I wasn't doing my part.

"Love letter from Eliot?" She leaned against the door and smirked at me.

"Ha and no. Just a note to myself for something I have to remember to do when I get home." I picked up a rag and prepared to do battle with cleaning tables. "No slowdown yet? I really thought we'd at least have the lull like we did yesterday."

"Nope, and I heard from the staff that it's busier than yesterday. Has there been a line all day? I heard someone say no one has left to get breakfast or even coffee elsewhere."

"Huh." Not that I wasn't thankful, but it was pretty well-known that if your favorite place was crowded, there was no shame in going down the street to another diner and getting your fix. I'd done it myself. And as much as I would love to serve everyone in town every morning, there just was no way we could do that, even if we were a relatively small town.

"Is there a lot of talk still?"

"You'd know that if you'd been out filling coffee instead of trying to make toast. I thought we discussed you not being on toast?"

"Yeah, I was trying to look busy because Ryan and Lon from the farm supply place were talking about some property that might be up for sale now that Roderick was dead. I guess I wasn't paying attention, and I hit the toast button again instead of grabbing it out and putting new bread in."

She rolled her eyes at me and then laughed. "Are you like this at home, or do you just reserve it for us? I don't remember you ever being so absent-minded."

"Maybe it's older age." Of course, we were both only just now twenty-seven, so I'd never say that out in the dining room since most people were over sixty and would not take kindly to my joke.

"Nice one with the older and not old." She tucked her hands into her pockets, and her shoulders rose toward her ears. Well, crap, here it came. I braced myself.

"Look, I know you want to help your dad, and I get that finding the dead Roderick was probably traumatizing, but do you really think you should have your hand in this? Or even your nose?" She bit her lip. "I was kidding yesterday about already having a job, but you really do already have more than enough to do. I'm just concerned that all your questions at dinner had more to do with you doubting what we've done instead of truly doubting that I'm all in, like I have been since we first worked here."

Holy cow, that line of thought needed to be nipped, and right now, like cracking an egg with one downward smack. "No, and I do mean no way would I want to be anywhere but here and with anyone but you."

Her sigh could've blown over a forest. "Okay."

"Oh, Dani, I'm so sorry! I didn't mean to make you doubt us and the diner."

"No, no, it's okay. Just getting some flak from my mother, and with your questions on top, it sent me into a small panic. And you know I'm much better at asking than guessing."

"Understood. And please put it out of your mind because I'm not doubting us at all. Promise."

"Winkie swear?"

It was something we'd done when we were little kids, liking the pinky thing but having to make it our own with winks instead of hooking our pinkies together like normal people did.

I winked at her. "Swear with the winkiest."

She winked back. "Okay, phew! I feel better now. And I think I might have something for you, but I'm not sure exactly what it means."

"Whatever it is, I'll put it on the board, and we'll let someone else figure it all out. Of course, I want to help my dad, and it was not awesome finding Roderick like that, but I also think somehow someone is trying to involve me, or us, in this whole thing. I just can't let that happen without fighting back. You understand, right?"

"Actually, yes I do, and I'd expect nothing less from you." She took her order pad out of her apron. Ripping a ticket off from the bottom of the pad, she handed it to me. "Doris and Arthur were in, and they were talking about how Hildy and Roderick used to 'run together' as they put it. Doris thinks you should ask Hildy about what they did when they were young and their parents were hanging out together."

Not a bad idea, but I had a feeling Hildy would have to be handled with kid gloves if she hadn't already offered whatever information I was going to be asking for.

Time to talk to Eliot again—not that that was a hardship.

CHAPTER ELEVEN

I left Dani to do the rest of the cleanup since that was the schedule we'd put together when we'd bought the diner. I'd been there for most of the day already, and the end of the shift was all about cleaning and setting up for tomorrow. Really, I wanted to go home and go to bed, maybe snuggle with Stella Luna, but that was not to be.

I turned the order ticket over and over in my hand, not sure how I wanted to tackle this. While I'd thought I should talk to Eliot, he would be in a harder position than I would be. Hildy was my godmother, but she was his boss. If she didn't like the question, there wasn't much she could do to me but a bunch of things she could do to Eliot.

I'd just put out some feelers with her first before I brought Eliot in.

Approaching my car in the back of the diner, I was reminded that I also had that number for Karen in my pocket.

Whoever Karen was and whatever she wanted would have to wait because there was a lanyard from our diner stuck on the windshield under the windshield wiper.

Where were they coming from and who had them? Eliot's text from earlier about counting the lanyards resurfaced, and I vowed to check how many I had in the box I'd picked up from the printer. At least then I would know how many others I should expect to come back to me on my car, or near my house, or in other strange places.

It was unsettling. I looked around quickly as if I might see someone hiding behind a car waiting to see my reaction when I found it.

I didn't see anyone, which was both a relief and a disappointment, but I chose to focus more on the relief. I took a quick picture of it with my phone and then grabbed it out from under the windshield wiper. Getting into my car, I put the thing on my seat and then started the car, not knowing exactly where I wanted to go first. I probably should run it right over to my dad to see if they could check for fingerprints. I took another picture of it to keep just in case, and then I headed to the station. After dropping it off, my dad asked me if I'd counted them yet, and I had to say no. Vowing that I'd do it as soon as I could, I headed back toward my house.

Should I call this mysterious Karen to get an idea of what she thought I might need to know? Or should I head for Hildy first and see what she had to say for herself? If Karen's information was similar then I'd have a base to jump off from.

This sleuthing stuff was not for the faint at heart.

In the end, I chose to go to Hildy first. It was after lunchtime but before the big dinner rush at the restaurant. She might be more available while also not so deep into the night shift that she didn't want to talk about anything, much less a dead guy who she might have been involved with long ago.

The drive out to the inn was lovely on this fall day. Pine trees and oak branches swayed in the light breeze that Mother Nature provided. I rolled my windows down to air out the car and my brain. There was so much going on, and it felt like it was piling up faster than I could deal with it.

The main underlying issue was of course the lying part. I had to figure out when and how to tell Dani that financially I was not exactly solvent without having her freak out. Because she would freak out, and I'd bet my last five dollars in my savings on that. And she would have every right. When we'd first signed the papers for the diner, we were flush with all the money we'd both saved over the years hoping for this opportunity. We had sunk a bunch of money into changing the name then getting the restaurant itself remodeled and back to its former glory. Most of it had only been covered over by the vegetable lover, so it wasn't like we'd had to build any new walls or rearrange the kitchen, fortunately. But even removal of walls of live moss and the perpetual fountain the previous owner had put in wasn't exactly just taking it off and moving on.

Then we'd had to buy all the permits, open the bank account, and get a loan to make sure we had the kitchen stocked to the brim for the first few weeks. That hadn't gone as well as we'd projected since fixing it up had taken longer than I had anticipated, so we then had food on the shelves but no one to make it for.

But that was behind us now, and we were running full

throttle. I was so thankful people were coming in, even if it was just to catch up on the newest gossip regarding the death of a man in town, who might not have been a favorite of all, but definitely was favored by many.

And now I had to go see how much Hildy had favored him and if that had changed in the intervening years.

A thought popped into my head, and I shook it out before it could grab hold. Hildy was the killer. What if she'd been the one to kill Roderick for some transgressions? And then she tried to pin it on me with the lanyard because she'd figured no one would actually believe I was the culprit, and my dad would fight tooth and nail to make sure I was never even brought in as a suspect, much less convicted.

That was a bizarre idea, and I would not share it with anyone. I'd known Hildy all my life, and I knew without a shadow of a single doubt that there was no way she'd ever do that.

Thankfully, I came to that conclusion just as I was rolling into the nearly empty parking lot at the front of the inn. All the staff parked at the side, but out here it was fairly deserted. The last thing I'd want to do was go in looking suspicious of her before I'd even asked the first question.

I made absolutely certain my car was locked, hitting the lock button on my key fob three times before deciding I'd done all I could, and walked away.

The restaurant was as lovely in the daylight as it was in the evening. The stonework on the front complemented the dark wood doors that were banded with metal like a castle's doors. I always thought it should have a moat, but Hildy just laughed and called me silly. I would have put a moat in if I'd owned the place, but that was apparently just me.

Pulling the door toward me, I struggled for a moment before finally getting it to open. No noise greeted me when I entered and no hostess either. In fact, there was no one in the vestibule at all, and that was very weird. I considered calling out but thought better of it. I didn't want to disturb any of the patrons who were probably enjoying a more intimate late lunch, and they didn't want someone coming through the dining room yelling for Hildy while they sipped at their lobster bisque.

I stayed to the corners as I made my way back to the kitchen. No use in getting anyone riled up, or wondering what I was doing, or wanting to talk when I had a mission.

Gently pressing against the door, I listened for anyone coming around the corner or hustling by so I didn't accidentally knock a person over.

It sounded all clear, so I edged in and then just stood for a second. Whereas the din out in the main rooms had been low, it was high hustle back here. Sous chefs were chopping and chatting, waitstaff made side salads, and loaded up the enormous trays to carry out the door with plates balanced perfectly to be able to deliver the meal with little to no fuss. Dishwashers were chatting with each other as they pushed and pulled the used dinnerware through the steaming contraption that would clean in minutes what you'd cry over if it was in your own sink at home.

We had a similar vibe at the diner but not on this scale. Hildy had wanted me to work here after college, and while at first it had been tempting to consider, I had been sure that I wanted smaller, more intimate, but more fun in my kitchen. Terri might hate having to call out the numbers and ding the bell, but that casual flow and old timey feel was exactly what Dani and I had wanted for our establishment. This was a machine, a well-oiled one, but a really big machine.

And at the heart of it was Eliot.

The man was tall and big and yet so graceful as he moved from pot to pot, stirring and tasting and shaking his way down the line to make sure that all the entrees were moving in the right direction. He was a sight to behold, and if I didn't look away soon, I might start drooling.

Part of me wanted to think that was because the smells back here were rich with gravies and spices and herbs we didn't use. But the other part had to admit that it really was the man I was looking at and salivating over.

He glanced up just as I was going to look away, and a smile bloomed on his face that I hadn't expected. A little bit secret, a little bit saucy, a whole lot of charm. Whew, boy. Down, girl.

I smiled back and could feel the blush working up from my neck. Dang it!

Finally, I looked away and tried to pretend I was looking for Hildy, not trying to steal one more glance at him in his chef's jacket.

I heard a low chuckle and refused to look over to see if it was coming from him.

I stopped Maryann at the salad bar. "Do you know if Hildy's

in her office?" I asked, ignoring the way I could feel Eliot's gaze on my back.

"She's not in yet. Said she had something she had to do over at her place, and she'd be late. Do you need something? You could probably call her."

"Um, no, that's okay. I'll check in with her later." I headed right for the door again, bypassing Tobias at the sink and almost smacking Carlos in the tray as he came back from delivering food.

"Oops, sorry!"

"Hey, no worries there, pretty lady. It's always good to see you, and at least the tray kept me from getting slammed." He smiled too, but it most definitely did not have the same effect as someone who was still standing behind the stove.

"Thanks, see you around."

"I hope they find out who did that to Roderick. He was one of my mom's favorite people, and she was devastated when she heard."

Now what was this? Should I stay and ask? The question was on the top of my mind when Eliot let Carlos know his next order was ready to go out the door.

I glanced up one more time to find Eliot staring at me, so I flipped him a wave and didn't wait for him to return the gesture before bustling out the door and walking straight for the parking lot. I had nothing to offer anyone and yet no need to hide this time.

I'd find Hildy later. I wasn't going to interrupt whatever it was she was doing with my questions, without having some more information, and I knew just where to get that.

"Do we know anyone named Karen?" I asked my mom as I walked into the house I'd grown up in. So many wonderful memories here, and I loved being able to still make new ones. She and my dad had talked about selling the house years ago when I'd moved out into the dorm at college and decided against it. Since I was their only child and they didn't need the space anymore, it was a long conversation, but my dad had nixed the idea, wanting a home base that I always knew would be there, unlike when he was growing up.

I plopped myself into a chair at the kitchen table because that was always where my mother was. I didn't come by my delight in food and food preparation in a vacuum. While my dad was a cop, my mom, the nurse, had always been the homemaker, and she loved that.

Sarah Tapman had stood in this kitchen for over three

decades now. I had been a later in life baby after years of trying, but she'd made things for church bazaars and bake sales long before she had been dragooned into making snacks for my class for birthdays and Valentine's Day. And no, I did not sneak a second cupcake long ago so I could have more than anyone else. It was just the cards.

She turned away from the sink and dried her hands on her apron. She had a whole closet of them down here in the pantry, and it had become a Mother's Day custom to buy her a new one every year, and each year it was more outrageous than the last one. Today's apron had the word "What?!?!" on it with a black cat holding a bloody knife. It was also bright orange. Bless her for still wearing the thing I'd bought when I was in junior high school. It went very well with her silver and dark brown hair and always brought a sparkle to her light blue eyes.

"Karen?" She paused for a moment, looking up at the ceiling fan. "I mean, yes, of course we know some Karens. It would be hard not to since it's a common name, but I have a feeling you're asking for a different reason."

"Yeah, I got this paper with the name Karen and a number, and I'm thinking she wants me to call her, but I don't know who it might be."

"Some random person named Karen left you her phone number, but you don't know who it is, and she just wants you to call her? Does that happen often?"

"Not before Roderick was murdered, and people seem to think that I'm going to be the one looking into it?"

She shot her eyebrow up at me, and I knew what was coming next. "But aren't you the one who volunteered for that? To help your dad?"

"Well, yeah, sort of. But this is just weird now. I also keep getting my own lanyards popping up in random places like on my car. I don't know how they're getting them, and I have no idea who actually killed Roderick. It seems like it could be almost anyone."

Since Hildy and my mom were best friends and had been for almost their whole lives, I was not going to bring up that it could be something Hildy had done. It made me feel squicky to even think it, much less say it out loud. However, Mom would know all about how Roderick and Hildy had fit together years ago, and that way I wouldn't have to ask Hildy herself. Brilliance was my middle name. Not really since it was Barbara, but you get the drift.

"I do have a question beyond the Karen thing."

Mom pulled up a stool to the breakfast bar, the place where so many chats had happened throughout the years. This kitchen really was the center of the family, and it had always been that way.

"Okay."

"Someone told Dani today that we should look into Hildy and Roderick's past, and someone else told me that I should not mistake the sugar for the salt."

"People aren't still talking about the sugar and salt thing, are they? It's been so many years. It was a simple mix up, and it's not like anyone was poisoned. They need to let it go."

"Yeah, well, I don't think that's ever going to actually happen, but this felt more like a message. As if the person was saying if I hear sugary things, I shouldn't assume they're actually true but that it might instead be salty."

"Hmmm, I could see that. Do you remember exactly what was said?"

"That's as much as I could remember. She or he talked as soon as I answered the phone then hung up before I could say anything."

"Okay, so I can see why that would sound as if they were warning you instead of making fun of you. So, keep your ears open and your mind wide open. Don't believe everything you hear."

"Okay that makes sense, but about Hildy and Roderick. What were they to each other?"

"That one's a little harder to answer, sweetie. Hildy and Roderick kind of dated because their families had expected them to be together someday. But I never could stand that man, and I hated the idea of Hildy's whole future being tied up with a shyster like that. I told her, and she and I had a fight. We didn't speak for the three months they were together, and getting back on even ground with our friendship took time."

"How have I never heard of this rift?" And why did it seem like everything I thought I knew might not in fact be true, just with that one hiccup?

"It's not something we talk about much. It happened years and years ago. He was trying to talk her into starting some kind of business that seemed shady to me even when we were teenagers. But Hildy and her parents were fighting, and she didn't think she wanted to run a restaurant because she had dreams of being a fashion designer. He was giving her the possibility of a way out."

"A fashion designer? She would have been all 80s."

"Probably more 70s since even then she liked the last trends instead of the current ones, but yes. She had a college picked out and everything, but then something happened between them. I found her bawling her eyes out in the football stadium."

"Did she tell you what it was about?" I almost hated to ask since Mom hadn't volunteered the info, but if I was going to solve this and figure out what Dani's clue meant then I had to.

"I asked several times, but she wouldn't tell me. The last time, she snapped that it was none of my business. If she'd wanted me to know she would have said long before now. That was about twenty years ago, and it's never come up again."

Well, that was not good for my clue hunting. I did not want to ask Hildy to mentally relive something she wouldn't even tell her best friend about. Something that had made her change the whole course of her life.

Fashion designer? She had soared at what she'd ended up choosing, but did it make her happy? That was definitely a possibility for how to get into the conversation, especially if I started with sharing that I was nearly destitute until the diner was full on paying for itself. But did I want to go there when I wasn't telling my parents? Some more consideration was needed, and it didn't have to be done right now.

Instead, I sat with my mom and let her tell me about all the things that were going on with the garden club, and once I had the side room finished, she'd like to rent it for the monthly meetings. When I tried to tell her she could use it with the family discount, she scoffed at me and told me there was no need to do that. And if I did then I might not be a good businesswoman in the long run. I definitely did not want to bring up the money thing after that. So, I kissed her on the cheek, leaned in for one more hug, and then left

So, what next? Did I want to call this Karen and find out what she thought she had to say to me? Did I want to go back to the inn and see if I could coerce Hildy into telling me about her previous relationship with Roderick? Whatever had happened must have smoothed out at some point since she had been willing to hide him away from a jealous lover instead of throwing him to her like a snack for the roaring she-lion that was Delilah.

Or had she? I was going to have to ask. If nothing else, maybe it would get this horrible thought out of my head that my own godmother had set me up to take the fall for something I hadn't done and never would do.

But someone who had been so hurt by the man even if it was almost thirty years ago? Well, sometimes revenge could definitely be served cold like a shrimp cocktail on ice.

CHAPTER TWELVE

After I pulled into the parking lot again at the Poplarsville Inn, I sat in my car fiddling with the steering wheel. I really did not want to do this. I was very bad at confrontation. I could do it if I had to and had in the past when it was necessary, but this wasn't my case since I had no cases. And it wasn't my responsibility, but it was important. And if I didn't settle it in my own mind, I was going to have to tell my dad I thought Hildy might have a motive.

That would not go over well at the next family dinner.

As if thinking of him conjured him up, my cell phone rang, and for the first time today, it actually had a caller name attached to the number.

"Dad, how's it going?"

"I was going to ask you the same thing. I heard you've got some kind of ticketing system, and you burned toast this morning. Janis Fuller wanted to know if that was a punishable offense."

"Mrs. Fuller needs to keep her thoughts to herself. It wasn't that bad. Definitely not arrest worthy."

"Horace stopped me on the street to say that someone should have sent out the fire department."

I scoffed. "Now that is ridiculous! It didn't set off any fire alarms, and it was not that bad. People need to mind their own business."

"Not that you've been."

"Oh, nice one. You asked me to help. And now I can't seem to turn a corner without someone leaving me a message or a note or one of my lanyards."

"I turned the one in that you got today. Any more ideas on how they're getting them? Did you count them? How many are missing?"

I should have thought he would ask that before I offered up the info. Actually, I should have gone straight home after he'd asked earlier and counted them right that second. Instead, I'd been jaunting around asking questions and trying to get new clues and not handling the ones I had right in front of me. He was not going to be happy.

Dang it.

"I..."

He groaned after I paused too long. "Jax, come on. You need to be on top of things if you want to help."

I hadn't actually wanted to help except that it involved me. But he was right. I should have spent some time counting the darn things.

"I'll do it when I get home. I moved them to the trunk, but I have a few things I need to do before I can get to them."

"Don't forget."

That tone of voice still got me, a little sharp, a little warning, a little exasperation. I was not a child, but in my adulthood, I tried not to take it personally. It did nothing good to snap at him. Instead, I mocked him because that always seemed to derail any other conversation regarding what I should be doing.

"Yes, oh, perfect father of mine. I will of course follow your advice to the fullest. So it shall be."

At least that got him to laugh.

"Smarty pants."

"The smartiest. Now I have to go. I had a couple of clue-type things that I'm going to run down and see if they bear any fruit. If they do, I'll let you know."

I hoped it was vague enough that if I ended up with nothing, he wouldn't be disappointed or upset.

"If you'd rather not help out, I will understand, Jax. I just want to put that out there again. We have a police force who does this for a living. I'm not expecting you to solve it. I just thought it might help you process it to be a part of figuring out who did the bad thing."

I rested my head against the back of the seat. "I get it, Dad, and I do appreciate the opportunity to be a part of finding out who used something that was supposed to be fun for such a horrible act. I'm still doing all my own stuff too, but it's just weird that all of a sudden these people are coming out of the woodwork to talk about Roderick and what a jerk he was. I guess I never really interacted with him too much. Or when we did interact, it was not for something he thought he could get me to do. I think I'm a little out of

Dines, Drive-Ins, and Lies | 95

his age range, or at least I hope so."

It was bad enough with the sheer list of men who might have been wronged. Most were upwards from the sixties range. I would have hated to add a list of all the husbands of the under forty crowd.

"I get it. People have probably held on to grudges for years and really just want the opportunity to vent now that he's gone. Maybe they're just not afraid anymore that it might come back to bite them later."

Should I mention Hildy? I had already said something to my mom, and most likely she'd mention it to my dad later, but at this point I thought it was probably best not to say anything until I had solid information or knew for sure that it was nothing.

"Well, I should go and see what's next. I have errands to do and a cat to see to."

"Give Stella Luna a treat from me. My grandkitty deserves all the treats." For a hardcore policeman, my dad was a total softy when it came to my cat. If he was at my house, I didn't exist, and she would curl up on him for hours if he'd let her.

"Will do. And I'll call if I hear anything."

"Okay, and maybe stay away from the toaster if you're trying to eavesdrop on conversations at the diner."

I groaned as he disconnected.

So, did I go in and try to talk to Hildy or just call Karen and leave Hildy for another day? I highly doubted the conversation would go any better on Wednesday than it would on a Tuesday, so I took a deep breath and got out of the car. Now or never. I'd prefer never, but now my curiosity was getting the better of me. I really wanted to know what had been so cataclysmic that Hildy had changed her entire life after one afternoon with Roderick but wouldn't tell anyone what happened.

This time when I came into the restaurant, it was bustling out in the dining room just as much as it probably was in the kitchen. The dinner hour was rushing up on us and that meant tables were full as well as the lobby.

I waited in line again, and this time I was at least paying attention when the people in front of me were done putting in their name. I moved up to the hostess podium.

"Hey there, stranger!" Emily Broderick stood in her formal black cocktail dress with her auburn hair up in a French twist. Hildy might have put everyone else into a pink tux shirt, bow tie, and cummerbund, but the hostesses were given leeway to dress more elegantly, as long as it wasn't too short, too revealing, or too difficult to walk in.

This dress was a stunner, even though I was pretty sure it wasn't something Emily, who played volleyball and bowled like a champ, wore outside of her job here at the Poplarsville Inn.

"Hey, yourself. How are things?"

"Hildy is in a bit of a mood with all the stuff happening. The cops were here three times today, and she had to find a work-around for taking the garbage out because no one wants to enter the place where Roderick was found. We're all avoiding her, but other than that, it's just a normal Tuesday."

That did not bode well for the talk I wanted to have with her, but I was here already. And I couldn't exactly say I wanted a table to have an early dinner when I doubted my credit card could handle even the cheapest thing on the menu.

Forging forward it was then.

"I'm actually here to see her about that if you don't mind checking if she's available."

Emily rolled her eyes. "You're taking your own life into your own hands, but I'll go check and see if she has a minute."

Part of me hoped Hildy would send me away through Emily or text me to let me know I'd need to come back another day. Neither of those things happened as Hildy came walking out of her office with a stride that said determination but also weariness. She could be terse when she wanted to be, but she was rarely mean. I was braced just in case.

"Come on back. I asked for this, I know I did, so here I am."

I did not want to make her feel worse, but I didn't know how to avoid it. Did she ask for it because she'd done it on her own property, thinking it would be easier to cover up with me here? I hated that I'd even thought of the comment and was determined to prove my possible theory wrong.

I had to.

"I won't take long, I promise. I just have a few questions." Lies, all of it lies, and she was not going to be happy when she realized how much of a lie it was.

"Whatever you need, the sooner we get this solved, the sooner I can hopefully go back to my normal life. The sheer amount of people who want to tell me how horrible Roderick was, and how he might have deserved this, and why they would have done it if this other suspect hadn't is grating on my nerves."

"You too?" I asked.

"What do you mean, me too? Do you mean, I would have offed him myself if I'd had the chance?"

That hadn't been my intent, but if she wanted to answer that question, I certainly wasn't going to stop her. So, I shrugged instead of answering outright.

"Ugh! Get in the office and we'll talk."

I shuffled in ahead of her, finding myself in the same place as two nights ago, but at least this time, I wasn't surrounded by my dad and Eliot and nervous after finding a dead body.

When she took her seat behind the desk, she shook her head then pulled out one of the drawers. If it was anyone else, I would probably have told myself to beware of something deadly coming out of the drawer. But Hildy was my godmother and aunt, and she'd never hurt me. Of course, if she proved me wrong then no one would have known. Well, except my dad would have moved hell and earth to find me if she'd said I had run away or something.

She popped two antacids, then ripped open a pack of gummy worms, and stuck one in her mouth.

"You have all that amazing food at your fingertips, including chocolate peanut butter pie that should be illegal, and you're eating gummy worms? One of the most processed and manufactured candies available in the world? They're like plastic mixed with sugar."

She shoved another one in her mouth, as if to prove she could do whatever she wanted, and chewed.

Then she held the bag out to me. And I took one because of course I did. One did not simply say no to gummy worms. "I loved when you used to make that dirt cake with chocolate pudding and Oreos and more crushed Oreos and then make it look like the worms were coming out of the dirt."

"Fine memories," she said, then closed her eyes, and leaned back in her office chair. "Has anyone ever told you how I got this restaurant?"

A leading question or a misleading question? I wasn't sure, but I supposed I was here for either if she wanted to share with me. I wished I had something to write this all down on, but I didn't. So I'd have to just remember it, though I wasn't always very good at that.

She opened her eyes and looked at me.

Right, I should have answered the question. "The story I was told involved you being a third-generation restaurant owner, and you loved it so much and wanted to run it so badly that when you were old enough it was given to you. Then you did even more amazing things than anyone had expected, and here we are today."

She gave me a skeptical look, but I shrugged. That was the story I'd always been told. Well, except for today, but even then, I hadn't really been told a story, just told that the one I had heard before might not be the complete story.

"Your mom has never said anything else?"

Oh, that one was trickier to answer though my mom hadn't actually said anything other than she didn't know what had happened to change Hildy's mind from fashion to food.

"It's not something we talk about often. Now, I am thinking I didn't have the right story? I've never asked again because I thought I'd been given the truth from the beginning." Oh, nice one. No real lie. But still not saying much of anything. I would have patted myself on the back, but I didn't want to give myself away.

She held me in her stare for another few seconds and then closed her eyes. With them still closed, she started talking. "There's a reason I would hide Roderick from anyone who was looking for him to yell at him. There's a reason I protected Roderick no matter the circumstances and never asked why I would have to do that."

"Okay." I didn't know what else to say, but I felt I was supposed to say something. And I didn't want to tell her she didn't have to finish because I wanted to know, murder investigation or not. Call me curious.

"Years and years ago, he saved me from making a terrible mistake and ruined a chance for himself at the same exact time. He stood up for me in a situation that could have gone horribly wrong. Because of that I decided to do what I was supposed to do instead of what I thought I wanted to do. And my life was so much better that way. I could never thank him enough for what he did, and so whenever he needed me to hide him or get him out a scrape, I'd do it, pretty much every time. It was nothing bad, usually just women he should have kept his hands to himself with, but they made choices too. However, if the husband came after Roderick, I would see if I could smooth things over with a conversation, sometimes over a meal they wouldn't turn down."

So, she'd bribed them with lobster to leave Roderick alone? I wasn't sure how I felt about that. Not too good, regardless. I just wasn't sure how much not too good, like basement level or a few steps from the first floor.

"I'm not sure what to say. I mean I get it but..." And this was the big one... "Why?"

She closed her eyes and squinched them together until the wrinkles around her eyes looked less like crow feet and more like fissures in the side of a rock that were moments from splitting into thousands of fragments.

"There was an issue when I was younger."

Ah, perhaps this was the big breakup and the crying at the empty football stadium. I waited for more of the story, but she didn't say anything else, and a tear leaked out of the corner of her right eye. I couldn't do this to her. There was no way she would have killed Roderick. Nothing he could have done recently that would force her to strangle him in the back of her own restaurant and blame it on me. For one thing, she had been in the dining room pretty much the whole time, and she had been the one to ask me to go find him. But she also asked Eliot, who didn't want to look into anything beyond where the most recent catch of halibut was from, to look into this. No way would she have used her charm to pull a former policeman into the hunt for a killer if it really had been her.

"I'm sorry. You don't have to tell me about it. I can see it's hurting you." I rose to see myself out.

"Please, sit. I have to tell someone. With his death, so many things seem to be coming back up, and maybe it's time to tell my side of the story."

Gah, I just didn't know if I wanted it to be me she told it to. What if she asked me not to say anything, and then my mom asked how my sleuthing had gone? That would be horrendous to choose between the two of them.

"Okay," I said because I couldn't just leave her here like this.

"It was when I was in high school."

So, it was going to be the story of the crying in the empty football stadium. Part of me hoped she'd keep her eyes closed, so she couldn't see if she said something I already knew from my mom.

She opened her eyes though and focused on me like a laser. "This doesn't go beyond this room. I'm sure you're checking in with your dad, and I also know someone has to think I might have been the one to do it. It's a little convenient that I sent you out back to find him and give him your keys, and yet you found him dead and with one of your own lanyards."

I tried hard not to let my face heat up or change in any way. Had everyone been told that it was my lanyard that strangled him? I wasn't sure, but I wasn't going to miss what she had to say. I assumed I'd done okay with my neutral facial expression when she continued.

"I was set to go to a fashion design school and had a patron who was interested in helping me get there. Since my parents were angry that I wasn't choosing to take over the restaurant like they'd thought I would from the time I was born, I had to make my own way."

Keep that face neutral, Jax! I hummed in my throat to show I'd heard her but didn't want to say anything yet.

"So, Roderick took me to see this guy that he knew, who was looking to expand what he called 'his empires.' He was interested in seeing what I could do, and he had a lot of money. So, even if my parents wouldn't help me pay for college, he said he would. But he wanted to interview me first and see what my plans were after I graduated."

"Oh." I had a feeling I might know where this was going, but I wasn't sure, so I kept my mouth shut after that one word.

"I went in to talk with him, and Roderick stayed outside his office to talk to the secretary about some investments he was also hoping to make. He always was one for thinking ahead in business, even when we were in high school. Always had his eye on some prize out in the future where he didn't have to be a farmer and could instead be considered *nouveau riche*."

Another tear leaked out, and I grabbed a tissue from the box on the corner of her desk and handed it to her.

She dabbed and sniffed then continued, "This man—I won't name names because he's not around anymore—he wanted something for his time and his money, and it was something I wasn't willing to give, even though he tried to take it."

My stomach rolled at the thought of what that probably was. I wasn't going to ask for clarification.

"I screamed bloody murder, and Roderick broke the door down to stand between us. The man was yelling and cursing, and Roderick hauled me out of the office without a backward glance. But I know he never got the dream he wanted, and then neither did I. I told my parents I'd changed my mind after I bawled my eyes out on an empty football field because it was the only place that felt safe after that encounter. And Roderick and I remained friends, but not like we were before that. I was so thankful he'd saved me, but he hated himself for putting me in that position in the first place and for it ruining everything he'd wanted to do for himself going forward." She sighed. "I tried to talk with him years later and apologize, but he scoffed at me and told me he wouldn't want to be in business with someone like that anyway but never wanted to talk about it again."

"Wow."

"So yes, I protected him whenever I could, and I'm pretty sure I'd do it again if he hadn't been killed. But now that he has, I feel like something is missing from my life, and I never got to say goodbye."

And then she bawled her eyes out for real. I didn't know if it was to the level of what she'd done in an empty football field when her dreams had been killed and her person had been threatened, but it had to be close.

Eliot slowly opened the door and peeked his head in. I shooed him off with a quick hand gesture, and he pulled the door closed again quietly.

Hildy was not my suspect, and there was no way she would have killed Roderick. While that meant I was back at square one, it also meant that one of my very favorite people was off the hook. Phew! I felt so much better!

However, now it was time to go call Karen and avoid my mother, so she wouldn't know I knew a secret I couldn't tell her. Add it to the pile, right on top of the fact that I was failing monetarily.

CHAPTER THIRTEEN

I wasn't sure what to do next or where to go. While Karen was waiting for my call, she might have to wait a little longer. I was raw from what Hildy had told me and had decisions to make but didn't know where to start.

I had the evening and so many things I'd considered moving from my to-do list to my to-done list, but now I had more information than I knew what to do with. Yet, I didn't know what was important enough to share and what wasn't. I was certain that if I told my dad Hildy had not done it then it would be enough. He probably wasn't considering her a suspect at this point anyway. But I still added her name to my list at home, then crossed her off, and put the word *reasons* next to her name.

"What are we going to do, Stella Luna? I should call this lady, but I don't even know why or what I'd do once I talk to her. What if she tells me something really weird, and I don't know what to do with it?"

For her part, Stella meowed at me and then curled up against my thigh on my chair. I'd bought this chair specifically because we would both fit. I wasn't little and neither was Stella Luna, and we liked to sit together but not with her draped over my lap. Because she didn't like being moved once she settled in, and I needed to get up and do stuff, I couldn't just sit there all night like my dad would if he came over to visit.

To prepare myself and also procrastinate, I finally pulled out the lanyards and set them on the counter. I glanced at the phone number for Karen over and over again, messing up the count on the lanyards and having to start over several times. But eventually, I got it right and came out with exactly nine hundred ninety-eight. The only two missing were the one the killer had used to strangle Roderick and the one I'd found on my windshield.

Finally, I bit the bullet and took the number out of my

pocket, grabbed my cell phone, and dialed it. I hesitated one more second before hitting the green call button, and then hoped I wasn't going to regret my decision.

"Took you long enough!"

I tried but couldn't place the voice, not that I knew everyone in town, but there were certain people I would have known from word one. This was not one of them.

"Am I speaking with Karen?" I asked, settling into the chair with the notebook on the arm and Stella Luna right up against my side with her paws pushing at my waist and her head twisted in what had to be an uncomfortable position, but one she loved anyway.

"That's not my real name, but I thought you might like it more if I said Karen, maybe get a chuckle. But then you took forever to call, and I wondered if I should have told you who I really am."

"And who are you really then?" Because I had a feeling that whatever she told me would not only need to be triple checked but maybe even quadruple checked before I even breathed about it near my father.

"Ha! No, I'm not telling you now because I don't want to have anything to do with this slimy mess."

"But you still have something to tell me?" Or had I called for no apparent reason, and she'd only answered so she could be irritated with me for not calling sooner? My head hurt.

"Look, I don't want to be a part of *this*, but that doesn't mean I'm not part of *something* if you get what I mean."

I really had no idea, but I didn't want to tell her that and have her hang up on me. So, I made what I thought might sound like an affirmative noise while I waited for her to spill, so I could get off the phone and maybe make myself some dinner that didn't come off a griddle.

Maybe an open-faced hot chicken sandwich. It was easy-peasy to do in the microwave, which made me very happy. Oh, now that sounded delish…

"And that's why you need to look in all them jukebox things that you had in storage. There's one that's broken. Find that one and I bet you find something that might just help." Then she hung up on me, and I stared at the phone in shock.

I wrestled with whether I should call her back and admit that I'd been dreaming of feeding myself instead of listening to what she had to say, but I figured that would not go well. She probably wouldn't answer the phone, anyway, thinking that she'd already done what she needed to do, and the rest was up to me.

In the end, I decided to go with what I had heard and keep her phone number in case I needed clarification after I found whatever this something was in one of our jukeboxes. I only hoped that whichever one she had been talking about was actually still in our possession. I was almost positive we still had them all. The vegetable guy had tried and failed to sell a few before he'd given the restaurant back to Jeb, who then let us buy it from him.

I wondered briefly if the original owner might know what the woman had been talking about, but he was dealing with some pretty hard medical issues right now. I wasn't going to ask him vague questions when I could just go there by myself and check out the many jukeboxes we had on the tables.

Right after I ate that hot chicken sandwich…

I waffled a few hours later because I did not want to go to the diner by myself after dark. I'd done it a bunch of times when we were getting ready to open. Dani and I had been in and out of that place at all hours, depending on what we had time to accomplish due to still working other jobs and renovations and all the other things it had taken to get our business moving in the right direction to open our front doors.

But I did not want to find another lanyard on the front door or have someone call me randomly while I was in the diner and scare me while I was alone.

But I didn't want to wait until tomorrow after everyone left and after working a long shift, either. I wasn't going to be able to do it while we were open for customers.

In the end, I called Eliot, hoping to find out when he was going to be done with work and what it would take to talk him into coming over to help me go through the jukeboxes. I looked at the clock and realized that Dani would already most likely be in bed, and I didn't want to interrupt her sleep since she was opening tomorrow.

I'd apologize tomorrow for not including her if we found anything.

"Hey, what's up? Did you need something?"

That voice. Yikes. I calmed myself down by slow blinking and then launching into what the fake Karen had told me and asking when he was done with work.

"Whoa, whoa, I don't even know where to… what?"

"I blanked out while the woman was rambling on and missed the part about what was supposed to be in the jukeboxes, or at least one of them. We have them all as far as I know, but I don't want to go there by myself tonight, and I don't want to wait until tomorrow in case it's something important. So, when do you get off work, and can I convince you to escort me to my diner to do some sleuthing?"

"Do you promise not to make me any toast?"

Oh, my word! It had become a full-on grapevine gossip thing. I should have figured on that. It always did. I groaned. "Yes, I promise to stay far away from the toaster. Have you never made a mistake?"

"Well, there was that one time, but it ended up making the recipe so much better, and now I do it deliberately all the time."

"Of course."

He chuckled, and I loved the sound of it. No matter how much I shouldn't be noticing that kind of thing.

"I'm actually clocking out now. Seems everyone is spending their eating-out money at some diner where all the gossip is hot and the toast well done."

"Sounds like the best place to eat in the world."

"I wouldn't know, but I might just have to try it out."

"Any time and the toast is on me."

He chuckled. Oops! I probably shouldn't have phrased it quite that way.

"So how long do you think it will take you to make your way over to the best diner in the world?" I petted Stella Luna and prepared to apologize to her for having to leave her so late in the evening. Normally, I'd be turning in now and letting her knead the bread in bed before she decided to curl up behind my bent knees and fall fast asleep until it was time to feed her in the morning.

"Give me fifteen minutes and I'll be on my way. I want to check in with Hildy before I head out. I haven't really seen her at all tonight, and that's unusual."

I held my tongue when I really wanted to tell him I had probably upset her, and that's why she'd hidden away for the evening. But that might cause him to ask why she was upset, and that just wasn't my story to tell.

"Okay, I'll leave in about fifteen minutes, so I'll get there a little after you. You can park in the back, and we'll go in that way."

"I'll text you when I get there."

"See you then." I checked the clock, and it wasn't actually as late as I had thought it would be. Yes, it was dark outside, but that was just because of the time of year, not necessarily the time on the clock.

I took some time in the bathroom, freshening up as my grandmother used to call it, before petting a yowling Stella Luna and making sure she had food and water and that treat my dad had told me to make sure I got her from him.

She wasn't a happy camper, but at least she'd be a comfy camper. That was about all I had to offer at the moment as I headed out to my car with my keys in hand.

Normally, I strolled around in the evening with not a single worry, but ever since this murder had taken place and the lanyards and notes had cropped up, I'd taken to checking out my surroundings far more than I had before. What was that rustle in the tree? Did I just see a shadow in the parking lot out front?

The answer to both of those were negative as I logically knew they would be, but that didn't stop me from worrying, getting in my car as fast as I could, and then shutting and locking my doors as quickly as I possibly could.

The drive to the diner was short.

I still got there before Eliot, but I pulled into the lit back lot behind the diner. I couldn't go around being scared of everything and everyone, and it wasn't even full-on nighttime just yet. My dash clock said it was nine but only because I'd forgotten how to turn it when the clocks changed.

He should be here any minute, and I was on lookout because I did not want to miss him pulling up and then be scared if he knocked on my window. There was only so much stress I could take in one day, and that would be one thing too many.

I saw headlights turn the corner and almost got out of the car to say hi, but whoever it was did not stop and, in fact, sped up as they passed the diner in the long row of attached businesses. I ducked down just in case, knowing that it probably wouldn't make a difference, but not being able to stop myself, regardless.

Of course, that made it so I had no idea who was driving the car or even what kind of car it was. I really needed to up my sleuthing game, or I was going to be a failure at this before I even really got started.

Another car rounded the corner, and I stayed where I was, not ducking but ready to memorize the license plate if I had to.

This one though was Eliot, and watching him get out of his SUV and run a hand through his dark hair was not hard on the eyes or senses. I'd have said it calmed me right down, but I'd be lying.

I did, however, compose myself before getting out of my own car. He didn't come over once he could tell I saw him, and that made it much easier to get myself under control. No hopping out like some teenager who just realized the guy she likes works at the movie theater, so she would stay there for hours on end, watching all the movies she had no interest in and buying bag after bag of popcorn just to see him, even though she never ate them.

Yes, that had been me back in the day, but I digress.

"Hey there." He walked the short distance around the end of my car and met me on the stoop outside the back door. "Did you bring any tools to work on the jukeboxes with?"

"Everything should be inside. We did work on several that weren't working right before we opened, so we probably don't have to check every single one of them. I'd like to start with the ones we didn't touch."

"Whatever way you think is best."

I liked a man who knew when to follow my lead. "And then if we don't find anything, we can go back and do the ones we didn't check."

"Yep, makes sense. Show me the way." He gestured for me to go first, and I appreciated that too, although he really couldn't have gone in front of me since I had the key.

Down, Jax, down.

I opened the back door lock and hit the alarm in under thirty seconds. Flipping on some lights, I walked through the back room and the kitchen then into the front, trying to remember which jukeboxes were where. I was not the best at remembering things like that, regardless of my assurances earlier.

But Dani had a flow chart with all the tables and what was on them, so I backtracked to her locker to see if I could snag that and use it to map out our plan of attack.

When I opened the door, though, an avalanche of things fell out. Blankets, towels, and a few stuffed animals, along with four sweatshirts and an entire stack of order pads. What on earth was she doing?

I'd ask her tomorrow, though, because the chart for the jukeboxes floated out after the swoosh of air created by the avalanche. I stuffed everything back in the locker and jammed the door shut as fast as I could.

"She's not going to be mad that you messed with her stuff?" Eliot asked, eyeing the locker.

"Will she even be able to tell that I messed with her stuff? She must have a system of some kind for keeping it all from falling out that I just don't know about, and she can take me to task tomorrow if she really wants to. For now, we're going on a jukebox hunt."

The door must not have latched properly because the whole thing swung open again, and the avalanche was not easy to stop cascading over the entire floor. Awesome.

I groaned but bent over to start picking things up and Eliot helped this time.

"Any reason why she might think it's necessary to have all this stuff packed in here? Do you not have a supply room of some sort?"

Yes, we did, and it was the room we were trying to turn into an event room, the one with the avocado paintings. I had no idea why Dani had all this stuffed in here. While the first time I was ready to gloss over it, the second time I paused to really see what I was returning to the locker.

Order pads with doodles on them, napkins that looked like someone had chewed on them, aprons with bleach marks. What was the connecting thing here, and why was she hiding them? I could only assume that was what she was doing since I hadn't seen any of this stuff and had not been told our supplies were being wasted like this. Or maybe they were coming in ruined? I didn't know, but I put it on my mental list to talk about it with her when I saw her tomorrow.

"So, what's the plan here?" After everything was back in the locker, Eliot stood with a screwdriver in one hand and a piece of paper with my notes in the other.

"You're all set to investigate jukeboxes, sir? Looks like you have all the proper tools as outlined in the manual." I smiled at him, letting the things in Dani's locker settle in the back of my mind. I could do nothing about them right now, and she was most likely on her way to bed. Sending her off to dreamland with tense words and what she might take as accusations wouldn't be the best rest. Plus, I had some of my own secrets, so it wasn't like I could really chastise her if I wouldn't chastise myself. And I wasn't willing to do that at the moment, probably really not ever, but I kept feeling like the day of reckoning might be coming sooner than I'd prefer.

"The person on the phone didn't tell me exactly which one it was." That was not exactly true since she might have but I hadn't been listening.

"So, we just go through each one. We're looking for some kind of clue, but we don't know what it might be, what it looks like, what it could signify, or what to do with it if and when we find it."

"Well, that sounds horrible when you say it like that."

He chuckled, but it sounded more derisive than jovial.

"Look, I am completely new to this whole sleuthing thing in general, specifically in the case of trying to find a murderer. I know all the shows like to cast the quirky, inquisitive person as super clever and a bit lucky, as well as being able to see the unseen when the time is right in the storyline. Unfortunately, you just have me, a lot unlucky, definitely nosy, and quirky as all get out, but not particularly clever most days. So, I'm doing my best."

"You're absolutely right, and I'm sorry for saying it like that."

Again, something I hadn't heard from a man in a long time unless it was my father. Absolutely right? Sorry? How was this man not being actively pursued by every single female in town?

Although that made me pause. How did I know he wasn't? How was I sure that he didn't have a girlfriend or even a wife? Although, I couldn't imagine Hildy nudging me to spend time with him if he had a significant other. And it wasn't like I could ask that now without seeming very strange—way beyond quirky—so I put it in the back of my head with all my other unanswered questions just waiting to be asked when the time was right.

"Are all the jukeboxes out on the tables?" he asked, bringing me out of my thoughts and back to where the action was.

"No, there are several that we weren't able to get working no matter what we did."

"You probably weren't looking for any kind of clue at that time, I assume."

"You would assume right on that. And if it didn't work as soon as we plugged it in, we put it aside to mess with later because we had enough to at least get started."

"So where should we start? I'll follow where you lead."

He almost made it too easy, but I wouldn't take advantage of that. Instead, I used a flashlight to guide us to the side room. I didn't want to turn on all the lights in the dining room because I didn't want to deal with passersby wondering what was going on or for people to get super excited that we might be open late for one night of wild hash browns.

The side room was spacious, but it didn't currently have any windows, so I didn't hesitate to flip on all the lights and then search out two chairs. Eliot dragged a small table to the center of the room and then started hunting for the random jukeboxes. He'd find them in boxes and crates and sometimes just sitting on a chair or table alone.

I had planned on telling him where to look to help, but he was already halfway through getting them all and probably didn't need any guidance from me. Good enough, and honestly, I was fine with that because my head was too cloudy right now with all the things I was trying to remember, not forget, and ask when the time was right. Those on top of wondering who had killed Roderick, and why it wasn't until he was dead that everyone started airing their grievances. Had he been that powerful? Were people really that scared of speaking out against him when he'd been alive? Why?

Eliot brought a jukebox over to the table, pulled up a chair, and got to work. Unscrewing the back of the Wurlitzer with his handy screwdriver, he hummed as he revealed the insides. "I've never even thought about how these were constructed."

I hadn't either until I had to do maintenance on one at a table and found the interior to be fascinating while also convoluted. Gears and flippers and electronics galore greeted me then and Eliot now.

"Nothing unusual here though," he said. "You're sure the woman didn't tell you what to look for?"

I couldn't evade anymore, and it seemed like it might actually be more important than I had realized when I'd first missed it. "Like I said… I blanked out when I was on the phone. I only caught the end of what she was saying, and then she hung up on me before I could ask any questions."

"You didn't call her back for clarification?"

I knew he was going to ask that. "I just had hoped I could find it without having to bother her again. Whatever it is."

"Well…"

"Yeah, yeah. I'll call her now." Dang it.

Taking out my phone, I tried to compose what I would say to her before she answered, but I came up with nothing clever. So, I just went with my gut when she said hello.

"Look, lady who is not Karen, I'm sorry for bothering you after our last call, but I didn't catch everything you were saying. Now that I'm at the diner, looking at these things, I realize I have no idea what I'm supposed to find."

She chuckled and then full out laughed. At least she had picked up. "I kind of figured you might call back since you didn't ask anything else and seemed to have drifted off. Thinking about that new man of yours?"

I had no new man, and how would she know about him even if I did? I couldn't tell who I was talking to. The voice didn't sound familiar, but not everyone's would, especially if you didn't know who you expected it to be or where you might know them from.

"Can we cut the mystery stuff? Can you please tell me who you really are, and what I'm looking for?"

"You can have one or the other. But not both."

"Why not?"

"Or I can hang up now." There was a pause, and I was very afraid that she actually had hung up.

"Wait!"

"I'm still here, but I don't want to get in trouble. This has nothing to do with me now, and it didn't then. I'd rather not be involved at all, but something was telling me I needed to at least help here. Now which do you want? And choose carefully because I don't think you're going to get another chance."

CHAPTER FOURTEEN

Nothing quite like being put in a position where you have one choice but need both. This lady, whoever she was, played hardball, and I wasn't going to be able to get around her.

"The what," I said grudgingly, still wishing I could push for both but not sure how to do it. Also, I knew finding the clue was probably more important than knowing who it came from if I could find it.

"Good choice." She sighed, maybe because I'd let her off the hook, and she hadn't been sure I would at first? "There's a key in the back of one of the flip cards. Someone, and don't ask me who because I don't know, stuck it in there years ago. You find the key and then find what it belongs to, and it might help you."

Cryptic, as in very cryptic. But if she didn't know more then I didn't want to press too hard.

"You're sure you don't want to tell me who you are? It might help figure out where the key belongs."

"Nice try but there's no way that would help you in any form. So, find the key, find the keyhole, and then see what comes next. I'm getting rid of this burner phone now so if you try to call it will be dead. Good luck, Jaxxy. You've got this." And the line went dead.

Jaxxy? There were only a handful of people who called me that. I would have to think of who those people were, but that in itself was a clue. One I could consider after I found the key and the keyhole. No pressure, though.

I relayed the information to a very patient Eliot, who had continued taking backs off the jukeboxes. "She strikes me as a woman who knows enough to be dangerous but maybe not enough to help much," I said.

"A key and then we have to find the keyhole? That could be anywhere for anything. I just hope it's not a standard house key. I'm not going all over the town trying to unlock people's doors. We might have a pass to some extent because of your dad and people trusting you, but I guarantee that would not go well even with the first house."

"But at least we have a lead now."

"Yeah, so why don't you sit down and get to work with me?"

I glanced over, and he'd moved the second chair to face him across the table. I wasn't sure if that was better than being right up against him, but since I didn't have another table, and I couldn't really move the chair anywhere else, I took a seat and found my knees touching his.

Just fantastic. Because another distraction was exactly what I needed in the middle of all this chaos.

"She didn't say anything about what song page it was in, did she?" He seemed completely unaffected by our closeness, so I told myself to do the exact same thing, even if I had to fake it until I made it.

"I'm just happy she told me what we were looking for at all. And no, she said nothing about the page. Only that it's in the back of a flipper or something like that."

"How many of these are there?"

"A lot." And there were. I just really hoped we wouldn't have to remove every single one off the tables before we found what we were looking for.

"Would it be possible to just call Jeb and verify that there is a key, and we're not off on a wild goose chase?" he asked.

I'd thought about that, but Jeb could be a cagey one when he wanted to be. "I'd rather have irrefutable proof, like the key in my hand, before I say anything to him. It's possible he'd deny it outright and then not want to talk about it when I did find the key. I'd rather hit him with everything all at once."

"You know him better than I do."

I was starting to doubt if there was a key and if it would reveal secrets leading to a killer.

We worked in silence for a few minutes, moving our fingers along the back of each card in hopes that we'd feel a ridge or something that would tell us we had finally found the outline of a key. I did not want to have to rip open every page because I hadn't been kidding when I said these could get some good money if we found a collector. But they would fetch far less if I destroyed each one in pursuit of something that could have been a joke, even if I didn't believe that Karen—who was not Karen—would do that to me, Jaxxy.

The name pinged in my brain again, and I tried to remember at what point in my life people had called me that and why I had made them stop.

It was a hard-to-place memory, but I felt around the edges of it with my mind as I opened yet another jukebox and again found nothing out of the ordinary. Shoot!

The thought kept flickering, but maybe I was trying too hard to divide my energies between too many things.

"Do you really think we'll figure out who killed Roderick?" I asked without looking up from my job.

Eliot sighed. "I don't know that it will be us necessarily. It's rarely only two people. It happens as a collective from many different parts and departments and information from people. The cops put it together, and even then, you don't always get a confession. You have proof, and someone can refute it or shine a different light on it."

I felt like we might be getting dangerously close to that thing that had made him leave the force. Part of me wanted to know and push to find out what had happened, but the other part of me reminded myself that he was helping when he didn't really need to. Alienating him by interrogating him would not aid my cause.

"I don't want to pry, but I do have good listening ears if you ever want to talk," I said, keeping my eyes on what I was doing in order not to mess it up.

"Appreciated." And then he shouted in joy. "Found it!"

He held it out triumphantly, and I was thankful to see it didn't look like a normal house key. It was something smaller, like for a hanging lock, or a post office box, or a safety deposit box. So, we were away from houses, but there were near infinite possibilities for what the key could go to, including a shed in someone's backyard. And that put us back with the invading people's spaces and hoping they didn't call the cops on us.

All while still running a diner and making sure I didn't run out of money. Excellent.

Perhaps I should talk to Jeb before tackling other people's property.

Maybe the universe wanted to test me on my resilience because, just as I thought that, I heard a crash in the front of the diner, and my whole body froze. What the hell was that?

"Stay here."

Eliot had to be kidding. I was not going to stay in the side room while he rode into some potentially horrible situation without me. It hadn't stopped me last time with Dani, and it wasn't going to stop me now. I wasn't a damsel, and I'd had plenty of distress that I'd saved myself from. Maybe not all of it, but I'd done a pretty good job of surviving so far.

I was only two steps behind him when my breath caught in my throat. The entire front window lay in shards on the counter that held the register. I couldn't see behind the counter, but I would bet everything I still owned, no matter how little that was, that the entire space was littered with glass.

And there was a brick on my counter right next to the register.

"Who did this? More importantly, why did the person do this?" Eliot asked.

I'd like to know that too.

"Hmm," Eliot said, but in a way that sounded less like thinking and more like curiosity tinged with skepticism. Don't ask me how I knew that off one noise, but I wasn't wrong when I watched him take a square of fabric out of his jacket pocket and turn the brick over.

He angled it so I could see it too, and in thick black marker, it said, *STOP*.

"That's not very original," I said.

"But it could be effective. How are you feeling about being an amateur sleuth now?"

"Not as good as I thought I'd feel trying to bring about justice." This no longer felt like just me innocently looking into some murder, and I wasn't happy about it. That window had cost a fortune.

"You can back out now if you want."

Boy, did I want but I also did not like being intimidated, and if someone was going to try to scare me away like that, then I wasn't going to go for it.

And I wanted to know who the person was because I wanted him to pay for this damage. Oh, my word...

"How am I going to pay for this?" I whispered to myself. "Freaking Smitty and his freaking grubby, snatchy hands!"

My voice must have gotten a little louder than a whisper

though. Either that or Eliot had supersonic hearing.

"Who's Smitty, and why are his hands snatchy?" He pinned me with a gaze that I couldn't look away from.

Oh, but I tried, believe me I tried. In the end, I winced, and he shook his head, looking away first.

"A reciprocation on your offer... If at some point, you do want to actually talk about that person and whatever it is that he did to make you not be able to afford to replace a new window at your thriving business, I wouldn't turn away from that conversation."

I winced again because that was probably the nicest thing I'd heard from a man who wasn't my father in a very long time, and that was actually quite sad.

I blew out a breath, shook it off, and stared at the brick like it was my only issue in the whole wide world.

"Did you see anyone skulking around before you came back?" I asked. "Because I didn't."

"That doesn't necessarily mean anything. Even with streetlights, there are plenty of places to hide and then run by to do the bricking."

"True."

"I did kind of see someone, though I doubt it was him." Eliot turned the brick over in his hand like maybe it had more to tell. Part of me very much hoped it didn't have any more threats.

"Would you know the guy if you saw him again?"

"Like the one who kept walking past the window the other morning?" he asked. "Or Smitty?"

"We're not broaching the subject of Smitty presently, and I already told you about the guy who kept walking in front of the window yesterday morning. He works at the train depot. Did you see him again? Do you think he's the one who threw the brick?"

"I'm not entirely sure since I was in the back talking with you. So really, it could have been anyone. The guy pacing and casing could have been a look out for the person who actually did it. He could be someone else entirely, maybe looking to come in and rob you. Maybe he was considering asking you on a date and kept waiting for me to leave so he could ask."

I shot him a narrow-eyed glare and chuffed out a breath. "Not helping."

"Oh, but I think I am." He turned the brick over, and it had more to say than just *STOP*.

No one wants to hurt you, but we might have to if you don't back off.

"Well, that's a little more direct than the one word on the front."

"And it's signed."

"No, it's not!" I went to grab the brick, and he held it up and away from where I could grab it. I was about to climb up his body to get it like I used to when my cousin would try to play keep away from me, but I realized that probably was a very bad idea and would result in a situation I was not willing to wade into over a brick.

"No, it's not signed, but I wish it was." He smiled at me, just one side of his mouth kicking up in a way that made my insides flutter, just a little.

Dangerous, that was what he was, and I was not looking for dangerous.

"Okay, so we have a brick and a broken pane of glass. I'm not a happy camper, and I want whoever did this to pay for it." Sticking my hands on my hips, I checked out the floor behind the counter, and it was indeed covered in broken glass. Thank goodness we had already closed for the day, or things would have been even more horrible with clean up.

I grabbed the dustpan and brush, but Eliot stood in my way.

"We're going to have to call your dad."

CHAPTER FIFTEEN

I froze in place and closed my eyes. The very last thing I wanted to do was call my dad, right after trying to find the money to replace a huge plate glass window.

"Or we at least need to call the police if you don't want to call him specifically," Eliot continued, perhaps seeing my distress. "This is vandalism and needs to be reported. I know you don't want to, but we're going to have to. It's the responsible thing to do."

I knew that, but I didn't have to like it. "Crap."

"Yeah. Why don't you just call the police in general and let them handle it as a low priority?"

"I'd better call Dani too and at least leave her a message. We'll have to contact the insurance." My head was starting to hurt. "And a busted-out front window isn't exactly low priority if we want to be open tomorrow. Crap!"

"Have any plywood lying around or maybe a big sheet of plastic that could go up, at least to keep the elements out?"

"Right, but what am I going to do about keeping real intruders out?"

"You could sleep at the register, or better yet call your dad and see what he can help with."

I very much wanted to avoid that at all costs, but I was coming around to thinking I was being ridiculous. It made far more sense to do the correct thing, instead of the independent thing that was not very smart, even if I felt it could be easier.

"Fine, but you call the cops. I'll call him just to give him a heads up as a dad, not as part of the force."

"Good call. And whoever Smitty is, I hope you can smack his grabby hands and get back whatever you lost."

I nodded at him because I was already waiting for my dad to answer. He and my mom should probably be in the middle of watching whatever series my mom was currently streaming, but he'd be fine answering the phone and not in bed, so those two things worked hard in my favor.

"What's going on? Why do I feel a very bad twinge in my back right now and think it has to do with you and your situation?" he said instead of hello.

"Are you claiming to be physically psychic? Like you don't know what I'm thinking, but if your knee jerks, then that means I got the wrong kind of bread at the store?"

"Jax, what is it you want?"

"Eliot is calling in a vandalism claim to the police department right now. I didn't want to catch you off guard if someone was talking about it over the radio, and you caught it but were unaware."

"Vandalism? Like someone spray painted your house or your grass, or you have streamers of toilet paper sitting in your trees?"

I closed my eyes, even though he couldn't see me. "Um, more like someone just threw a brick through the plate glass window at the front of the diner, and the brick and glass landed on my counter."

There was a moment of silence, and then the cop came hauling out of the gate.

"I'll be right there, don't touch anything, and don't let anyone else touch anything unless it's a cop."

He was talking to someone else, probably my mom, so I ended the call and looked at Eliot. "He'll be here momentarily."

"Yeah, probably not before the gawkers."

And he was right as he gestured out the broken window, and there was a small crowd of people across the street on the opposite sidewalk. A few of them were talking amongst themselves, but one in particular stood out from the rest of the crowd in that she was staring right at me and smiling.

Denise Snyder. Did not recommend. Zero out of ten points. What was she doing here though and at this time of night? I didn't need to ask why she was smiling since that was obvious. She delighted in any trouble I managed to find myself in and had since we were in eighth grade.

Ignoring her and not engaging was always the best direction, but apparently, I was not willing to learn from last time. Or any of the other times…

I grabbed my keys from the next room, unlocked the front

door, and stalked across the street, not even looking to see if there were any cars. Fortunately, there weren't but that hadn't even registered until I was standing in front of her.

"Like what you see?" I asked, invading her space and blocking her view of my broken window.

"*Like* is such a neutral word. I prefer something a little stronger as in love or enjoy or wish I could find someone to thank."

I opened my mouth to fire back at her but felt a hand on my shoulder and paused, whipping my head around to see who had dared interrupt my harsh rejoinder.

Eliot. Eliot was standing next to me with his hand on my shoulder, and his face set in an expression of something like don't get involved or don't give her what she obviously wants. It was good advice, and I should have taken it.

Instead, I looked Denise over from the top of her jet black hair to the tips of her flip-flopped feet (flip-flops in late September!) and said, "If I find out this was orchestrated by you, or even by someone you know, be prepared to answer for it."

"Oh, I had nothing to do with it. I just think it was ingenuous. What did they break the window with if I may ask? It looks very thorough even if it appears to lack a kind of finesse."

"Don't," Eliot said, and this time I listened. I highly doubted anyone knew it had been a brick unless they'd been the one to throw it. I'd been around my dad long enough to know that sometimes you held back information just to see if the person who'd done it would slip up and mention it when they shouldn't know unless they'd been the one to do it.

"Come now, it must have been something heavy, maybe a crowbar or a sledgehammer? Leave nothing behind, no evidence of the crime except the broken glass?" Her giggle rode my last nerve, but I found it within myself not to respond. I'd thank Eliot for that later.

"Let's go wait for the police. I'll have to make sure the insurance gets the information too." I turned to walk away and didn't look back.

Good for me.

"Ohhhhh, she makes me want to smack something with a spatula," I said under my breath just loud enough that Eliot would be able to hear it. I took my time walking across the street, not wanting to appear as angry as I was inside. She could only get to me if I let her, and I wouldn't let her again. But I was totally going to put my dad on her tail to see if somehow she had something to do with Roderick's death. I might lack any evidence at all and have no reason to believe she would be involved, but I was willing to use some resources to harass her a bit, just in case.

The police showed up as we entered the diner, and when I glanced out the broken window, Denise was gone. Good riddance but that wasn't going to remove her from my list of possible suspects.

In fact, it moved her right to the top.

"Are you okay, Jax?" my dad asked as I walked through to the side room where Eliot and I had been set up minding our own business, kind of, when the brick had been thrown. I needed a minute out of the chaos to regroup and get myself back under control.

"I'm fine, Dad, just irritated, and Denise was outside getting a good chuckle. If you need to start somewhere, maybe start with her for both cases at this point."

"Denise? What was she doing here? I thought she had left town after not getting Jeb to sell to her instead of you." He made a note in his notebook and then glanced up at me. "Did she say anything that made sense or gave herself away?"

A sigh gusted out of me, and I shook my head. "No, she's just being mean, but I want her looked at anyway, or I can do it. I wouldn't be surprised if she had something to do with all of this. It's right up her destruction alley, after all."

And I wasn't completely wrong. Denise had been one of those kids who got whatever she wanted, whenever she wanted, and woe betide anyone who might have wanted something for themselves. From specific cheerleader uniforms to special seats in a classroom, she'd wielded her sword of "My family founded this town three hundred years ago" as a weapon that she swung, not caring who she hit as long as it got her what she wanted.

And I had been tagged as her major opponent, almost her archnemesis in her story long ago, for reasons I still didn't understand. And quite frankly, I'd stopped caring when we were in high school unless she got in my face or was rabble-rousing to gain support against me.

When Jeb had taken the diner back from the vegetable lover, she'd started a campaign and had a petition that was supposedly signed to keep me, and by extension Dani, from buying the diner. Except you could tell that every signature was hers, just different words. But every E always had an extra loop that trailed off below the line, and she did it all the time on every letter E. It was hard to miss if you knew to look for it.

I grabbed the handkerchief Eliot had used when the brick first came in to look at the writing on the other side but didn't see anything that would say it had definitely been written by Denise.

No matter how much I wanted a dropped E, there wasn't anything that definitive. Crap.

How was I going to be able to prove it was her if she didn't stay consistent with her writing?

"What does it say?" My father came up behind me and took the handkerchief and the brick from me.

"I think it's just a warning."

I felt lame for saying that when his gaze narrowed in on me, and he shook his head. "This looks more like a threat." He shook his head again. "I know you want to help, and I get it. I also appreciate anything and everything you were going to give me, but your mom would skin me alive if something happened to you. How about you just pass along anything you might hear randomly instead of actually looking into things? Eliot can still work with us if he wants to, but I need you to be safe if I want to keep my marriage intact." He nudged me with his shoulder, probably to see if I'd laugh, but I was too irritated to laugh.

Who was doing this and why?

When I didn't respond, he sighed. "Tell you what," he said. "Why don't you just close things down for the night? Tomorrow is soon enough to look into this more. I'll bring down some plywood tonight and cover up the window. You can paint *OPEN* on the outside of it, and we'll see about getting Wendell down here to get a new glass in as soon as possible. I'm sure he'd be willing to wait for the insurance money after it's fixed."

"Should I just call in the morning?" I didn't want to, and I'd have to get up especially early to catch Dani before she was scheduled to come in and would see the plywood with no explanation. I didn't feel right texting her the information because it would catch her off guard and maybe throw her into a tailspin, which I most certainly didn't want to do.

We needed cool and calm and collected. Not chaotically in crisis. Thank you very much.

I looked around at the team of people moving through the diner and felt my shoulders drop. Even with insurance, there was still going to be a deductible, which I was certain we could afford through the diner's receipts, but I hated to do that. And it just highlighted that if anything else happened, I would be tanked with no recourse.

I could just go home and go to bed and not worry about this until I had to talk to Dani about it.

That flew out the broken window when she showed up in her pajama pants and a cardigan. I shut my eyes, so I could take a second to breathe before launching into damage control when I had my own damage to wade through.

"It's not as bad as it looks."

She shot me a glare that told me in no uncertain terms there was no way that could be true.

"It's not going to be that hard to fix?" I was not in love with the way that came out as an unsure question/statement, but there wasn't much I could do about it.

"This is not good. And I heard there was a brick involved. Someone threw a brick through our window. What the heck is going on? I thought we were a sleepy town with very little excitement, and someone is out to totally prove me wrong, and I do not like it."

"Wait, who told you it was a brick?"

"What does that matter? The brick is the thing that matters, not who told me." She crossed her arms under her chest, and I was at least glad to see that she'd put a bra on when the strap peeped out of the wide neck of her sleep shirt.

"Well, who told you matters because no one who isn't here was supposed to know about how the window was broken, and if they told you, then it might be because they were the ones who did it."

That stopped her in her tracks.

"I don't know. My phone was going off like someone standing at a bellhop station with unlimited access to ring the bell. I deleted all the messages as I listened to each one and got more and more upset until I finally decided to come down here and see what was happening and if you're okay." She stopped and grabbed my hand. "Are you okay? You didn't get hit by the brick, did you?"

"No, Eliot and I were in the side room with the avocados when we heard the crash."

That seemed to distract her. "Really?" she said, drawing out the word and giving me a sly smile. "And what were you doing in the side room that has no windows, and no one can see in if you shut the door?"

I rolled my eyes. "We were looking at jukeboxes if you must know and had just found a key, but we don't know what keyhole it goes to."

She wandered over to the lunch counter and took a seat. After crossing her legs, she swung the swivel chair back and forth like someone trying to play coy. "Apparently, there's a lot going on that I know nothing about. Care to fill me in?"

"Me too," my dad said from next to the toaster. "What's this about keys and keyholes, and why were you looking, and where did you find it?"

That was a lot of questions and not a lot of full answers that he was looking for—they were both looking for—so I did my best to answer but also keep it short. "I talked to someone who left me a number. I was supposed to find a secret that had been hidden in a jukebox. Eliot offered to help me look, so we came here, and right after we found the key, the window shattered. There's not much more than that. It's the basics, but it's all I've got."

My dad nodded to someone over his shoulder and guided Dani off the chair. "Since we don't know what that key opens, I'm going to leave it with you for the moment. We'll clean up when we're done, and I'll wait for Wendell to come in. He said he's got the glass now and can install it before tomorrow so you don't have to deal with plywood and people thinking you might be closed. You'll have to get someone to come redo the logo and whatever else you had painted another day, but at least you'll have something up with no issues."

Eliot broke away from the two officers he had been talking to in order to escort us out to our cars. "Ladies, if you're ready to go, then I'll make sure you are safe leaving."

"I'm assuming then that you're staying and will keep us up-to-date on anything you hear?" It was said as a question, but it wasn't meant that way.

"Yes, I will." Once he closed the door behind him, and we were in the parking lot out back, his whole attitude changed. "There's something very strange going on here, and if the cops think they're talking to one of their own, they might say something that they wouldn't say in front of you. I know that probably frustrates you to no end, but sometimes you have to play by someone else's rules if you really want to win."

I *harrumphed* and so did Dani.

"I get it. I swear I do, but you either get the info you want, or you stay here, and we get nothing. I guess that's your choice."

Another choice and it really wasn't any better than the last one, where I could have the not-really-Karen's name or the info on what I might find in the jukebox. Like last time, I took the path that would get me what I wanted even if it wasn't everything I wanted. Sometimes *some* was better than *none*.

That would be nice, but I could see Dani getting ready to revolt. I pulled her along with me as we headed to our cars. "Just follow my lead. I need to talk to you anyway, and it would be better to do it away from anyone in the midst of the clean-up. Dad said that Wendell will wait for the insurance money and charge us the deductible later, so we don't have to worry about that at the moment, okay?"

"Why do I feel like I have no idea what is going on?" she asked, and it was a valid question because I felt the same way.

"We'll figure this out. I know we will. Just come along and we'll get started."

I rolled down my window and gestured for Dani to do the same. "We'll talk tomorrow, okay? I'll come in to help with all the prep first thing in the morning since I'm sure we're going to be hopping now that something actually happened at the diner instead of just in connection with me. It might be best to be ready for the crowds, so we don't have too many complaints, and yes, I will choose something to help with that is not bread buttering or filling salt and sugar shakers. Maybe I'll stick to bussing the tables."

We agreed to meet here first thing in the morning, and neither would get out of our cars until we were both here and ready to make a mad dash into the diner. Not that it would help if someone wanted to bust our windows, but at least having a plan seemed better than nothing. And Eliot agreed to check in with us later in the day after he got up for work.

So, I went home, and I hugged my cat, and I worried about everything that could go wrong tomorrow, and even more about what the key was for, and what would be behind the lock if we ever found it.

CHAPTER SIXTEEN

I barely slept, and so I was not the nicest person when I woke up the next morning. But I was coherent and mostly rested after a night of freakish dreams. I always seemed to be running, either from something or to something, though I never ended up getting there, so I didn't know what I was trying to get.

"Ugh, Stella Luna, today promises to be a long day. I'm going to ask your grandmother to come see you today just in case I can't get away."

Sometimes, I thought Stella was certain she was a dog. She did not like being left alone for long periods of time, and when I used to leave for a weekend, I never left her to her own devices, or I'd come home to horrendous destruction that she caused while I'd been gone.

When I was younger, I had a cat who couldn't be bothered with me and could go days on his own if we were away. He preferred it that way. But Stella was a different kind, and I tried to work with that. Which meant I asked my mother to come over, give her a few pets, and maybe let her lie on her lap for a few minutes while I worked.

Today was going to be more than just regular working because not only would we probably have a bigger crowd than normal, but I also had to figure out how I wanted to broach the locker subject with Dani. I had considered doing it last night when we walked through the break room, but with everything else that was happening, I was afraid it would overwhelm her and me at the same time.

Why had she put all that damaged stuff into her locker instead of bringing it to me? Was she protecting someone? But who could it be?

I ran through the list of our employees while I tugged on some jeans and dropped a polo, embroidered on the pocket with the diner's name and the logo on the back, over my head. I'd get my apron when I got to the diner, and after I talked with Dani about what she'd been doing and if we needed help.

Even after getting dressed and brushing my teeth, I still couldn't come up with anyone who she might be protecting, or even anyone on our staff who might need to be protected. And more importantly, from what? They were bleached aprons and damaged order pads. What was the purpose of keeping them instead of just throwing them in the trash?

I did my hair up in a way that would be acceptable but not take too much effort, and I was ready to face the day, or at least I hoped so. I wasn't taking any bets just in case.

Instead of going directly to the back of the row of buildings to park, I chose to drive in front just to see how the glass had turned out from the front view. Other than the lettering not being present, it looked exactly as it had the night before. I was so thankful and would make sure to start the insurance claim today. Since it was o'dark thirty, I sat for a minute in the road and just looked at everything we'd created, and everything we'd done to make this diner awesome. No one was going to take that from us—not Denise, not a killer, not hateful brick throwers.

It was time to get proactive, and I knew just how I was going to do that.

After I found out what in the heck Dani was up to.

And speak of the devil, someone honked a horn behind me and flashed the high beams. When I pressed down on the gas, the car followed me around the end of the building and then parked next to me. Dani, looking a little worse for wear, emerged from the car but then seemed to get a burst of energy as she headed for the back door in front of me.

I scrambled out of my car and tried to get there at the same time as her. I was a few seconds off, but that just meant I had to wait ten seconds while she disarmed the alarm. I wasn't sure why I was absolutely determined to beat her to the back room until I saw she had opened a locker, and I realized I was going to use that as a conversation starter.

Except she opened a different locker.

"That's not your locker."

"Uh, yes, it is."

"No, you're over there. That's the one you chose when we

first bought the place."

"And it's the one that had issues with the lock, so no one uses it anymore."

"Except someone is." I knocked lightly on the metal door.

"What? Why? I told everyone to stay away from it. We have plenty of lockers for everyone without using it."

"And yet…" I opened the locker we were talking about, and all the things stuck inside tumbled out. Napkins covered the floor along with order pads and bleached aprons.

"What the heck is all this?" she asked, crouching down and scattering things around to get a better view of everything that had tumbled out.

"I was going to ask you that."

She shot me a look that was part irritation and part confoundedness. "And now I'm asking you."

"And so that means neither of us have the answer."

"Good call." She stood and stuck her hands on her waist. "But what is all this? I mean, obviously the stuff is ruined and really should have been claimed as a loss and then written off, but I don't get who's keeping it, or why they would, or how it's getting ruined in the first place. Did you notice this many supplies being gone at any one time, or do you think it's been a trickle over the six months?"

Another mystery. I was about tired of those. Glancing at the clock, I realized that the staff was going to start arriving at any minute. I had met Dani here, thinking we might need a few minutes to talk about what was in the locker before anyone else came in, but now we had to figure out who to talk to instead. I just wanted some answers rather than more questions.

Apparently, today was not going to be that day.

"Help me jam all this back in here. We'll keep an eye on who opens it throughout the day. Everything should fall out again, so I'm hoping we'll hear it before they can leave the room."

Dani handed me some of the aprons and rolled her eyes. "Your amateur sleuth is showing. Why don't we just have a staff meeting this week and talk about what we found and be point blank. That way we're not trying to figure out anything, and we're trusting our staff, who we love like family, to be honest with us. It might be something totally innocuous, Jax. I don't want to make too much out of it if there's a simple explanation."

Grudgingly, I agreed, "Fine, you're probably right, but I reserve the option to sleuth if we don't get some real answers."

"Sleuth away then, but let's not make it more complicated than we have to, okay?"

We had just shut the door and resumed getting ready for the day when Terri came in with a smile on her face and a skip in her step.

"It is way too early to be that happy," I grumbled, and she laughed.

"Actually, it's the perfect time to be incredibly happy. My daughter got engaged last night, and I'm going to have a new son, and then hopefully, they will provide me with grandchildren someday!"

"Well, that is something to be thrilled about then." I hugged her then stepped back. "We'll catch up in just a minute if you want to fire up the grill."

I held up my hand behind my back to stop Dani from moving along with her. Terri left the room, humming to herself.

"What's up, Jax? We need to help her. She shouldn't be left to get everything going by herself, especially when both of us are here."

"I know that, Dani. I'm the one who made the two people at all times rule after all. But I wanted to check with you about something. Instead of a whole staff meeting, should we just ask each one individually if the locker is theirs? We could get the right person without accusing all the people at the same time that way."

She thought it over for a minute but not any more than that. "Let's talk this afternoon. I have concerns, but I don't want to go into them now with opening happening soon. I promise we'll talk about it this afternoon."

Why did I get the distinct feeling that we weren't going to talk about it at all? Hmmm.

But then I didn't have any more time to think about anything because the second Dani unlocked the front door, the chime that signaled it being opened went off like rapid fire.

And every one of the groups of customers had some version of an apology for what happened last night, but also gossip about who it might have been and why. None of them mentioned Denise as a culprit, but plenty named her as trying to talk with them about how sad the vandalism was, and that maybe if she'd owned the diner, that would have never happened.

Seriously, had she sent out mass emails and made phone

calls all night long? It had only been under twelve hours since the brick incident, and nearly every person who walked through the door had something to say about being talked to by Denise.

I finally asked Katherine Mosser, a friend of my mom's, if Denise knew Roderick, thinking that maybe she was on a warpath because her heart was broken over his passing.

"Oh honey, no, she hated him more than anyone really. She'd been with him for a short time when he tried to coerce her into something that she would never talk about. But it didn't get far enough for her to do anything but seethe at his treatment. He didn't really hurt her like he's done other women. It was more that he wounded her ego, and I'm sure you know how she takes to that kind of dig." She opened her eyes wide and arched her eyebrows.

Ah, so that was what this was. I'd wounded her ego by buying the diner instead of stepping aside and just letting her have it. Because that was what she'd wanted, and apparently Denise got exactly what she wanted.

Well, she wasn't going to this time. No matter how much dirt she tried to throw on us. She could spend all the time she wanted trying to make us look bad or have people doubt our services and our awesome food and running this place, but in the end, she was going to lose. I would absolutely stake everything I still owned on that, no matter how minimal it was.

I tried not to let her, or it, ruin my day, but by nine in the morning, I was losing the battle.

Or at least that was until we got a party of five seated, and then I got a call that another party was on its way. We very definitely did not want them sitting next to each other. For the life of me, I couldn't seem to get anyone to switch tables, so I could keep the two sets of diners from engaging in full-out combat in my diner once they arrived.

I grabbed Dani and dragged her into the back. "We have a situation. I need your help."

"Why is everything so dramatic with you lately? I remember you being much more positive and sunnier like our name before this whole murder thing happened. I'd like my old Jax back."

I groaned. "Look, I would too, but Delilah and her crew were just seated two minutes ago, and they're back there bashing everyone and everything. Which, fine, whatever, but my mom just texted me that Lydia Benningfield, Roderick's ex-wife, is on her way in with all her cronies. Mom's friend next door overheard her making a battle plan over the phone and wanted Mom to warn me. I'm afraid things are going to get dicey."

"Holy heck, what are we doing standing in the back? We need to get on this as soon as possible. Jax, this could be a full-on midday showdown if we can't get them away from each other." She peeked her head out between the double doors separating the back from the dining room.

"We should be able to get someone to move along, shouldn't we?" I asked, peeking out above her. "Dale and his buddies have been here since we opened three hours ago. Surely, they're ready to move along. How much coffee can one group drink?" Dale waved his hand in the air, and Jennifer came over to top their cups off. Gah!

"Incoming," Dani said and then straightened her hair and her apron and sailed out the doors like the mothership.

Okay, she could handle the new party while I made sure the old party didn't see what was going on. Coffee refills would be safe enough and giving our specials for the day if they hadn't already ordered.

I straightened myself, though I hadn't exactly gotten mussed since I wasn't allowed to do much of anything anymore in my own establishment.

Their loss. I was good at what I did when I wasn't distracted, which I definitely was right about now with so many different occupied seats on this Ferris wheel of chaos.

I sailed out of the room, too, but felt more like a dinghy than a mothership. "Ladies, how are we doing today? Can I get you all some more coffee? Has anyone been by to tell you about our specials?"

"Behind you," Jennifer said, and I heard the snap of a tray holder and then her lowering the tray to the stand. Specials were not needed then, but I could still do coffee and keep the focus on me. I definitely wanted them looking at me instead of paying attention to the chattering going on at the front door that had just opened, spilling in several women from what I could hear.

"Coffee?" I said louder. "Tea? Chocolate milk, Mary? It's on the house."

Delilah zeroed in on me and my words. "Everything is on the house?"

"Well, no, just the second chocolate milk. We normally charge for that, and the coffee and tea are endless refills already." I should have kept my mouth shut. Obviously, I couldn't even offer refills correctly without getting myself into trouble. Where had my business savvy gone? I hadn't studied at college for nothing. I knew how to conduct business, but this whole thing was really messing with my mojo.

"So, if we all get chocolate milk, then we can all get unlimited refills?" Delilah, forever looking out for the freebie. I should have thought of that.

"Sure." What else could I say?

No one but her took me up on it, and they went back to talking amongst themselves as I kept an ear out for Dani seating the other party. I didn't want to turn around and look, but when I'd come out of the back, the only spot available for a bigger group of people was no more than three tables away, which was not far enough.

I told myself it would be what it would be but couldn't help cringing when Delilah raised her voice and started talking.

"Roderick left me everything. We might not have been able to make it to the justice of the peace, and I might not have the marriage license I would have liked, but he assured me that if anything were to happen to him everything would be mine."

There was some *oohing* and *ahhing*, a couple of cheers, and a joyous laugh, that last one from Delilah.

It did not go unnoticed three tables away.

"Roderick and his ridiculous promises. The only things left are debts, and that son of his who thinks he's going to get something but will end up with nothing too. I didn't even get my half of our money in the divorce five years ago, and I know for certain he spent every penny of that. He'd even asked me last week if he could borrow money from me for a dinner he was hosting—for all those women who ignore the fact that they aren't the only ones he's romancing." This from Lydia. Her table made sounds of commiseration, and I did not chance looking behind me to see if they were making eye contact over here.

"I'll be back with your chocolate milk." I scooted away before anything else was lobbed across the enemy lines.

I did however stand off to the side just so I wouldn't miss anything.

"You know," Delilah said to her group but definitely loud enough to be heard by the Lydia crowd. "It's such a pity that women who have been tossed aside for good reason don't seem to understand how life works. If only they'd get on with their own business instead of always trying to nose into what is no longer theirs. I bet the world would be a much better place if those women would just get over it, admit that they weren't enough to keep a good man, and then go on with their pitiful lives." Pontificated by the woman who obviously was not paying attention to the fact that Roderick had been with several women per Jasper in the course of one day. Who did she think she was playing? Especially when it appeared she was the one who probably got played.

Lydia scoffed but didn't look in Delilah's direction. "It does take all kinds, doesn't it? I get that Roderick could be a charmer. He was an even better one when he thought he was going to get something out of someone, like an inheritance or access to their bank account. I guess maybe he even kept some women around to be able to roll through town in the Jaguar their daddy bought them in 1992, like with Delilah, but really it was just for a place to land. With me, he at least actually ponied up and went through with one of the many promises he made. Not that it benefited me other than when we were divorced, and I could have his checks garnished. I don't see that he was making money anymore, and that doesn't matter at this point since I remarried. But while I'd like to feel sorry for anyone caught in his web, there's one maybe two?" She cocked her head to the side. "No definitely one that will only get what she very much deserves, and that is a big fat zero, as in nothing. Unless she wanted his debt. I suppose they'd be happy to honor a fake proposal and future marriage that didn't happen if she would be willing to take on all his issues just to make it legal. Honestly, it's probably all he would have ever wanted."

"How dare you!" Delilah stood from her throne at the head of her own table and threw down the paper napkin that had been on her lap.

Uh oh. Might be time to step in.

Lydia snorted and turned her back on Delilah. "You know, I'd wonder about the patrons in here except that every other table seems to have pretty decent people. In fact, every table has some decent people, just not all the people at the table are decent."

"You horrible person!" Delilah shrieked.

"Did you hear something? I feel like someone is trying to tell me something, but it's at a pitch only dogs can hear."

Oh yikes.

Should I step in or leave it be? Delilah might have stood and thrown the napkin, but I didn't see her making a move to actually come out from behind the table. Even if she did, there really wasn't much to do. Not to mention people were drinking coffee and looking around to see what was going on. Once they landed on the battleground of tables twelve and nine, they seemed to be riveted to the back corner where the insults were flying, but only from Delilah as Lydia kept her back turned and the smile fierce on her face.

Delilah finally ended up just sputtering. I took that moment to bring her the chocolate milk she'd requested, and she drained it in one long swallow then handed the glass back to me. "Refill," she said.

"Can do."

I walked back to the milk machine and kept an eye on the two tables. Lydia had moved on to other subjects while Delilah seemed lost as to what should happen next. I could almost see the wheels spinning under her ultra-styled hair. Should she walk over to Lydia and make her pay attention to her? Should she let it go and keep talking as if Lydia wasn't there and perhaps a little quieter, so Lydia wouldn't respond to everything she said? Should she leave and call this one a draw, even though it was clearly a loss for her and a win for Lydia?

Decisions, decisions. And quite frankly, I didn't care what she did. As long as it didn't involve physical contact, I thought it was probably best not to get involved.

A table opened up once the talking had settled down into just the two groups chatting amongst themselves. I didn't hear any more bombs being lobbed, and that must have made the men at table eight decide it was time to get on with the rest of their days.

Not two minutes later, a new set of people came in, and Jennifer seated them. I didn't know where Dani was, but I knew she would have waited for a different table to open up before moving them right into the direct line of fire.

Because leading the group was Roderick's son.

CHAPTER SEVENTEEN

There was no way for me to divert the group. Jennifer was already laying down the menus and telling them today's specials. It was a group of five men and two women. A mix of ages sat around the table, with Kenneth Benningfield taking the seat at the head of the table and seeming to preside over the group, as if now that his father had gone, he was the head of whatever he thought Roderick had been running. I recognized a few of them but not all of them. Kenneth's friend, Tobias, sat near the other end of the table. I knew him vaguely since he worked for Hildy in the evenings. That light brown hair and his slightly tanned skin were hard to miss. I wondered what they were doing here at this time of day, instead of going to Hildy's restaurant, since I'd never seen Kenneth or Roderick in here before.

Roderick's son wasn't a bad guy. He was a little younger than me and rarely caused any real trouble in town. But his dad's shadow had been big, and there were rumors Roderick had deliberately cut him off from any and all financial assistance in an effort to get him to grow up. From what I could tell, he hadn't, at least not as of last week when I saw him trying to walk out of the farmer's market with a loaded basket and a cashier trotting after him telling him they hadn't put anything on "running tabs" since the late 1900s. I hadn't heard how that had ended, but maybe I would today. Or maybe this was just a huge disaster waiting to happen, and I should have watched more closely at the front door instead of trying to eavesdrop on the two ladies' groups.

Either way I was stuck.

After Jennifer left, I waited to see what kind of group these people were. They could have been having a sort of celebration of life, though Roderick had almost never come here before his passing, so it wasn't like they were honoring him by eating at one of his favorite places.

What were they doing here then? Not that I minded seven people and the hopefully big check they were about to start. As long as Kenneth didn't try to hand me one of his dad's credit cards.

I made a beeline for the cash register and left a note to check the names on all credit cards being used because, really, I needed to make sure that whoever paid for Delilah's table also had a credit card that would run correctly.

Ah, the life of a diner owner. What had I loved so much about this a year ago?

But then when I looked up, there was a commotion at the new table, and Delilah, who had not been ready to actually confront Lydia physically, was apparently quite okay with doing so with Roderick's son.

"What are you doing here, and why are you with Brady Adams?" She struck a pose, the shoulder pads of her lime green blazer taking up most of my field of vision.

Who was Brady?

"Ah, Delilah, you were next on my list to visit. I'm glad I caught you here instead. I'm going to be representing Kenneth in a transaction, so I don't think I'll be able to handle that thing we talked about before. So sorry, but I'm sure you understand."

A realtor? A lawyer? A contemporary of Roderick's since both his girlfriend and son knew him? Business associate? But he wasn't a woman... His chiseled face and bright blue eyes were a dead giveaway, something he shared with his son.

"No, Brady, I do not understand, and if you are handling anything, it better be me."

"Did you get the deed then? Because Kenneth assures me the lawyer let him know it's passing down to him since there were no changes made to the will."

The deed? I felt like I should be closer, but there was no real reason for me to walk up to the table and insert myself into any part of this conversation. I was going to have to roll with it and see where it went. I did get out my order pad, just in case something came to light that I wasn't aware of. And what deed were they talking about?

"But I was told—"

Brady cut her off. "Were you actually told by someone who has true authority, or were you just made one more promise that didn't come through? Again?"

That took the wind right out of Delilah's sails. I could almost see her deflating like a shiny lime green balloon. Part of me felt for her no matter how much of a pain she could be at times. No one deserved to be treated like that and lied to endlessly. However, she hadn't exactly shown herself to be the nicest of people earlier, so maybe karma was shifting some gears and taking payment for some debts but not all.

In the midst of this verbal sparring, I had forgotten about Lydia and her table, but they made themselves unavoidable when she appeared at Brady's elbow, equidistant from both Delilah and Kenneth. It was like a triangle of grave consequences waiting to explode.

I looked around for anyone to help me. While it hadn't been physical and had been pretty manageable up to this point, currently I was not feeling the same vibe.

"Please tell me you're not talking about the land Roderick's family has owned for the last three hundred years." Lydia laughed derisively.

"You're not welcome in this conversation," Kenneth said stiffly, avoiding eye contact with Lydia. I was trying to remember when she was married to Roderick. Had Kenneth lived with them? Was he young enough that she would have been an actual stepmother?

"I don't need an invitation, Kenny. Please, continue with what you think you're doing with this hundred-acre wood."

Kenneth flinched at the Winnie the Pooh reference.

Brady ran right into the conversation that I had a feeling was not going to turn out how he assumed it would.

"We're ready to bring our town into the 2020s, Lydia, even if you want to remain in the 1900s. I am certain that we would all benefit from a lovely new neighborhood filled with new shops, and new homes, and new people who would bring a boost to our economy that we seriously need."

She nodded along with his words but then shook her head at the end. "And you think you're going to do that with Roderick's land that you're certain he left to Kenneth?" The way she said it made my already doubtful nature bloom into full-out absolutely not.

Brady bristled and straightened the blue tie at his neck. "Yes, we're already in the process of getting the permits and clearance. Kenneth will be an amazing caretaker and businessman. He understands the risks but also the benefits the way Roderick never did. And hopefully, my son Tobias will follow Kenneth's example to grow up enough and take ownership of his life, so that he can also help."

"Sure thing, partner," the younger man said while rolling his eyes.

Little bit of tension there.

However, there it was. This Brady guy had been in talks with Roderick and had been shut down, but now that Roderick was dead, Kenneth stood to make millions. Or at least that was what Brady was selling him. I doubted that was actually how it would happen.

Even if the land was available which I also doubted.

"Well, good luck with that." Lydia went back to her table, dismissing everyone in Delilah's party and Kenneth's party without a single gesture.

When she resumed her seat, there was a lot of whispering and quiet laughter, but no one looked over at Kenneth's table again. I wrote *land* on my order pad and decided to ask Eliot how I would look something like that up. I might have been a master when it came to spreadsheets, and even building a basic website from a template or looking up old recipes to try them out here, but research of this level was way beyond my scope.

Speak of the devil and he will appear though. Eliot stood at the front door waiting to be seated. What was he doing here this early in the morning? Although it really wasn't that early when I glanced at the big Cadillac clock. Almost ten, when I felt like I'd started this packed day less than an hour ago.

But so much had happened that I needed to process. Thank goodness for the order pad.

I hustled to the front before anyone else could get to Eliot.

"Just one?" I asked, grabbing a menu and a set of silverware from the bin at the front counter.

His smile was a little cheeky and a lot welcome. I could stare at him for hours probably, but that was not a thought I should be entertaining right now.

"The counter's fine." He glanced toward the back of the diner where my three warring parties sat. "I might have some info on that whole thing back there. I told Dani to leave me up here until you were available, so we could talk without interrupting your day."

So thoughtful, but now I felt bad for not realizing he'd been standing here. Plus, I wasn't sure why Dani wouldn't have let me know he was waiting.

Although, to be fair, I had been embroiled in some avid watching of the unfolding drama, so that gave her a pass and me too most likely.

I apologized anyway. "Sorry about the delay. I guess you got to see it all play out in real time?"

"Not the whole thing since Stan at table one just told me that I missed the first showdown between Lydia and Delilah, but this land part was something I've been wondering about."

"Me too. So, what did you find out?" I used the big plastic-covered menu to hide my mouth as I asked.

"No one is getting that land except the county."

"What? The county?"

"Keep your voice down." He rolled his eyes, and I definitely felt like the amateur I totally was.

"Sorry about that. The county?" I whispered. "Should we tell them and see what the fallout is? Maybe with them all in the same room, something will crop up because I'm thinking that Kenneth might need to be very high on our suspect list. Do you think he'd k—"

Eliot shook his head sharply, and I cut myself off.

"Not here?"

"No, not here and not now." He nudged me with his shoulder. "Now, I'd really like some of those pancakes I keep hearing about and maybe a milkshake. I hear those things are right next to heaven. And maybe a biscuit with sausage gravy."

"Super special coming up then." It wasn't really a thing, but I could make it happen. It was my diner after all. At least for now as long as nothing else bad happened.

Five minutes later, Terri dinged the bell with a vengeance. Even Dani looked up with narrowed eyes, and I reminded myself to field that with her instead of letting her plow into Terri. I headed her off as she was arrowed straight for the kitchen and the grill.

"Don't do it. I told her she could ding as much as she wanted. She's just frustrated no matter how happy she said she was about the engagement."

"The dinging is driving me crazy."

Terri hit the bell three times in quick succession again. I kept myself from staring at her because it would only add fuel to the fire, and she seemed hot around the collar enough for all of us.

"We asked for the dinging." I shrugged.

"We asked for responsible dinging not dinging with

abandon. There are limits to these kinds of things."

"Well, don't tell her that yet. Just let her have her day. She'll settle down."

As if to prove my point, Terri only hit the bell twice on her next go around.

"This is on you," Dani said under her breath. "If anyone complains about the excessive dinging, I am totally sending them to you as the complaints department."

"I'm willing to take that punishment to keep our best cook happy. Now, I have a plate to deliver to one Eliot Myers and a milkshake to make, and then I need to figure out what to do next with the groups in the back since none of them seem to be leaving. At least they aren't hovering at each other's tables."

Dani shifted her gaze to my left. "Looks like the Delilah contingent is on the move."

"Someone better be paying that tab. Don't let her leave without payment."

"Jennifer's on it."

And she was, cornering the table in the archway from the farthest dining area to the front door.

With the way the booths were set up along the whole wall and the lunch counter on the other side, bracketing the space and leaving exactly one chute to the door, Delilah wasn't going to be able to get past Jennifer without shoving her out of the way. I doubted even Delilah would do that.

Although it looked like she was going to try. Until her sister scoffed and shoved Delilah out of the way. "Here. And give yourself a good tip for having to deal with all these ridiculous people."

Helen Westbrook was normally the quiet one living in her younger sister's shadow. But sometimes that wore thin from my guess, and perhaps she was someone worth talking to about Delilah. If I could introduce it as a fact-finding mission for her sister instead of trying to pit one sister against the other.

I put it on my to-do list on my order pad. I was running out of space, but that only made me feel like I was actually getting somewhere instead of stuck in the middle of nothing with no answers. Even though technically, I had no answers. It was convoluted, but it made sense in my head, and right now that was all that mattered.

Jennifer brought the check back quickly, and Helen nodded

after checking the total. Normally, we would not let waitresses write down their own tip. The customer should do that and sign the credit card slip, but this was going far better than I had expected, so I let it slide. Just this once.

I lifted my hand to wave the party out the front door, thought better of it, and pretended to tuck the hair behind my ear. Better not to push the limits of friendly interaction when really, she was more like a rupturing volcano.

If Delilah had truly believed that everything was going to be hers when Roderick died, then had she made that happen—causing a commotion in Hildy's restaurant itself to get him out the door and right into the sights of someone who was willing to kill for the woman?

Or had she stolen the lanyard out of my car, strangled him, then came in, and made a commotion to give herself some more time before he was found?

Did she know enough about Hildy and her absolute need to save Roderick from his own mistakes that she had bet on Hildy sending me out? But how could she have counted on me finding the body? Plus, there was no way the lanyard could have been a weapon of choice. It had to be totally by chance. It wasn't like I had announced they would be in the car and invited anyone to take them who thought they might have an alternative use.

Although, she had ties with many people in town, and Hildy was predictable in her defense of the man. Delilah might have even been fine with someone finding Roderick hours after she stormed in, started yelling, got fed by Hildy to keep it down, and then left, all with no one knowing what she'd done until after the garbage was taken out. I really hadn't had to be the one to find him, but she could have thought her luck was on the high roll when I did.

I wasn't sure why she would have wanted to set up such an elaborate scheme, but I couldn't rule it out either.

Although if she had hired someone—scratch that—if she had promised someone something after she finally got some money of her own, then the killer could have made the decision to use the lanyard, and she would have still been able to make her grand entrance and know that Roderick would most likely be hidden by Hildy.

Convoluted, so convoluted, but murder was rarely simple. Or that was what I had learned from all those hours of listening to murder podcasts.

Helen turned at the last moment as everyone else preceded her out the front door and gave me a quick and terse nod. She sent one toward the lunch counter too, and I figured it was probably for Eliot, though I couldn't be sure. He was one of five people sitting on the swivel chairs, waiting for their orders to be delivered. Down the counter from him, a girl had a textbook out in front of her as she sipped her milkshake. The young guy sitting next to her only had eyes for her. An older man with the newspaper sat to her left sipping coffee and closing his eyes with every taste. And a guy I'd gone to high school with was digging into his breakfast with glee while he played some kind of word game on his phone. I knew most people in town, and I couldn't really see any of them killing anyone, much less Roderick. They were all lost in their own worlds, and only Eliot was looking at her, but he didn't nod back.

Yet if not Eliot, then who since no one else was looking at her?

The vibe in the diner changed to something happier, almost like a switch had been flipped as soon as Delilah was clear of the glass door everyone exited through. There was a calm that seemed to wash over the space, as if she and her cohorts had taken all the negativity with them in one fell swoop.

I breathed a sigh of relief and smiled at Terri as she dinged the bell just once for the biscuits with sausage gravy that were ready for Eliot.

I turned to deliver them to him and then got to working on his milkshake. I hummed under my breath, ready to start making sense of some of the notes I'd been copiously taking and hopefully find out where the key could be used. I made a mental note to talk with Jeb to see if he remembered the key as I stuck the stainless-steel tumbler under the blending wand of the old-fashioned milkshake mixer. Yes, he was dealing with medical issues, but this would just be a simple question of whether he remembered who had placed the key there, and maybe why they would have done that. Nothing too weighty.

I turned to hand Eliot his milkshake and then nearly dropped it as Delilah screamed back into the diner in full-hellion mode.

"Who did that to my car? Jax, you will pay for this!"

CHAPTER EIGHTEEN

It was like déjà vu from the night when she'd come into the Poplarsville Inn with irritation in her voice and mayhem on her mind.

I had to admit that, for just a second, I hoped she was not having anyone else killed and put into our garbage area out back.

But then her words registered, and my heart got stuck in my throat.

"I am not leaving until you have someone clean my car, or I will sue your establishment. I really want it to fall completely on you, but since your friend Dani had the stupidity to sign on with you as a co-owner, then she's just going to have to accept the collateral damage. You both can take the fall for this. This happened on your property, and you will be held responsible for the damage, and you will *pay* for the damage! I won't be disrespected like this! I won't! It's too much!" And then she started crying.

I was at a loss as to what to do. Her sister stayed outside the new glass window with her arms crossed and a scowl on her face. For me? Or for Delilah's behavior?

Neither was good. Didn't I just ask for nothing bad to happen? And no matter where she'd parked, all parking was public property and therefore not my financial responsibility. But I certainly didn't want to start with that reminder.

"Delilah, I'm sorry for whatever happened. We'll see what we can do to help."

"I don't want your help! I want you to fix it! *Now*!"

Was her car damaged? Because it wasn't like I had touch-up paint or a suction cup to pull out a dent just lying around waiting to be useful. I might have a flat tire patch in my car out back, but I wasn't going to fix that either when it wasn't my responsibility. If it was something small, I might help but not claim that it was mine to do from the beginning. She'd probably haul us into court and demand payment for her property damage and more money for pain and suffering for having to deal with it.

Why was this happening to me? All I wanted was to run a little diner, entertain the townspeople, and make a tidy profit while feeling secure in my decisions. So far, I was at zero for any of those.

Eliot silently got up from his plates of food, went out to the sidewalk, and then hung a right.

Dani came flying up to the counter and smoothed a hand down Delilah's arm then held her hand and murmured things to her. Just as long as it wasn't claiming responsibility, I was fine with that. Some people who had been gathering their coats and things from the booth to leave after the exit of Delilah the first time, put their stuff back down and resumed their seats for the second act apparently.

Wonderful.

For my part, I took my apron off, laid it carefully on the front counter, and then followed Eliot out to the right. What I saw when I rounded the next corner at the end of the building wasn't exactly what I would have thought would cause that kind of wailing and gnashing of teeth.

Maybe I was wrong though. Eliot walked around the car and then turned around and did the same from the opposite direction. He used a finger to swipe at something on the windshield and brought it to his nose. I would not have done that without knowing what I was dealing with, but then again, how would I know without touching it? One point for Eliot and his continued goodness in most situations. I'd thank him for that by taking care of his check.

"What's the damage?" I asked quietly, not that anyone could miss the not very nice words that were scrawled over every window—every surface really—of the whole sedan. It was a Jaguar but had definitely seen better days, even without the cursing and name calling currently gracing her windshield.

"Soap. It's just soap, but there is a lot of it."

"I'll go get a bucket of hot water." I turned to leave and headed back to the sink where we had plenty of steamy water.

"You're sure you want to do that? She might take it as you claiming responsibility for something you aren't responsible for. It's a valid concern."

I took him in from head to toe in one glance. He did have a point, but it was also just soap. If it made things not so aggressive in my diner and smoothed out the edges for her on at least one thing, then I was willing to do it. "It's not that big of a deal. And if there's more damage than just the soap, I'm not against calling my father again to have him come check things out and make sure it's reported as vandalism."

"Maybe we should do that anyway." He took his phone out of his back pocket and made the call while I turned back toward the diner and my bucket of hot water. I wanted gloves too just in case.

As I made the left to round the corner, I came face-to-face with Lydia.

"Oh, uh, hi." Not the best of hellos but for right now it would have to do.

"You know, she probably did that herself. Whatever it is that's wrong with her car. She's been a chaser of drama and notice since she was little."

And what was the right response to that? I couldn't exactly tell her I was very aware I was playing into her hands without sounding like a dork for doing so. Instead of answering, I just shrugged.

"Were you aware Roderick and I were married when she started coming around?" She leaned against the brick wall with her ankles crossed, looking out across the street. "She wanted him and had wanted him for years but had never been able to actually catch him. And then we were married, and I thought we were happy. I thought he'd finally figured out how to settle down and be the person I knew he could be if he let go of all the posturing." She closed her eyes and drew in a breath. "He was a good man at his core but had sucky circumstances when he was growing up. I could have sworn he'd finally learned it wasn't about pushing every boundary to get someone to notice him because I saw him." She released the breath and shook her head. "But then she started coming around, and she didn't want him to stop posturing and preening for anyone and for everyone to look at him. She thought he was her equal, and if he wasn't doing it anymore, then she couldn't either, and that was unacceptable to her."

I still couldn't find the right words to participate in this monologue, so I let her keep going with a nod.

"So, I found them in a compromising position. I knew as soon as I opened the front door to the house that something was wrong. Roderick looked so sad when I came into the dining room and found her laid out like a Thanksgiving feast on my dining room table. I didn't think they'd actually done anything yet, but I couldn't fight her if he wasn't going to help me, so I gave up."

"I don't know that you gave up," I finally said. "You can't save someone if they don't want to be saved. And no matter how much we think someone else is capable of being a better version of themselves, if they don't believe it, then we can't always carry them to the finish line. They have to do that themselves."

A tear leaked out of her eye, and even though I didn't know Lydia very well, I stepped forward to hug her. It seemed like the right thing to do. She held tight as soon as I stepped in.

"I really thought we'd make it." She sobbed into my shoulder, her body shaking with the force of her crying. "I really thought he wanted to be everything I knew he could be."

I patted her back and left it there. I didn't have the answers for the universe, and I wasn't even going to try. I had my own stuff going on, and that included wiping down a car absolutely covered with insults and soap.

I released her and put a hand on her wrist. "I'm sorry for your loss, all of it. I know what it's like to have to face reality instead of living in what would have been a dream come true." Boy, did I and my bank account know that.

"No one's said that to me." She sniffed and wiped at her eyes. "Everyone has been so glad that he's gone, from his son, to people who had called themselves his friend, to people who went through the divorce with me. I know it was messy, and I never did get my payout, but I still feel like a widow, and no one has said that I'm allowed to cry over it. Just that I should be thankful I wasn't still married to him, and thankful he and his issues are gone. I don't feel that though."

Which made sense. Even if she'd hated him in the end, she might still need to grieve. It would be difficult if no one else thought you should be doing that.

She gripped the back of her neck and shook her head slightly. "Anyway, phew, sorry about that. I should take myself home and just chalk this up as a day I shouldn't have come out of the house. I have those every once in a while, and my current husband doesn't exactly understand why someone who shafted me over hundreds of thousands of dollars would be worth me being sad over."

The part of me that often held a lot of compassion for people wanted to offer to be her sounding board. The other part of me—the one who was finally realizing my own mental health was worth a lot, which meant I didn't have to save everyone either—just smiled at her as I shoved down the urge to give her my phone number and tell her she could call me any time.

Maybe if she'd tell her friends what was bothering her, what she was struggling with, she'd have support she didn't realize they'd give.

And oh, I was not even going to go there since that spoke to my own situation. I was most definitely not in a place to deal with that right now. I still needed to get the bucket of hot water and then probably talk to Eliot about how to clean the car. And that was after I talked to the police who had just driven by without sirens and turned the corner to approach Delilah's car. The faster I got it cleaned, the faster she'd be out of there.

I wasn't surprised to find her sitting at the lunch counter, drinking another chocolate milk. She drained it as soon as I came in and slammed the plastic tumbler on the counter like she was asking for another shot of whisky in the Old West.

Not my circus, not my monkeys, but I definitely knew the clowns…

After filling up my bucket of hot water, I lugged it out the back door and around the end of the building. I was not surprised to find my father waiting for me or that Eliot was still there. They stopped talking as soon as I came into view though. What were they talking about? Did I even really want to know?

I decided I really didn't, so I continued trudging along and set the bucket down at the front of the car.

"Is there anything you need here, Dad, or can I start wiping it down? I'm going to be out of chocolate milk if I don't get Delilah on her way with a clean car."

"Some pretty nasty words on there," he said, flipping his notebook closed.

"Yeah, I saw that, and I have no idea who would have done it, but it's not my business." I just barely cut myself off from saying not my circus. It was one thing to think it, but another to use it out loud when talking with the police even if that policeman was my dad.

"Not your monkeys, I get it," he said with a smile.

I smiled back at him, but it only kicked up one side of my mouth. Delilah drove a sedan, and it was low to the ground, but I still was going to have a tough time reaching the roof if there was writing up there too.

"You'll stick around?" my dad asked. I thought at first he was talking to me, but when I glanced over, Eliot nodded while looking in my direction. What? Were they best buds now, trying to keep yours truly on the straight and narrow? I did not need a keeper, and I certainly didn't need those keeper duties passed from one man to the next.

It wasn't worth mentioning because I'd just get some tired line about caring about me and wanting me to be safe. I wanted to be safe too, but it was also broad daylight and in the middle of the town.

Although, the more I thought about it as I started with a sopping wet sponge to get the majority of the soap to come off in one wet swipe, someone had done this in broad daylight and in the middle of town. And yet no one seemed to know how or when or who.

Or at least no one had reported it, which could be a whole other set of shenanigans. Few people liked Delilah, maybe just the ones who had come in with her to breakfast, but even that number would be decreased by at least one if you wanted to count her sister out of the Go Delilah camp.

While every once in a while I wished I had a sibling, it was times like these that I thanked my lucky stars Mom had thought I was perfect so why try for a second.

I swiped, I scrubbed, making sure not to mess up the paint because heaven forbid I scratch the car, and I swabbed. Eliot said goodbye to my father and then came to stand near me on the passenger side of the car.

"You didn't happen to bring out a second sponge, did you?" he asked. Which was very nice of him since I was the one who'd offered to do this and hadn't expected anyone else to help.

"I did, actually, if you want to roll up your sleeves and dive into this soapy mess."

And it was a soapy mess. Someone must have used bar after bar to write all these words on every available inch of the car. No corner or bumper was spared.

"Whoever did this must really hate Delilah." Eliot took up a post on the other side of the car and started in at the front fender.

"Either that or it's some kid who was paid enough to think it would be fun to draw with no holds barred on a car with soap. I've heard of weirder enjoyment."

Laughing, Eliot agreed and got back to work.

We didn't talk much after that, which was fine with me. I wanted to get this done as quickly as possible and move on to the rest of my day. And maybe Delilah would be nicer to me after I did this favor. Though I wasn't really banking on that happening.

Eliot and I met up at the back of the car. He was much faster than I was, and his side looked a little cleaner when I went around to check it out.

"Does it pass your inspection?" He started on the taillights with a grin.

"You missed something on this one door handle, but I can get that for you."

He looked shocked when he darted his head around the side of the car to look at where I was.

I laughed and appreciated that levity in the middle of all this mess.

"Oh. Ha. Ha."

"You did great. I really appreciate the help. Dani and I are super busy, and I feel bad leaving her with Delilah, but this had to be done. And it was done much faster with you helping."

"No problem. Happy to help."

"You want some assistance on the other side?" I asked.

"Nope, I'm pretty much done. Except..." he trailed off, and I wondered what he had been about to say. I came to stand behind him, and my gut clenched.

Because behind the license plate frame, held in with the pressure from the plate itself, was another one of my lanyards. Dang it!

CHAPTER NINETEEN

"What in the literal weirdness is going on?" I wanted to scream the words, but I kept them at a low volume so as not to bring more attention to myself. I already felt like I was doing detention or something after getting caught vandalizing property. Of course, that was not true, but there'd been a few snickers as people passed me on the sidewalk and admired my ability to clean a car. One had even offered me cash if I'd come clean his car.

No thanks. I wouldn't be doing this one either if I didn't think it might earn me some points when I started questioning Delilah about Roderick's untimely death.

But first I needed to deal with the fact that yet again I had found one of my own lanyards at the scene of the crime. I had counted them and found only two were missing, but that couldn't be true now that I'd found another one. I turned it over and over in my hand. Nothing had come from either one. My dad told me they had been wiped clean, so I doubted I was messing up fingerprints. And even if the cops sent this one out for prints, it would have been touched by so many people—between the people who'd made them at the printers to those who did a quality check to those who boxed them.

There was no way to tell who might have done this, and that person would have to be in the database as a previous offender to be called on for this one. Besides, there was no way to tell when exactly the lanyard would have been put there. It could have happened the night Roderick had been killed. Maybe someone took the lanyards out of my car, killed Roderick, and then left one for Delilah in an effort to connect the two. It could be possible. Not probable, but possible.

And I was not taking that to my dad.

"You done?" I asked Eliot, feeling a little defeated by not having any solid info to give to my dad, and no real idea who had killed Roderick to even point the police in the right direction. Honestly, I had nothing except some jokester who thought my lanyards were some kind of calling cards for their bad and horrible behavior.

Should I count them again so I could be prepared for the possibility of how many more times this could happen? I didn't know. I thought I'd counted them correctly last time, but I couldn't have if there was yet one more out of my stash. And I also needed to make some phone calls.

Maybe Dani would let me go home early.

"Are we done then?" I asked again. "I don't think it's worth taking the lanyard to my dad. It hasn't helped in anything, and it's just like all the others. They mean nothing, they say nothing, and they're just irritating as all get out."

Eliot stood up and gave me a long look. "They do have some significance if you keep finding them every time something is done regarding this murder. I'd at least tell your dad." Eliot dropped his sponge into the bucket. The water was dirty and soapy. Definitely something I'd be flushing down the toilet and not emptying into any of our sinks.

"How about you tell my dad since the two of you looked especially chummy when you were talking until I came on scene, and your mouths closed up tight."

I had not meant to say that, but once I had, I definitely did not expect Eliot to laugh at my snarkiness.

"Worried we were telling tales about you? I'm sure he's got a whole library I'd like to read."

"You'd... you'd read a library of my misspent youth?"

"And anything current too." He picked the bucket up. "Although if you'd rather give me your take in person, I'm here for that too. Now lead the way to where you want to dump this. I have a feeling we might need to start looking a little harder into the connection of the lanyards and who might have had the opportunity to steal them. Plus, I was thinking, and one of the things I talked to your father about was that they had viewed the limited footage available from the inn from the back, but I don't know if they looked at any on the side where your car was. Maybe we can get a line on who took the lanyards out of your car in the first place."

"That's a really good idea."

"Don't sound so surprised. They're getting the extra footage to look over."

I groaned. "Of course I'm not surprised you are smart. I just wish I had been smarter. I should have looked at that days ago."

"Are you a professionally trained detective or police officer?"

We walked next to each other, and Eliot kept the bucket on his opposite side. So, it didn't accidentally splash me as he swung it? That would be so sweet. Like to the point where my teeth might ache.

"You know I'm not."

"And yet I am, and so is your father, and we didn't look at those tapes ourselves. Don't worry about it. Investigation is two parts research and finding things and about five parts intuition and luck sometimes. What matters is that your dad is exploring all the avenues and taking everything we give him very seriously. Not everyone does that for civilians. And they can be your greatest asset if they're telling the truth."

It sounded like there was more to that statement than just the words. "And is it often that they're not telling the truth?"

His gaze shifted to the ground and then to the left, anywhere but to me. "Yeah, that happens more than I'd like to admit, and I believed him… I mean them."

Definitely more to the story and statement. But I wasn't going to push it. He hadn't when I'd made that comment about Smitty, so I wouldn't now. "I'm here if you ever want to share that story."

"I see what you did there."

I smiled at him, and we continued on down through the back door. The locker we'd found stuffed with things caught my eye. Since no one was back here, I glanced through the swinging doors and also made sure no one was right outside them.

"I asked Dani about the locker, and she says she hasn't used it since we opened, so she's not the one shoving all the things in there. I wonder who it could be?"

"Do you have cameras back here, speaking of watching a video?"

I shook my head. "No, we never thought we'd need something like that, and it was just an extra cost we couldn't justify."

"Maybe you need to consider doing it anyway. It's not too expensive. They might be perfect." He pointed to the corner of the ceiling after putting the bucket down. "Or you could ask everyone who is back here if they've seen anyone go in that locker."

I nudged the bucket toward the bathroom with my toe. "Right, but the whole telling the truth thing rears its ugly head with that again."

"It does, but maybe then you'd know if something is really going wrong or just a miscommunication or mistake. It could be something totally above board, you know."

"I suppose." I tapped a finger to my chin. "I'll think about it. For right now, we need to get that water down the toilet and then let Delilah know she can stop consuming my chocolate milk like it's free."

"But it is to her right now."

Chuckling, I gave him the point on that one. "It is, but I'd like it not to be, and the faster we get her out of here, the faster she can stop doing chocolate milk shots like they're coming in a thimble."

Eliot offered to dump the water while I went to share the good news with Delilah. But when I went to the lunch counter, she was already gone.

"She left right after someone called her," Dani said as I approached her at the register. "I don't know who she was talking to, but it seemed urgent. I tried texting you to let you know she was on her way to demand you hurry up, but you didn't answer."

Pulling my phone out of my pocket, I realized it was still on silent as we asked everyone working here to set their phone. This place was busy enough without also having notifications dinging left and right while food was being delivered.

"I found another lanyard." I kept my voice down, so hopefully no one else would hear me.

Dani did not get that hint. "Another one!" she practically yelled.

"Keep it down!" I tried whispering again. "I think I need to count them again to see how many we have and how many are missing. I did that and thought I had a correct number, but with this one showing up, I'm wondering if I was wrong. And I would feel better having at least some idea of what might be showing up in the near future if this person is using it as a calling card."

"That is entirely too rude of them. What kind of calling card is that? It's not like anyone would think it was you if you vandalized something and then left your own lanyard. No one is that stupid."

She threw her hands up in the air, almost hitting the wall, then caught herself.

"I wouldn't think so either, yet they keep leaving them. What's the purpose? What do they think they're accomplishing by leaving the lanyard every time they make a move? Maybe it really is just to irritate me. Maybe it's to throw me off by wondering where they're getting them instead of who has them."

That actually made a lot of sense, and I put the thought in the back of my mind to discuss with Eliot later. When had that become a thing? I wasn't sure, but I did know I wasn't against it.

"Do you need me for the rest of the day, or are we good now?" I looked out over the room and figured that the back was probably pretty empty, as there wasn't a ton of noise coming from that direction. Then again, that could have been because everyone had their mouth full back there, but I doubted it.

"I think we're good if you need to take off. We'll be closing in a few hours anyway. Did you get a chance to talk to anyone about the locker?"

This time she did keep her voice down. I appreciated that more than I could say.

"Not yet. Eliot thinks we might want to consider putting a camera back there, but I hate to do that without letting everyone know they're being filmed. I would feel like we were violating people's privacy in a work place if you know what I mean."

"Yeah, I know what you mean. No one wants to watch someone else adjusting their underwear after coming out of the bathroom."

"Precisely," I said with a nod.

"I'll ask around. Most of them will be here today and tomorrow, and it might be better coming from me, someone who isn't sleuthing after a murderer. They might think you are looking for connections, and I can just tell them that between the brick through the front window and the vandalism of Delilah's car it might be a good idea."

"Good point." I sighed. "When did life get this complicated? I just wanted to own a diner, serve up some home-cooked meals, and have full access to as many pancakes as I could handle. I haven't eaten one in days now. I'm all wrapped up in looking into people's pasts, finding out who they associate with now, and listening endlessly to gossip, hoping someone will say something that allows me to connect the dots on a map the size of Texas."

She placed her hand on my shoulder. "I know you're just complaining, and I'd do the same thing in the midst of all this, but I do want to remind you that you can step out at any time. I'm sure your dad appreciates your help, but he really can't expect that you'll keep this up just because it's stuff that it would take him longer to do."

She very much had a point, but I very much had a counterpoint. "I know, and I very well might take him up on that unspoken invitation, but I also want to know who wants us to be blamed for everything that's going on. My brain keeps trying to make connections with all these dots, and it's going to drive me bananas if I quit now."

"I don't doubt that. I just might remind you every once in a while that you're doing this when you don't have to."

I took a moment to hug my best friend and thank her again. I did take her up on her offer to let me out early since I was tired from cleaning that car from top to bottom. I didn't know where Eliot had gone, but when I glanced out the back window, I saw him standing near my car.

"Nothing better to do than hang out waiting for me, huh?" Of course, I was joking, but my traitorous heart gave a little flutter, even though I told it very clearly not to. With so much going on and so much unsteady around here, the very last thing I needed to be doing was mooning over a guy I barely knew and who barely knew me.

"Eh, after I finished my delicious meal and that tasty milkshake, I had some time and thought you might want to go over the lanyard thing. Or maybe talk about who this might be and why. I wasn't here for the whole thing this morning between all the tables, but maybe you heard something that might connect some more dots."

"I was just saying to Dani about connecting the dots. Is that the right way to look at it?"

He shrugged and stuffed his hands into the pockets of his jeans. "I don't pretend to know the way things work. I only know what usually worked for me until it didn't."

Someday, I was going to hear the whole story of why he'd quit the force and moved a hundred miles away, but maybe someday wasn't today. First, I'd have to have enough courage to push him on it. I'd offered earlier, and he hadn't said no, so there was hope that maybe that *someday* might be sooner than I would think.

"Do you want to come over and go through the things I

have? I can duck back into the diner and get any tips and gossip the wait staff have picked up throughout the day, and then we can maybe stop in at Hildy's to find out if she still has the parking lot footage."

"I used my time while I was waiting for you to come out to talk with her about that. She thinks she has the footage of the corner of the building, which should cover your passenger side in the video, but she didn't have time to go through it to see if it's right or not. They're getting slammed over there too. I didn't want to offer to help out until I knew whether you were available tonight or not."

Really, could he be any more thoughtful and accommodating? It was almost scary to think this might actually be his personality. But I thought I had read Smitty right too, and I couldn't have been more wrong.

"Let's run by my house first then the inn. If they're busy now, I doubt it's going to be any better during the dinner rush, and this way we can get in and out of her hair before they fill up this evening."

"I'll follow you over."

And he didn't always have to lead? Holy heck, where had he been all my life?

No, no, no! This was the wrong time and the wrong place even if it wasn't the wrong person.

Settling into my car, I closed my eyes for just a moment as I switched on the ignition. I had many things to concentrate on. None of which had to do with starting a new relationship when I'd just gotten out of one that I was still dealing with the consequences. And it was possible that Eliot was just this perfect because we were playing in his sandbox, even if he didn't think he belonged there anymore because of a mistake I doubted he was the only one to make.

I opened my eyes and backed out of the parking spot then pointed my car toward home. Had I washed the dishes? Would Stella Luna have destroyed everything in her wake? She did that sometimes, and other times, I'd come home after six hours to find her in the precise spot I'd left her in before sunrise. It was a crapshoot either way, and honestly, I wasn't trying to impress Eliot, so the state of my house was a moot point.

That's not to say I wasn't incredibly grateful when I opened the front door to see that it looked just as nice as I'd left it this morning.

Stella came to see me as soon as I crossed the threshold, but when Eliot came in behind me, she darted for him like he was covered in catnip. She twined herself in and out between his ankles, purring louder than I had ever heard her purr before. It sounded like she had a megaphone around her neck.

"Friendly," he said, bending over to run a hand down her back as she made another figure eight in front of and behind his ankles.

"Do you like cats?" This could be a deal breaker.

"I do. I haven't owned one in years, but they usually tend to try to be friendly to me. Not necessarily this friendly, but friendly." Stella gave up on the infinity symbols and instead started kneading the dough on his pant leg.

"I can move her."

"No need, it's fine." He petted her again and then waited for her to stop kneading him before he walked over to my breakfast bar. As soon as he sat down, Stella gracefully leapt from the tiled floor onto his lap. She circled a few times and then, having made an appropriate nest on his lap, she settled in. If I knew my cat, and I did, she was not going to move even if he tried to get up. And what little I knew of Eliot, he wouldn't even try. What a pair. And why did that make me jealous of a cat?

Moving on because I did not want to explore that too much...

"I'll just bring everything over to you. That might work best." I left before he could answer and went into my office to gather the notes and order pad slips, the pictures I'd taken where I'd found the lanyards, and any research I'd done. Which wasn't much but it was something. At the last minute, I also grabbed my laptop, just in case we might need it.

"Do you want something to drink?" I asked as I laid everything out on the surface in front of him and tried to arrange it in a way that I thought would make sense.

"Not yet, I'm fine. I had this awesome milkshake earlier made by this very wonderful person, so I think I'm good for the time being."

I so wanted to lift my eyes to see if he was teasing, but I just couldn't do it. I hummed in approval instead and kept my eyes on what I was doing, namely making a mess of things by spreading them out, then putting them back in piles, to then spread them out again but differently.

"It's not a science, Jax. Why don't you leave it in a pile, and we can go through each thing one at a time and put them in the appropriate piles? That might be our best bet."

Made total sense. And why hadn't I thought of that? I reined in my frustration and tried again.

"Okay." I straightened my pretty impressive stack of materials and then grabbed the first order slip off the top. "Barbie is getting new boobs."

"Ah, um, good for her? Didn't we go over that one already? Do you think it's more significant now and should remain in the pile?"

I snickered because of the ridiculousness of that being my first piece of any kind of evidence and also because of his answer. "Should I put that in the 'might be of consequence' pile?"

"Let's call it 'could be significant if we find a different dot to connect to' if that's okay?"

"You're the former cop, not me. We're going to go with whatever you think is best."

"Yeah, well, I don't always seem to know what's best, so let's meet in the middle and make decisions together. I don't outrank you to be honest."

I lifted my gaze to his and found a true sadness in his green eyes. Maybe I should ask him after all. But no, I wasn't ready to spill my secrets just because he did, and I knew I would feel compelled to do just that if he shared only because I'd asked.

"Okay, so Barbie's new assets are in the 'need a connecting dot' pile. I do have some information that has to do with why the farmer's market is discounting their cheese."

That surprised a laugh out of him. "Really, is that a true topic of conversation?"

"My customers talk about all kinds of stuff. We're not making deals like they do at Hildy's place over fifty-dollar plates of scallops. We're talking weather and if the farmer's almanac had it right last Tuesday which, by the way, it pretty much always does."

"Good to know. Let's put the cheese conversation in most likely not connected."

"Can do."

We kept going through each slip one at a time. Issues with gutters and how people didn't like the new light they'd put up on Main Street because it didn't register that you were sitting there until a second or third car came up behind you. Talk about the construction going on in town, and how it was making us grow more than most of the lifelong residents wanted. I sorted, and we laughed at some of them, but he also had insight into some things that I would have never considered.

"Put the one with the info on banking mistakes over to the pile with the closer to home tidbits," he said. "Since so much of what we've heard seems to have to do with money, that's always a pretty good motivator for offing someone that could be more significant than we think."

"Okay."

"And I don't think it's written down on any of your papers, but we might want to consider the mix between two different people thinking they're getting this land and not being aware that it was already promised to the county." He took the hand he had been resting on Stella's back and used it to turn a piece of paper over. He held his hand out, and without asking for it, I handed him a pen. He scribbled a few notes. I tried to make out what he'd written, but it was worse than looking at a doctor's signature.

"Care to explain?" I asked.

"So, I was doing some research this morning before I came into the diner. I wanted to see if there was anything in particular in his past that might spark a death outside of all these ladies that everyone seems to think he's got on leashes. Narrowing down the search field will help. Not that we're going to cut the ladies or their husbands out of the equation. But if we can prove that everything else is on the up and up, I'd rather wait to make sure nothing else makes sense before we tackle that list Jasper gave you."

"Makes sense. So, the land. What did you find out?" And why did I feel like such a slacker for not having anything substantial to add? There were a ton of papers and slips and napkins with scribbles in the probably not-significant pile and very few in the could-be pile. Was I wasting too much time gathering every single thing instead of only keeping things that made sense?

"Now, wait, when you had written that the shoo-in is Linus, what did you mean?"

I looked at the handwriting because I did not remember writing that down, though that didn't necessarily mean I hadn't, only that I didn't remember.

"Um, well, let's see. I've listened to so many conversations over the last few days, and that kind of looks like my writing, but the

I is dotted differently than I normally do." I bit my lower lip and tried to think of anything that might have to do with Linus. Was that a person? An operating system for the restaurant business? A software for a computer? An app on the phone for something? I ran over and over everything I could think of, and nothing was popping.

"I'm sorry. I don't know what it means, and to be honest, I don't remember writing it."

"If you could think a little harder that would be wonderful because when I was researching the land and how it's going to the county, the name Linus came up as the developer who wants to try to buy it off the county, even though the paperwork filed says that it is to become a conservatory. And I heard Hildy talking about how she can't get someone named Linus to leave her alone about buying her restaurant."

Well, then, maybe it was a real clue out of all the mess of other false leads.

Go figure.

CHAPTER TWENTY

We kept going through the notes, looking for anything that would connect to that particular Linus dot, and found a few things that might but nothing concrete. Eventually Stella Luna got bored and jumped off Eliot's lap to go play with her stuffed mouse in the living room.

As soon as his lap was free, Eliot was up and stalking around my kitchen. There really wasn't another word for it. He was a man on a mission. When he went past the first few cabinets, he looked at me as if asking permission to open them. I nodded yes as I kept trying to paw through the data to see what else could help us.

After the fourth cabinet, I waved my hand at the whole kitchen and said, "Make yourself at home. There's nothing too exciting, but there's also nothing to hide. Have at it."

I took the seat next to the one he vacated at the breakfast bar and continued sorting things, now having more of a system of what should probably go where. The real info pile was only growing a little bit while the other piles were nearly falling over with the stacked papers. I hadn't realized how much we'd gathered until this moment. We might not have a lot, but we certainly didn't miss a single thing as far as I could tell.

Out of the corner of my eye, I appreciated the way Eliot's black T-shirt and blue jeans contrasted so completely with my turquoise cabinets and cream trim. I'd been going through a coloring phase when I'd updated the kitchen and got roped into this color combo that I still loved, but it didn't match much else in my small house.

I returned to my pile creation until Eliot pulled open the door to the refrigerator and scoffed.

I glanced up and nearly snickered at his look of horror. I knew what he was seeing—almost nothing in there. I ate most meals at the diner, and since there was only one of me, sometimes it was hard to prepare meals that were a single serving. So, I tended to keep a small pint of milk, a block of cheese, a couple of eggs, and some bread in the fridge and not much else. If there was anything I hated doing it was throwing food away because it had started rotting and could no longer be used.

"Please tell me your pantry is in better shape than this." He shot me a look, and I shrugged.

"You already looked in my pantry." I pointed at the two long doors to the left of the stove.

"That is not a pantry. That's a collection of paper plates and holiday platters that probably haven't seen the light of day in years if ever."

"I assure you it is a pantry. Maybe not the one you keep or really anyone keeps, but it's mine, and I'm not ashamed of it."

"Ha," he said, "you should be. However, it's just more of a challenge for me, and I accept it."

I giggled because he sounded both offended and interested at the same time. I sat at the breakfast bar with my chin in my upturned hand while he rummaged in my freezer. That had a little more going for it since freezer burn didn't bother me as much as contemplating cutting the mold off a block of cheese or seeing my white bread go green.

"The utensils—"

"I found them already. You keep to what you're doing over there, and I'll see if I can wrangle this into something edible over here."

"Yes, sir."

He shot me a narrow-eyed look but smiled a wicked smile and turned his back on me.

"So, while I'm looking at all this information, is there anything I should be researching online? Like deeds or Roderick? He probably had an extensive digital footprint with all the things he'd been into, right?"

"Hmm, sure." He rattled some pans and started mumbling to himself. I heard something about virgin olive oil and my can of spray oil, and that was about it.

"So, if I just put his name in, do you think I should follow some links to the different places he's listed? Or will that get me into trouble the way I might not want to be in?"

"Okay."

That didn't answer my question, but I had a feeling he was

lost in the ether of food creation. I wished him good luck with the limited selection I had on hand.

The first few links were just pages Roderick had set up for himself, talking about his life and the things he'd accomplished but skewed toward whatever organization he was trying to be a part of. Like he mentioned his extensive knowledge of fishing and put the logo and the link for the national fishing conglomerate in the area on his page. Another he had photographed himself with a bunch of beagles and talked about being a rival to the Dog Whisperer and then linked to the AKC. One more had him dressed in a suit and tie, expounding on his financial expertise, and inviting people to pay him for advice to grow their money with a twenty percent stake for him. He hadn't linked that to anything, but it looked like he'd just made it a few days before he'd been killed.

I moved to the next page of links and found some social media links that looked interesting. I waded through them, but nothing looked like anything more than the others—him putting forward a picture of himself that wasn't true and making claims that there was no way he could back up.

And then I found a group online that required you to fill out a survey before you could join. I bypassed that for the moment to see who was in the group and what they were talking about. I was astounded when I found my mother's sister's name in the register, and when I looked closer, all the group members were female and about ninety percent of their husbands were on the list that Jasper had handed me. Or at least that's what I thought until I pulled the list out from one of the piles and compared, finding that ninety-five percent of the women on the list had husbands on the group list.

What was this, and how did it affect what I knew?

Now I really wanted to get into the group. Clicking the link for the questionnaire, I was met with a slew of questions that seemed to have nothing to do with each other. What was my favorite color? Did I have my own bank account? Was I ready to make a difference in the world by making other people's lives better? Did I like flowers? Did I wear dresses? If I had to compare myself to a movie star from before 2000, who would it be?

What the heck was this? I took a screenshot of the different pages and saved it to my desktop. I looked up and was going to ask Eliot what he thought, but his face was a storm cloud of disapproval, and he had a generic box of macaroni and cheese in his hands. I hid my smile as I lowered my head back to what I was working on and left him to fend for himself in this strange territory of someone who didn't really ever cook at home. He'd either figure it out, or I had a great restaurant I could recommend we go to if he got a discount for eating at the inn.

I answered the questions to the best of my abilities and got an auto-response that my answers would be taken into consideration, and I would be added to the "Bevy of Roderick's Bower" if I was found acceptable.

Okay, that was ridiculous. But what was more ridiculous was that my aunt was a member. I had to know what it entailed and why. And if I couldn't get in because Roderick was now dead and not taking new applications, I was going to have to figure out how to ask her.

I glanced up and found Eliot smiling. No more swearing and no more grumbling to himself. No, he was full on smiling and looked to have gotten over himself. That was either going to be a blessing, or it would be delivered as a sermon on the responsibilities of being an adult living on my own.

"One of the ways I coped with what happened was to challenge myself to make something delicious out of nothing. When I was trying to work through what had gone wrong with the last guy I had a hand in convicting, it helped."

Okay. I put the paperwork down and gave him my undivided attention. There was a tension in the air that made me feel like this was important, and if he was going to share, I needed to be listening.

"I would take things from the grocery aisles that were obviously as processed and manufactured as possible, and then I'd make them into something that a person would pay a hundred dollars for a taste."

I chuckled. "I don't have a hundred dollars if you're going to charge me in my own home to eat food you're making with my own ingredients."

"That's what I like about you, Jax. You have an answer for everything even if you think it's the wrong answer. You'll defend it no matter what, and it turns out you're usually right. So here was the scenario. What would you have done?"

"Lay it out for me. I'm all ears." And a ton of trepidation. What if I got it wrong, and he didn't finish cooking whatever was starting to fill my house with the most divine aromas?

"There was a bank heist. I had the guy on camera, walking

out of the bank with a bulging suitcase of something. When I rolled back the video, he had gone in with a very empty looking case, and there was a gun tucked into the back of his pants. Or at least I thought it was a gun. I did not expect him to try to tell me it was a banana to address his diabetic sugar low just in case he sank too fast."

"And you were supposed to believe that? Did he use it to threaten the teller at the bank? Did she think it was a banana?"

"See." He shook his head and smiled. "Good questions, really good questions, and ones I asked myself. We even found some of the money that was stolen and were able to match it up from the place it was spent to a building where he had made purchases. I thought I had it all. I even had an inmate who was his cellmate who said my guy had told him how it all went down. He gave me details that there was no way he would have known unless my guy did it. We hadn't released that information to the public for the very reason that anyone who volunteered something like that must have insider information."

"That makes sense. I thought the same thing today. If whoever did this mentioned that it was a brick that came through the window when my dad told me no one had been told that, I would be suspicious. Although Dani said she heard about the brick but can't remember who said it."

"Precisely, though sometimes information does leak or someone says something near someone else that clues them in. It happens. But the kind of details the inmate had were far beyond guessing what flew through a window to break it. I'm talking caliber of the gun, where the one bullet that was shot had embedded in the deposit slips, and the fact that he was left-handed."

I tucked my arms around me and waited.

"So, we get to the trial, and it's all set. He continued to protest his innocence, but most people usually do, especially those who are guilty. We had a strong case though. My fellow officers and I had done everything we could, looked at the arrest and the evidence a hundred times to make sure we were not putting the wrong guy away. And the jury believed everything the prosecutor laid out because it was airtight and solid as anything."

He took a deep breath and paused to stir whatever smelled so incredibly lovely on the stove in a big pan I hadn't used probably since I'd moved here four years ago.

"And then it all collapsed. He was released with new

evidence that we apparently missed. The judge let him off without even a slap on the wrist. He expunged his record, made me formally apologize for getting it wrong, and then my guy got to go back to his life from before. He sued the department for wrongful pursuit and defamation of character, and they paid him with few questions. I'd screwed up. I'd believed someone who I shouldn't have, and my career was over."

Here were all the details to fill in the abbreviated story Aunt Hildy had told me. Still… "That's not possible."

"And yet it happened."

I wanted to defend him until the cows came home. I might not know him better than other people, and we'd only met a few days ago, but there was no way Eliot would get something so wrong. It just didn't feel possible.

"So here you are cooking in my kitchen with limited supplies, trying to read clues and make guesses off our limited information because Hildy asked you to help."

He laughed, but it was a darker sound than I heard before. "I doubt I'll be much help, and if I come to any conclusions, then you might want to quadruple check them or have your dad make sure he would have come to the same conclusion independently before you go after anyone. It's the only way to be sure."

"Eliot…"

With a flourish, he dropped spoonfuls of whatever was in the pot into my shallow bowls I sometimes used for cereal if the milk was starting to age out in the fridge. The second it was on the counter in front of me my mouth started watering uncontrollably. What on earth had he done, and what had he done it with?

"Dig in while it's still hot. I might be a crap investigator, but the pantry is my playground, and I think I hit this one out of the park."

He fixed his own bowl and then grabbed the generic shaker of parmesan cheese out of the door of the fridge before sitting down. "Tell me when," he said, sounding an awful lot like a popular Italian chain restaurant waiter.

His shaking skills were something to behold, and he'd nearly drowned whatever this was in cheese before I finally said to stop.

"I was wondering if you were so afraid of the pasta that you would rather eat an entire bottle of fake cheese than eat my food."

"No, no, my word, no. This smells like heaven." I pulled

Dines, Drive-Ins, and Lies | 171

napkins from the holder in front of me and started using my spoon to take off the mountain cap of the cheese and get down to a much more manageable sprinkling. "So, what is this?"

"Taste it then tell me if you know."

I was not a fan of tests, having often failed them in school even if I knew the information backward and forward. But he seemed to find joy in this even after telling his very rough story, so I indulged him. It wouldn't hurt me if I got it wrong.

I dipped my spoon in the edge of the bowl where a reddish-brown sauce cradled delicious looking noodles and shredded chicken, I was pretty sure. I didn't think I had any other meat in the freezer other than chicken, and the noodles at first glance looked savory. But when I tried to remember what I had on hand, all I could come up with was packaged ramen or that box of mac and cheese.

Still, I smiled and planned to gush over how awesome this was no matter how it tasted. That was one lie I was absolutely fine with telling.

Except when I brought the spoon to my mouth, there was absolutely no way of stopping the complete and utter moan of yumminess. Oh my stars. This was… "Perfection. How on earth did you do that with nothing here? Are you magic? How bad do you think Hildy would hate me if I tried to steal you from her? We're thinking of staying open for dinner but don't have much of a menu except breakfast all day, but this… this is divine."

"For real divine? Or you're just saying that because you feel sorry for me being so completely wrong at the job I thought I'd retire from, so you're being nice to me?"

Instead of an answer, I slowly slid his bowl away from him, put the spoon I'd already eaten off of into the pasta, and took a bite from there too. I licked it therefore it was mine. These were the rules.

A laugh burst out of him, but this time it was real and filled with joy and maybe a little relief? I wasn't sure, but I liked it. I liked even more that he pulled me in for a quick hug and kissed the top of my head before hopping off the barstool and dishing up another bowl for himself.

"Thank you for trusting me enough to tell me what happened," I said. "And I'm sorry that's how it went down. I don't think you did the wrong thing. I think something happened in there that skewed the data to his favor, and you got annihilated in the process."

"Well, I appreciate your vote of confidence there, but that

chapter is over, and this one is rocking if you loved my soup this much. We'll leave it there for the night. Eat up. We should go check in with Hildy and see what she's got on tape, and then I'm thinking we might want to call it a day. It's been a long one, and it hasn't necessarily been an all good one."

He was right. So, we stuck to funnier topics for the rest of the meal. Things like why I didn't feel the need to even have good sugar in the house, and how I could stand generic parmesan.

We headed over to the inn in separate cars because he would probably want to go home after this as he should. Tomorrow was another day. With everything that he'd been able to put together regarding Roderick, I was very tempted to tell him about Smitty, and what had happened, if just to get it out to someone. No one else knew, but maybe I also wanted to see if he had any ideas on how I might be able to get my money back.

But again, tomorrow was another day.

Hildy's was a bust since the only video she had was grainy, and it showed literally just my driver's side taillight and the lanyards that had been in the passenger side. I did write myself a note to count them again when I got home, and then I drove there by myself, reminding myself I did not want a relationship. I wasn't ready for a relationship. And even if Eliot seemed perfect, there had to be something wrong with him, some aspect I wouldn't be able to handle. We just needed to get to know each other better before I found that thing I couldn't live with.

But that night my dreams were filled with him and his smile and his voice. I woke up not remembering exactly what I'd dreamed about but feeling very happy about the feelings they had evoked.

"Down, sister," I said to myself in the mirror as Stella Luna jumped up on the counter to see what I was doing.

She must have thought I meant her because she went right to the floor, searched out the shirt I'd been wearing last night, and dragged it to the couch then made a nest on it. Silly cat.

But it did smell like Eliot when I sniffed it. Maybe she wasn't so silly after all.

Today was a busy day, so I left her with the living room light on and a kiss on her head then went to work. Dani was off today, so I had all day there. We had talked about hiring a manager to help, but for right now that was out of the budget. Yet, if the crowds kept coming like they had yesterday and were today, then we might need to rethink that.

Finally, three rolled around, and I said goodbye to everyone. I stood at the crack in the doors as each left to see if anyone looked at the stuffed locker or tried to use it, but no one even gave it a glance. I was going to have to find a different way of doing recon if I wanted to solve that little mystery.

In the meantime, I went home and pulled my computer back up. I had not yet received approval for my request to join the Bevy, but I had driven past my aunt's house and saw her car in the driveway earlier. I took a chance and called her cell phone to see if I could figure out how to ask her if she'd been cheating on Uncle Ralph with a loser, and why on earth she thought being in a group of women fawning after a loser jerk of a person was a good use of her time. But first I'd ask her if she wanted to tell me what they talked about and what the allure was for someone to join—something I just didn't understand.

"Hey there, stranger," Aunt Sadie said as soon as she answered the call.

"Hi there! Are you busy? I don't want to keep you if you're in the middle of something."

"Nope, nothing going on. Ralph is out bowling this evening, and I have nothing to do, so I'm just wandering around picking things up and then putting them down again."

We both chuckled at her lame joke, and I asked all the requisite questions like how the family was, how my cousins were, what new escapade her youngest had gotten himself into lately (he was trying to get into the flag team at the high school) and then how her job was. It took about ten minutes, but it was worth it to not come off as looking for only one thing and leaving her hanging if I didn't get it.

"So, Aunt Sadie…"

"Yes, sweets? What's up? Not that I don't love phone calls from you, but you usually text. So, what's going on?"

Now I really didn't want to ask. I did not need to know if my aunt had once had an affair with a guy who didn't deserve to even breathe her air.

"Just spit it out, Jax. It can't be that bad. And it's between us, so I'm not worried."

"Were you involved with Roderick before he died?" There. I spit it out like she'd told me to, and she started sputtering like I had been afraid she might. Dang it!

"Involved?" Her voice rose a few notes. "Involved?" Make that an octave.

If she started screeching, I was going to have to hang up, and then I'd try again later, maybe after I grabbed some cake from the diner and perhaps one of my now delectable milkshakes. Like a peace offering for irritating her but also a transition to still needing the information.

But she blew out a harsh breath and hummed for a moment like she was channeling some kind of better energy or maybe just the will not to break her voice box.

"I'm sure you have reasons for asking, and it's not on you that this is an embarrassing situation, and one that I'd rather never have to think about again."

"I am sorry for upsetting you. I just don't really have anyone else I can ask who I know will tell me the truth."

She sighed, a gusty one this time instead of harsh. "This has to do with his death then I take it?"

"Yeah. I'm getting slammed on all sides with rumors and clues, and I don't know how to put them together. But then I came across this social media group last night, and your name was on there, along with a bunch of other ladies in town, and I couldn't tell what it was for." Best to leave it there. No speculation needed.

"It was a horrible decision on my part, and one that I will probably regret for the rest of my days. It's something your uncle and I do not talk about. It's the past."

Maybe I should just leave it there, I thought. I highly doubted any of the ladies had killed Roderick, and all I was doing was bringing up bad memories and making my aunt, my favorite aunt related by blood, uncomfortable. It wasn't worth it. I had other avenues to pursue, and if my dad saw the info for himself and wanted to interview people, then he would do more footwork before just shooting in the dark at any moving target.

"We can leave it there," I finally said. "I hope you have a good day, and again, I'm sorry for hurting you when I didn't mean to."

"No, it's valid and if you're asking, then God knows your father probably will too when he gets around to it. I'd rather deal with it now than wait for that phone call or request to come in."

"Okay." I wasn't sure what else to say since this was not my story, and I had no idea what questions to ask to make it easier for her to tell hers.

"A couple of years ago, your uncle and I were going through a rough patch."

Did I really want to hear this? I was afraid I didn't if that was the way she was going to start it. But I kept my cringe to myself.

"Not in our marriage, that has always been solid."

I released the breath I hadn't realized I'd been holding.

"But financially we were nearing a bind after one of the kids got into some trouble and had to pay the consequences."

As much as I was curious about who that was and what they'd done, I reminded myself that it had nothing to do with what I needed to know and could lead to a whole other uncomfortable tale that I might want to avoid being witness to.

"Anyway, Roderick had emailed me a few times asking if I'd be willing to go into business with him. His projections were good but not over the top, his charm was on full force, and I thought it might be a good and fast way to bring in some needed cash without overtaxing myself."

"I'm assuming that was not at all what happened."

"No, it was a scam from the very beginning. He was selling land he didn't own and then ghosting people left and right. Even if you could corner him, he somehow slithered out from under the questioning and any responsibility. When I read the contract word for word, it was actually well done and on the up-and-up, but it was akin to selling you swampland in the state of New York. Nonexistent. And it wasn't the only scam he was running. He had another with beauty products that your Aunt May got roped into, and another involving crypto currency that my friend Doris plunged her whole savings into. But every time he managed to weasel out of being held accountable for his acts. That group was originally about keeping ourselves informed, warning everyone about what might be next, and making sure no one else got bamboozled. We set it up with the intention of keeping each other safe but called it something nice, so he wouldn't feel threatened."

"The questions to get in were strange."

This time she laughed, and a weight lifted from my shoulders.

"Yeah, well, it was code. Only those who knew the right answers would be allowed in, and that was only because we told the right people the right way to answer them." She paused. "I didn't even realize it was still running. Did you answer the questions?"

"I did."

"I'll have to go check out your answers." She snickered, and I felt better about the whole thing, but I still had more questions.

"So now that we're in a better place, I'm sorry again for upsetting you. Do you think anyone in the group would have wanted Roderick dead?"

"Honestly, yes and no. I think they would have been fine if something had ushered him into the fiery depths of hell, but I don't think any of us would have actually done it and certainly not with a lanyard, and not one from your diner. Did they find out how whoever it was got it?"

"I have no idea, but I'm still looking. I've counted them again and again, and I'm not missing as many as I've found, so I don't know if there are more out there or not. There was no damage to my car that anyone found, but I keep finding them in creepy places. If I can't figure out how many they took, I don't know when that might stop."

"How many did you order?"

I should have known she would ask that. She was my mother's sister, and their minds ran along the same track more often than I wanted to admit.

"One thousand. I counted them, and I was missing two. But now I've found three, and I don't know how they're getting them."

"You're going to want to make sure that any information you can get on your own is solid before you jump off into the next thing."

"I'm doing my best. I will try to see what else I can find when we get off the phone."

"We can do that now if you want. I love talking with you, but your uncle is due home in a few minutes, and I'd like a little time to settle my brain about my part in things. At least he didn't ruin me like Jane and Sandra."

"Is it better now at least? Did you recoup your money?"

"Not recoup but at least I stopped bleeding it out to fund his lifestyle. And with him gone, there's no one else who will get hurt."

I could think of at least three people who were not going to go unharmed by his demise, and they had all been in my diner yesterday. Maybe it was time to stop stalking the small-time players. Really start talking to the ones who had a serious motive and most likely a good opportunity to exact their revenge or make it so what they thought they'd get after his passing was in the works, even if it wasn't.

CHAPTER TWENTY-ONE

To prepare myself for the conversations I might get to have if I was brave enough to actually approach the key players, I did some more research. Instead of just Roderick's name, this time I also used some keywords like business and con man, and that exploded my search engine. The results came rolling in within seconds, and none of them were good.

The sheer number of businesses and cons the man had started and then abandoned was extensive. I started a spreadsheet after I got to page three of a word document, and I wasn't even on page two on the search results. A hundred lines later, I marveled at how he had gotten away with so much with little to no backlash. But then I got to page three of the search results, and the threats and horrible reviews were plenty.

And for each one, he would answer and goad, never apologize, never repent, never change tactics, just sneer with his words, and give major attitude to those he'd hurt.

My suspect list grew seven times in fifteen minutes.

I sent a text to Eliot because I wasn't sure what he was up to, and as much as I didn't mind talking with Aunt Sadie on the phone, I was much better at texting when contacting other people.

He winged one back within seconds, saying that he was looking into the land because he had thought Roderick was just donating it to the county out of the goodness of his heart and wanting to make sure his death did not benefit anyone, but it looked like that was not the case. He'd get back to me later.

Just as I was shooting another message back to him that we'd talk when he was available and inviting him to come make dinner again and promising that I'd have real things to cook, a knock sounded on my door.

Was he on his way somewhere else, and since we were texting, he thought it best to just stop in instead?

With a big smile on my face, I opened the door and was greeted by a huge bouquet of red roses. They had been placed on the small side table I had out there to set down my tea if I wanted to read on the front porch. Looking left and right I saw no one who would have delivered them. It hadn't taken me long to answer the knock, and I would have thought that I got here in time to at least say thanks to the delivery person.

Instead, the bouquet sat in all its glory on the table, and no one was in sight.

I brought it in, a little nervous now. I would have loved to just be so excited to get such a pretty arrangement, a little giddy that someone had paid for me to get them.

But with the way things had been going recently, I wasn't nearly as trusting as I had been even a week ago, much less three months ago before Smitty had run off with my money.

I placed the glass vase on the breakfast bar and walked back and forth in front of it, avoiding the barstools Eliot and I had sat on last night.

I'd had such an amazing time with so little effort, and that was new to me when it came to the dating scene. Not that Eliot and I were dating.

Before I fell down that rabbit hole, I approached the flowers. They could have been from Eliot. Maybe instead of thinking he should stop by to talk instead of text, he'd thought it would be a great idea to send me a flower arrangement. Maybe it was to say thanks for listening to his story and believing him. Maybe they were actually for Stella Luna due to her obvious affection for him.

Maybe I should just open the card that was sticking out of the flowers and see what was in it and stop maybe-ing.

Lifting the flap on the card, I closed my eyes and pulled it out, hoping it was something good. Even if the flowers were for Stella that would be better than some of the other things my mind was trying to conjure up.

I opened the card, and my heart stuttered. If I was going to *maybe*, then maybe I should have figured that no one nice was sending flowers, and I should have been prepared for maybe getting a threatening note with the blood red roses.

I threw the card on the ground as if that would save me from the message that had been written. Stella Luna immediately pounced on it, threw it over her back, then darted around and picked it up again to throw it again. It was a game for her but a metaphorically stab in the heart for me.

She didn't want to give it back to me when I tried to get it out of her mouth, but I was bigger, and I was going to win. I tapped her on the nose, and she turned and threw the card again. This time I caught it in midair, and she trotted around looking for where her new toy had landed.

In my hands. Right where someone who wanted to scare me off had made sure it would land and land with a one-two punch.

Okay, they were only words, and I was safe. No one was actually going to hurt me, and I was more determined now than ever to find out who was behind all this. They needed to pay for their crimes, including ruining a perfectly beautiful bouquet with hate and threats. Threats to take me out if I didn't show up alone at the drive-in tonight to get the real info or stop searching for things that were none of my business. But they miscalculated and made those things even more my business by making it personal, more personal than the lanyards as far as I was concerned.

Picking up the phone again (how many phone calls had I made today? Too many), I dialed the florist. Margie had made me my very own corsage for Winter Formal in high school when I went with a bunch of my friends instead of waiting for some boy to ask me out. We'd all giggled and laughed and *oohed* and *ahhed* over the selection of flowers as we put together what we wanted instead of waiting for some offering from a boy who might not really want to know the first thing about us as long as we looked pretty on their arm.

It rang four times, and I was almost certain that I was going to go to voicemail when a harried Margie answered with an abrupt, "Hello."

Before I could get a word out, she tried again. "Sorry, sorry, good afternoon and thank you for calling The Florid Florist. How can I make your day brighter today?" She sighed like that had taken it all out of her, and I considered hanging up. But I had things I needed to know.

"Margie, it's Jax. Things not going so well over there today?"

"That easy to tell, huh?"

"A little yeah. When you answered, it sounded like you were ready to deadhead someone."

"See, you still remember terminology from when you

worked for me that one summer! You should have come here instead of going to the diner."

It was a conversation we'd had a few times, but as much fun as I had that one summer, the diner was always where I knew I belonged. "Sad for all of us, I'm sure, but what's going on over there that is making you so agitated?"

"I was supposed to get a delivery of those cards people fill out to put in the small envelopes and I'm missing an entire box. The printer is saying they delivered them all, and that it's not their responsibility if I lost track of a box out of ten."

"That lacks customer service etiquette."

"Seriously, they might then also be lacking a customer if they don't fix this. Those cards are not cheap."

No, they weren't, but neither were my lanyards. Who was stealing these things and why?

"Did you have a bouquet going out to me at all today? Did anyone call in and ask for a bunch of red roses in a purple vase?"

I heard keys clicking on her computer. "I have a new assistant since I couldn't talk you into being here. I don't see anything in the system though. A big bunch of red roses? Hmmm, nope."

"Are the roses missing out of your inventory, or are you all accounted for in those?"

"Give me a second." I heard her clunk the phone down on a hard surface, and then she moved away, talking to someone about getting the daisies ready for Roderick's funeral wreath. I wondered who was paying for that. I hadn't come across anyone who would make a wreath out of weeds at this point, much less pay for it to be made with real flowers.

"Nope, I don't have any missing roses. They're all accounted for."

Dang it! "Okay, thanks for checking and good luck on finding your missing cards."

We hung up and I filled in the information on my excel spreadsheet on another tab. I could transfer all my questions to the other tab to keep them in one place. They were stacking up faster than used coffee cups on a Saturday morning.

But they all seemed so random, and that was one of the biggest issues. It wasn't like I had one direction to look in, and it was just a matter of picking out which person in the locked room had done the strangling. There was a plethora of bad things Roderick had done over the course of his life. It could have been revenge served on ice. It could have been a crime of passion. One of chance where someone who was having a bad day and hated Roderick saw him skulking around out back. The person could have decided to take the opportunity to run to my car, pick the lock, grab a lanyard because they had no other weapon, then strangle him and leave him for dead in the garbage enclosure, figuring someone would find him at some point during the night.

Argh!!!

Okay, I needed to get myself into order and then see what there was to find. I wanted to offer my dad something, and right now I had a lot of nothing. Hmm, unless I took Eliot with me to the drive-in tonight to see what on earth there was that I needed to know so badly.

Since it was Tuesday night, there wouldn't be anyone there, so no one else would be in danger, but I was most certainly not going by myself. I was not too stupid to live. Seriously.

I texted Eliot again, knowing that he was only on for lunch today. I wanted to run the drive-in idea by him. He would probably put his cop hat back on and say that it was ridiculous for us to go. I almost wanted him to do that. I could call my dad and tell him someone was going to be at the drive-in tonight, and he could go over there and catch them in my stead. But I was all in now, and I didn't want to send him off on some wild goose chase if I could chase that goose on my own and offer it up on a platter garnished with herb potatoes and a carrot or two for flavor.

I got on social media and took a chance before I brought anyone else in. I took a picture of the flowers with the card and envelope in front of them and thanked the person who'd sent them, and said I'd see them tonight.

A little dangerous? Perhaps but I was getting annoyed that someone was playing with me. I didn't take well to that kind of thing. We'd see what happened from there. In the meantime, I was going to search my car to see if I'd missed any between the seats.

Of course, as soon as I saw the car in the driveway, I couldn't help but notice that there was a lanyard stuck under the windshield wiper. I yelled in the back of my throat, hoping that whoever was taunting me was watching, so they wouldn't be too surprised when I brought a hammer down on their head. This was ludicrous, and those things had not been cheap. I was done with finding them damaged and in the wrong place, which was anywhere but in the box I'd picked up from the printer the day of our celebratory dinner for being open for six months.

After taking a picture of the placement, I stalked back in the house and dragged the box out. I gave Stella Luna one of the lanyards to play with as I stared at the box of the biggest headache I'd had in years.

We were participating in a hometown day coming up next month, and Dani and I had decided the lanyards would be a great thing for people to use during the festival, so we'd invested in them. They had the logo running along the entire ribbon that would go around the person's neck. Not in a strangling way, obviously. They were long and had a metal clip at the bottom to hold on to a badge or a card or whatever you wanted to put on it. We'd considered using them for the diner instead of name tags but had decided against it because the lanyard would swing away from the body and land right in someone's coffee if you weren't careful. We didn't want that added stress on our servers.

The lanyards really were pretty—no matter how much I hated seeing them right now. They reminded me of everything that had gone wonky the last few days.

Except Eliot. He hadn't been wonky.

I cut myself off from daydreaming before I got too far into it because I had things to do and no time to daydream.

At the risk of inundating Eliot with texts, I sent him a quick message letting him know I'd found another and taken a picture. Then I sat down with my spreadsheet again. If I had nine hundred ninety-eight lanyards, then where were these extra ones coming from? Had no one actually broken into my car? The police had told me they didn't find evidence of a break in, but I really didn't think I had forgotten to lock my car, so how else could they have gotten a lanyard? What did it all mean? Had I been operating under false info all along?

That sucked to even consider it, but I had to.

So, if no one had stolen the lanyards out of my car, then they would have had to bring it with them to the crime scene.

That was a revelation that deserved its own tab in the spreadsheet.

I typed it in and then sat there staring at it.

The only way they could have done that was to get the lanyards from the printer.

Well, I guess I knew where I was headed before sundown and our showdown at the drive-in a few hours from now.

The drive to the printer didn't take long. I tried to formulate how to ask questions without giving away my real purpose there and tipping my hand before I was ready.

I tried and discarded a number of ways to ask how many they made and why there were extras. But if I went about it that way, there was every possibility that if it was someone at the printer—for whatever reason—they'd know I knew, and it could all come avalanching down on my head.

Instead, I sat in my car in their small parking lot for a minute going over other scenarios.

Someone pounded on my window and scared the heck out of me.

Kenneth Benningfield. Roderick's son. He laughed at my expression of terror and then gestured for me to roll down my window. I decided that I'd rather get out of the car and meet him face-to-face, not in a confined space. He wasn't quick to move when I started opening my door, staying right up against the car, and making it almost impossible for me to get the door all the way open. The smile on his face was nothing short of mischievous. So, I used my shoulder to crank the door out, and if he hadn't moved so quickly, I would have had the satisfaction of knocking him in his nether regions.

Now it was my turn to smile, and it was big. I stood up from my car as he huffed out an irritated breath. At least he could still breathe. That could have been iffy a few seconds ago if he hadn't been fast enough.

"What do you want, Kenneth?" I had to admit my voice was not very nice, and my attitude was on full display, but I wasn't sorry.

"I just wanted to thank you for keeping things mostly civil yesterday in the diner. That could have gone very wrong if you'd let Delilah at me or Lydia for that matter. Brady and I have a lot going on with this land deal, and I need my wits about me to make sure I do the deal in the best possible way."

I had nothing to say to that really since I hadn't done anything, and if he truly knew that he wasn't getting the land, then he might have gone about things in a different way. As it was, that was not my story to tell, but since I had him here, I did have some questions. They weren't on my spreadsheet, but I was confident I could remember the answers if he actually gave me any.

Leaning back against my car, I crossed my arms and my ankles. "So, your dad left you the land, and you're going to sell it to Brady?"

"No, I'm not selling it. I'm just going to develop it like it should have been developed years ago. But Hildy always told Dad that it was a bad idea because she wanted her restaurant to be the only one out that way, and she liked the fields better than a bunch of houses."

"And your dad wanted you to develop it, even though he never did?"

"Yeah. I don't know what was between him and Hildy because he always seemed to listen to her instead of people who wanted what was best for him. But now that he's gone, I can finally do the thing he should have done years ago. The thing that he was going to talk to my mom about the night he was killed."

So, not only did Kenneth think he was benefiting from his father's death, but he looked relieved that he could be the one to make the deal. Interesting. And it struck me as odd that Roderick would have been meeting up with his first wife to discuss that.

"He was meeting your mom?"

"Yeah, they've been talking about getting back together, and since she has some say in the land and what it can be used for, she said he wanted to talk to her, so we could move forward."

But Roderick had to have known that was not going to happen. So why had he made dinner plans with his first wife? And why did people keep getting added to my list of suspects?

"You think your mom could have convinced him?"

"Come on, Jaxxy, you know he was never going to cross Hildy. No one ever does. She might be nice and all, but at her core, she's just as ruthless as anyone I know. She gets what she wants by intimidating and making people feel stupid for thinking anything but what she thinks. Even Brady won't cross her, and he'll cross just about anyone for what he wants. With Dad finally gone, she can't make me do anything I don't want to do, and she can't keep me from doing anything I want to do either. Developers have been trying to get their hands on that land for years and years, and Dad would talk about how we could be swimming in money if he hadn't made some promise."

Some promise? Was it the same one Hildy talked about

when they were younger? It didn't quite fit the story she'd told me, but that didn't mean it wasn't true.

"So, what all are they putting up?" Might as well act like I was interested while I processed the rest of what he had said.

"Apartments, houses, townhomes and in the middle, there will be these shops and restaurants that have houses on top of them. It's going to be like its own little city, and I get to pick whichever place I want. I won't have to depend on anyone to give me somewhere to sleep anymore. It's going to be awesome."

Wait, so Kenneth didn't have anywhere permanent to live? How did I not know that?

"You're benefiting a lot from this." I watched his face because I had yet to see any sadness over his father's death.

"You could say that, but you could also say I'm finally getting a chance to live the way I would have all along if my father hadn't always been up to one scheme or another. I want to go on the good path here. Do you know how hard it is having a father that no one likes and almost everyone can't stand? I want to bring a good thing to this community. I want to actually do something good for once. And now that Roderick Benningfield and his wayward ways are gone, I can actually do that." He saluted me. "Wish me luck? I'm going to pick up an order I placed last week and see my girlfriend for a few minutes. Talk to you later."

His girlfriend worked here? Even more interesting.

CHAPTER TWENTY-TWO

I lingered outside the print shop for a few minutes, waiting to see who Kenneth was talking to and whether I knew her. Unfortunately, he wasn't a small guy, and whoever he was talking to was completely covered by his broad back. There was nowhere in the parking lot that I could walk to and get a better view with the way the windows were set up.

Dang it!

At the last minute, I decided that instead of hanging back, I might as well just walk in. I could see from there. *Duh.*

But when I went into the storefront, there was no one on the other side of the counter from him.

Clarissa Nolan, the owner, and someone who I'd worked with over months of back and forth regarding our new logo, looked tired when she approached the counter where I was standing.

"Hey, Jax. Please tell me there was nothing wrong with the order you picked up the other day. I can't take much more going wrong around here."

"Oh, um." I was not sure what to say since technically there was nothing wrong with the order itself, but I did need to know who was using my design and my concept to kill people and threaten others.

"No, nothing wrong with the product itself. I just wanted to, um, check to see if you ever have like mock ones made before you actually put in the full order?" That was the best I had come up with after trying to get the information I wanted from a bunch of different directions without it being true north or my true question—how did someone get some of my lanyards if I had them all, and why did they use it to kill a man behind a restaurant? That felt a little too blunt.

"Not usually. Sometimes the lady on the printer will run a few extras in case any of them are damaged. Did you have any that were damaged?"

Part of me wanted to ask her to define damaged because the material itself was strong enough to have strangled someone without breaking, which was pretty impressive on its own, but it had caused a lot of damage too.

"There were four that I know of."

"Did you bring them with you so I can look them over? We can try to replace them, but I'd need the faulty ones. I just need to be able to give them to Jane so she can see what's happening and fix it."

I highly doubted my father would let me have the murder weapon to hand over to her just so I could keep up this fake dialogue.

"I'll have to ask Dani if she has them. Thanks."

"You need anything else?"

I looked around the small storefront at the many blank templates that you could use to make brochures and T-shirts and swag galore. I didn't need any of it, and I couldn't make a purchase without running it by Dani since you couldn't order just one and have it be cost effective. But I was still waiting to see if whoever had been talking with Kenneth came back.

"Um, well, perhaps some pricing on something."

She stared at me, obviously waiting for me to say how many and what I was looking at, but I had nothing. My mind had blanked out.

"Yeah, let me talk with Dani, and I'll get back to you. I'm not sure, and I don't want to take up your time."

"Okay, thanks." And she walked away. Fine then.

I went out to my car with no more information than I'd walked in with, but I did have things to look into, like Kenneth and his claim to want to do better and the absolute belief that he was getting the land. I couldn't imagine having a dad like Roderick, and I did get what he said about how hard it could be but from the opposite direction. When your father was one of the best, it wasn't easy to always feel like you needed to be even better, and mistakes were not something I did well. Take my current money situation. One of the biggest holdbacks to letting anyone know I was in trouble was that I didn't want to disappoint my parents or have people know I was stupid enough to let someone have access to my accounts. So, I kept it to myself and would work it out alone instead of asking for help. I knew that, and I knew that it was not the smartest way to go about things, but I just couldn't seem to make myself do anything different.

I sighed as I went around the back of my car to look in my

trunk for a coat. The wind had picked up and was brisk enough to want to have my arms covered.

Someone grunted and groaned off to the left. Were they hurt? I couldn't stop myself from checking out the situation.

And when I came around my back bumper, I saw a small redheaded woman lifting what had to be a very heavy box, making some noise but without a lot of straining. She stood straight and then just walked it in like it wasn't an issue at all. And Kenneth held the door for her. Kissing her on the forehead as she walked past.

Ducking back around the corner, I tried to decide what to do. I knew that face and that hair. Her mother worked for us at the diner. Alice Connelly was a wonderful woman who had fallen on hard times when her husband had up and left in the middle of the night, taking everything they owned with him.

She walked to work and still had a teenager at home. What was this one's name? Meredith? Mercy? Hailey? Hilary!

Hilary was the girlfriend? And what had she done to make Kenneth's situation better? He'd said she'd helped him, and that with his father dead, things would get better. She obviously was strong. Could she have taken a lanyard from here, found Roderick when he was outside the restaurant, and strangled him? Maybe hooked the lanyard around his neck and then stepped with her back to his and pulled tight so he couldn't move until he died?

I'd seen it on TV, which of course was not reality, but I was sure it could be done that way for someone who was determined.

But how had she known he was going to be in the back? How did she even know he was there?

I had so much to think about and so many unanswered questions. But if it was her, I should be narrowing down my search and looking for things that only would point toward her. Or was that the wrong way? Eliot had said that you had to keep an open mind and not get caught up in one suspect if there were others, and we still had the drive-in meeting this evening.

What to do? What to do?

I returned to my car because Kenneth was coming back from the side, and I didn't want to get caught spying on him and his girlfriend, no matter what I thought they had done.

With Daddy out of the way, I was hoping they wouldn't have anyone else they needed put in the ground for them to be happy, so no one else should currently be in danger. Which left me some time to decide what came next. And I didn't want to make that decision without running it by Eliot.

On the one hand, that felt like a good decision, and on the other hand, I was a little irritated that I didn't think I could move without him. I did not need a man, and he did not need to be needed.

I groaned at myself as I turned the ignition on in the car. This wasn't about me. It was about a murderer, and of course I should go to someone who knew far more about how this worked than I did. And I wasn't going to my dad because I had no evidence whatsoever on this Hilary girl, only a few clues that I was running string around to connect when it could be completely wrong. I didn't want to be completely wrong.

As I drove away, I caught a glimpse of Hilary in my rearview mirror. She stood with her hands on her hips and a scowl on her face. For me? Well, if I could prove that she'd killed Roderick so that her boyfriend could have what he wanted, she would be even unhappier looking at me in the witness stand as I testified to send her to jail for the rest of her life.

But that time wasn't right now. Right now, I left a message for Jeb to start a conversation about that key Eliot had found in the jukebox, and then we had a drive-in to stealthily sneak around and hope we wouldn't be the stars of our own last show there.

"I don't think I've been to a drive-in for years and years." Eliot had picked me up at my house, and we'd driven together. I'd filled him in on everything that I'd done today. I wouldn't have said he was exactly happy about my stalking, but he didn't yell at me for being careless or stupid, so that wasn't a bad thing as far as I was concerned.

And now we were at the drive-in with its huge expanse of flat grass dotted with car-sized rectangles of gravel. Each spot had a pole with a radio attached to it. I used to love coming here. My dad would park the car so we could all sit in the back with the hatch up and the radio hanging in the window to carry the sound for whatever double feature we were seeing. I usually fell asleep in the back and would miss the ending of the movie itself. Every time, I'd wake up the next day in my bed wondering how I'd gotten there. My mom would laugh and just say they had to carry me in because I was out like a light.

That was one of the best memories of my childhood, and I was so thankful to have it.

"Do we have a plan?" I asked him.

"I don't even know what we're here for, so I don't have a plan. Do you have a plan?"

"I thought you were the former cop. I just own a diner. I have no plan."

We stared at each other, and then something popped through the air and suddenly the enormous screen at the end of the field shone like a beacon in the night. The radios all crackled to life.

"I know what you're looking for, but I don't think you're going to like it when you find it," a voice said.

Where was he talking from? I figured there was some kind of control room somewhere that the owner would use to make announcements or if there was an emergency and everyone had to leave, but I had no idea where that was. At the concession stand?

I glanced back at the squat building behind us, but it was completely dark.

"Do you know where they might be talking from?" I asked Elliot quietly.

He shrugged. "Nope."

"Why did I bring you again?"

"For my muscles and brains, I'm sure."

I snorted.

"I told you to come by yourself!" The voice sounded like it was verging on rage, so I was quick to react.

"I'm sorry! I wanted to, but with so much going on around the area lately, I just didn't feel safe coming completely alone. I didn't want to miss out on hearing what you had to say, so I made a compromise. This is Eliot. He's a chef at the Poplarsville Inn. He's just here for me not to feel so exposed."

There was some grumbling, and I couldn't tell if it was an exchange between two people or just the guy talking to himself. Either way, I looked at Eliot, and he shrugged again. Not helpful.

"So, what are we doing here? Why did you need me to be onsite at this deserted place to talk to me? About what? And why flowers?" I looked at Eliot and mimicked opening the door. He shook his head at me, but I felt like a sitting duck here in the car with no idea where the person on the speaker was. I'd feel better if I could run if I had to. So I got out of the car, and Eliot was quick to follow, even though he was swearing the whole time.

"The flowers were because most ladies like flowers from what I'm told, and I figured you'd bring them in the house easier than if it was a flaming bag of dog poop."

"Uh. Yes, you are correct about that."

There was a brief laugh and then more low volume heated words. I really wanted to know if he was talking to someone or just himself, but since I didn't know where he was talking from, I had no idea where to start looking.

"What should we do?" I whispered to Eliot. "We have to find out who this is. I'm almost willing to bet it's Kenneth, but I don't have much to go on other than that he thought he had the most to gain even if he gained nothing."

"I'm leaning that way too, but we can't make assumptions. We have to know for sure—with no doubt, not even the reasonable kind." He put his hands in his pockets and rocked back on his heels.

"What are you doing?" I asked, wondering if I should be doing it too.

"I'm trying to see where all the buildings are without being conspicuous, but it's dark out here."

"We probably shouldn't use a flashlight." Although I would have loved to have one of those ultra-bright flashlights right about now.

"No, we probably shouldn't." He glanced around the field and so did I.

"Look, there are really only three buildings. The snack shack, the bathroom, and that shed-type thing in the far corner. They're all dark, but I'm guessing whoever this is they're not in the bathroom, or it would echo."

"I agree. And I think if they were in the snack shack that we'd see lights."

But that left us with looking into a shed and having to traverse the field between where we were and where it was, about three hundred feet away. "Go us for our superior deduction skills, but how the heck are we going to get there without issues?"

"I have a plan," he said.

"Finally!"

He chuckled low and slow, and it sent tingles all over my body. A highly inappropriate thing to have happen when we were in the middle of a possibly dangerous situation, but I just let it happen then moved on as quickly as I could.

"Does this plan involve us running full-out? Because I have to say I haven't run in a whole lot of years." That was not a lie. If you wanted me to lift things, I could be your girl. Running was not an option though.

"I'll do the running, but first, I need you to do the distracting."

"And how am I supposed to do that?"

"By trying to guess who this is out loud. Start shouting names or facts and theories and see if you can get them to trip themselves up. Or lie a lot and make them correct you. Can you lie a lot?"

Oh boy, could I ever.

"What are you doing?" Whoever it was on the loudspeakers sounded like he was not happy that we hadn't been interacting with him while we talked amongst ourselves.

"Just trying to figure out why you'd want us here. What's the purpose?" I yelled. "We're here, and yet you're not giving me anything to work with. I'm pretty sure I know who killed Roderick if you were just going to give me any hints."

Eliot gave me a thumbs-up as he started sidling away toward the shed to the right. I started walking to the left so that whoever this was would hopefully keep their eyes trained on me instead of realizing what Eliot was up to.

"It's pretty simple, actually," I said, beginning that lying with a bang. "Roderick had something someone wanted, and he wouldn't give it up without a fight. So, this person killed him to make sure they could have whatever they wanted so badly. I think it might have been a misstep since the thing they wanted wasn't his to give. But we each learn at different paces, don't we?"

There was a growl that came through the speakers that put my teeth on edge. Maybe I was going too hard too soon.

Eliot was still moving stealthily toward the shed when I looked over at him. He rolled his hands like I should keep going.

Blowing out a breath, I continued, "See, the one thing I've been able to find in all of this was that Roderick ruined a lot of lives."

"HA!" Loud and clear through the speaker. I tried to see if I could also hear where it was coming from but got nothing.

"And in ruining a lot of those lives, he never paid for it, never made restitution. Heck, there's a social media group for women to warn each other about any new schemes he came up with so they could all be safe."

"There is?"

Now he sounded truly puzzled, so that meant I could most likely rule out any of the women who had been on that list. I wasn't going to rule out their husbands, but the women, yes. Although I wasn't completely convinced that the person talking through the speaker was actually a guy. I was reserving judgment on that.

"Yes, I assure you there is. And they all talk about the things that Roderick has done to them, or what they lost because of him. Kind of like a therapy friendship kind of thing so they don't feel so alone." I paused and stuck my hands in my pockets. "I could give you the address and the right answers to the questions if you think that might help you."

"I don't need help," the voice said, lashing out. "I just need you to take the tumble on this. It's not even really a fall if you think about it, Jaxxy. Tell your dad you did it because he could get you out of it and then let it go."

I was so startled I could not stop the guffaw that came out. Another completely inappropriate thing, but I couldn't help myself. "Are you kidding me? You think if I go to my father and tell him that I killed Roderick that he'll just be able to sweep that under the rug, let it go, turn a blind eye?" I scoffed, even though I probably shouldn't have. "There is no way on the green Earth that my father would do that. Not to mention there's no proof that I actually did do it. And I'm not a very convincing liar." Not true, but I was working with what I had at the moment. "Besides, why would I have done it? What's my motive?"

"You have to!" There was desperation in the voice now, and something that made me think I wasn't hearing the actual voice, like it was being sent through some kind of synthesizer.

"I don't."

"You do!" Louder this time but it also sounded closer. That double tone I'd been listening for earlier to be able to tell where the person was, came through loud and clear this time. I whipped around to pinpoint the real noise instead of the broadcast one.

And I realized we had not counted all the buildings on the property. The entry booth where you paid the fee to park and got your assigned spot was behind me and to my left. I had no way of letting Eliot know. He'd finally made it to the shed and had disappeared behind the back of the small building, but he was totally in the wrong place.

Apparently, I was going to try to see if I could in fact run.

It wasn't exactly a mad dash, but it was fast enough since the person in the booth was crying and not paying attention to where I was standing or if I was still standing there.

I wasn't sure who I expected to find in the booth, but it certainly wasn't our cook, Terri's, daughter.

Since she was still crying, I took a few seconds to text Eliot and hoped that if his phone was on silent that he would at least have it on vibrate. What was I going to do now? I could call the police, my father in particular, but I didn't even know what to tell him.

"Colleen? What are you doing?" Part of me wanted to bend over her and bring her in for a hug because she was obviously upset. The other part of me reminded myself that she was upset because she wanted me to tell my father I had killed a man and hopefully not get put in jail for it, but I wasn't going to do it.

"Oh, Jax, I'm going to be in so much trouble."

CHAPTER TWENTY-THREE

I wasn't sure what to say to that since I couldn't make her feel better by assuring her that wasn't going to happen. Peeking my head up over the counter, I got a brief view of Eliot heading our way.

"What is going on?" I looked her over and willed her to stop crying so I could find out what exactly had brought us to this point, out here at a defunct drive-in. Terri was going to be devastated. She'd ring that bell like a hungry chihuahua if this got back to her. But how could it not?

"I don't know!" Colleen wailed. Her gray eyes were bloodshot, and her face was puffy and pale. Part of me wanted to smooth her red hair back, but I didn't want to touch her.

And that was when I saw that she was handcuffed to the leg of the desk. Her wrist was bright red where the thing was clamped incredibly tight, and her feet were bound with another of my blasted lanyards.

"Oh, Colleen. Oh, my word, hold on. What happened?" I yanked on the handcuff without thinking about how that would do absolutely nothing except hurt her, and she cried out again.

"Ow!"

"I'm sorry! I'm so sorry! I didn't mean to hurt you." I yanked my hands back, making sure not to touch her again until I could figure out what exactly I was supposed to do. What in the world was going on?

"Jax? Jax, where are you?" Eliot wasn't yelling, so he had to be close. I didn't want to pop my head out again because I wanted to concentrate on Colleen. He'd find me soon enough.

"We're in the booth."

"On my way."

"What happened, Colleen? How'd you get here? What are you even doing here?"

"I don't know. Someone came up behind me when I was

walking home, and they stuck some rag over my face, and when I woke up, I found myself here. He stood behind me outside the booth and wouldn't let me see him, but he told me I had to convince you to turn yourself in for Roderick's murder, or he was going to kill my fiancé." And then the real sobbing started, which was totally understandable.

Who was this horrendous person who kept pulling all these stunts to move the finger away from him and onto other people? I had a few choice words that I was very much looking forward to saying when I found him.

"Do you have any idea who it could have been? Did you recognize the voice at all?"

She shook her head and cried some more. Should I call her mom down here? Should I see if I could get any more info out of her, or should I just call it a wash and let the authorities sort it out?

This one was a no-brainer. As soon as Eliot came up to the booth, I explained what I thought had happened and then stepped away to call my dad. If anything, I hoped he at least had keys to unlock the handcuff, and then he could take a statement.

I would spend the night going over every piece of evidence we had found, and I would figure out who this jerk was once and for all. He'd gone too far with this stunt. It was one thing for him to be running around trying to scare me and pin something on me. Pulling Colleen, one of the sweetest people I knew, into the fray was one thing too many.

A slew of cop cars pulled up at the same time from a variety of directions. I gave my dad what I knew, or what I could tell him, and then I dragged Eliot off to his car.

"This is the final straw. Whoever did this is going to pay and pay a lot for all the issues they're causing, on top of the horrible fact that they killed a man in cold blood. I want him to suffer, Eliot. Like, a lot."

He turned the ignition on in his little SUV and patted my knee. "I know, Jax, but we need more intel. We have to be sure who this is before we do anything else, or we could get more people hurt."

I chewed on my bottom lip for a minute before I could come up with an answer that didn't sound like I was screaming into the sky. "I know it was Kenneth. It has to be. And he knows Colleen. They went to school together. If he was able to grab her and disguise his voice, like he made her disguise hers over the speaker, then he could be the one pulling all these strings, hoping it will all just go by the wayside since no one had really liked Roderick in the first place."

Leaving the drive-in, he made a left and then got on the main road. "I completely understand, and I get that you want this done. But we still have that key that we never talked to Jeb about, we have the locker with all the destroyed supplies, and we have the woman who tried to get into Roderick's post office box." He sighed. "We can't just go running in and cornering Kenneth without some solid evidence, and even then, we should leave it up to the cops. This is their job, not ours."

Resting my forehead against the window I tried to formulate a plan that wouldn't irritate Eliot, since he'd been such a big help, but still get me what I wanted. The sooner the better.

Nothing came to me for the whole drive home, and I spent all the time between petting Stella Luna at my door to having to head into work the next morning going over every piece of paper and nugget of info we had.

Kenneth could have gotten the lanyards from his girlfriend, Hilary. He had dropped his father off at the inn for the dinner with his first wife, so he knew exactly where Roderick was. He also knew Delilah and could have easily called her and told her where Roderick was simply to get him to leave. Per Hildy, this wasn't the first time Roderick had gone out back to avoid someone, and most likely he'd joked about it with his son at some point. Heck, they might even have had a contingency plan if Roderick couldn't get out. Kenneth would have wanted to stay in his father's good graces if he thought he was going to get that land, or that he could talk his old man into finally doing what he said he wanted to do against Hildy's wishes.

And maybe Roderick had dragged his feet for too long. From what Brady had said, the market was ripe right now, and Kenneth hadn't taken very long to slide right in with the land developer to get things moving before his father was even put in the ground.

So, it had to be Kenneth. Now I just had to get him to admit it. Maybe over some hash browns and scrambled eggs.

With that thought, I got dressed and made peace with the fact that today was going to be horribly horrible on my energy meter. I might have to use some of tomorrow's energy to get through today. Then again, if I could finally catch who had killed Roderick, my days would open back up, and I could take off my sleuthing cap.

I let myself into the diner an hour later and immediately started the coffee. I wished just for a second that we had an espresso machine for a double shot to get me through. But Dani had nixed that idea, wanting to stay with the standard diner fare of days gone by. I'd agreed with her, of course, but right now I wished I hadn't.

Hanging my things in my locker, I took a second to pull open the locker with all the messed-up stuff in it. Eliot's point that we still had so many unanswered questions and clues rankled. Nothing fell out this time, even though I'd been braced for it.

The whole thing was empty except for a note.

Hey there, I see someone opened this and stuff fell out. Sorry about that. I've been trying to get together some items to donate for an upcoming play at the Little Theater in town, and I didn't want to crowd my house, so I left them in here. I finally was able to deliver them, so the locker is clear. If this is Jax reading this, sorry again. I should have asked before taking over one of your lockers.

It was signed Terri, and she had drawn a little bell and a smiley face on the bottom under her name.

Well, that was one mystery solved. Now I had another with her daughter being kidnapped, and I didn't think she'd want to put a smiley face on that one. But I had been thinking about why Kenneth would pull in Colleen. It wasn't like he had had her use her own voice. In that case, I would have followed her just because I wanted to save her. It didn't make too much sense, but then again, I was only here for the truth, and murder rarely made sense.

Fortunately, today was Terri's day off. I didn't have to worry about trying to keep my cool around her if Colleen hadn't called her from the station, where she was answering questions about the kidnapping. I really hoped she had been able to help my dad after he'd driven away with her in the front seat. More than anything, I hoped there would be some more reasoning behind how and why this had all happened. Maybe then he could use that information once I cornered Kenneth and got him to confess.

I had a plan this time.

The morning went relatively as I had expected it to. I thought my dad would stop by with an update or something, but he didn't. I did text him to see if he'd come up with anything and then sent another to Eliot to see if he was coming in.

I'd sent Kenneth an email asking if he'd come in to discuss his property idea with me, saying that I'd like to consider investing in one of the restaurants they were planning on putting into this micro-neighborhood. I totally lied like a champ about all the things I could see for the menu, and that we had the money to invest in top notch everything. If he believed that, then I had other offers to run by him for false hope too.

At about eight, there was a cascade of murmurs in the diner when Kenneth came in the front door. I'd held a table for him since seven-thirty just in case. I hadn't wanted to turn him away when he did finally arrive. Plus, everyone seemed to be hovering at their tables, just in case something new happened in our sleepy town that seemed to have far more secrets and scandals than I would have ever thought.

At least everyone was eating here and leaving good tips.

I fast-walked my way to Kenneth as he shut the door behind him. He'd dressed in a suit and tie in a navy blue that set off his light brown hair and blue eyes. I recalled the way he'd been excited yesterday and happy to do something that was totally different from the legacy his father had set up in his lifetime. I wished I wasn't going to try to get him to admit that he'd killed his father to make that happen.

But I had to. There was no one else who had as much at stake or as much to gain from Roderick's death.

"Coffee?" I asked as I seated him and handed him a menu. I would be the one waiting on this table. I let the other waitstaff know this one was mine, just in case things went sideways when I started pressing him for answers. I had kept it vague, or at least as vague as possible when I told them I needed information from him that only I could get.

I had really thought hard about how I was going to handle this. I could have sent my dad the info and then had Kenneth brought in for questioning, but I really wanted to see if I could finish this out. I'd admit that I wished Eliot was also here to help, but since he hadn't shown up yet, I was willing to move forward with my plan without him. The diner was full, and there was no way he was going to hurt me in front of all these people.

"Heading somewhere after this? You look spiffy."

He smiled, and you could definitely see his dad in him but not with the smarmy part. He looked like he genuinely was excited to be here and ready to start this next phase of his life. But was he willing to strike down anyone who stood in his way to get what he wanted?

"Nope, I wanted to thank you for taking an interest in what I'm doing by making sure I showed you that I valued your offer to listen." He unbuttoned his jacket, and his appearance fell apart a little when the vest, which had laid down nicely under the jacket, sagged. It looked like something out of his father's closet, and my heart sank. I didn't want Kenneth to be the killer. He was trying so hard and looked so proud of himself, putting together pieces of the dirty legacy he'd been given and attempting to make the most out of it.

I gripped the coffee carafe harder to stop myself from reaching out to straighten his tie.

Eliot chose that moment to show up. I had never been so happy to see someone walk in the door, and I'd been very happy to see a lot of people swing it open. He moved down the aisle between tables to sit at the end of the lunch counter, positioning himself so Kenneth would have to walk past him if he decided to leave through the front or back door.

"I'll be right with you, Kenneth. Breakfast is on me, so just look over the menu and let me know what you'd like the kitchen to make you."

There was that smile again, and I left before I could say anything else or try to make excuses for him.

I took myself off to the avocado room. Pushing through the door, I closed it behind me then turned to lean my forehead against the wood. What was I going to do? I was certain it was Kenneth, but his excitement and his earnestness was killing me. Had it also killed his father?

"You just do not know when to quit, do you?" a man said behind me, and I froze.

CHAPTER TWENTY-FOUR

To say I was unable to move and completely unwilling to turn around would have been an understatement. The fact that whoever was behind me had shoved me up against the door, and stuck something that felt very much like a gun against my back, was also a factor in me staying exactly where I was.

"Nothing to say?" he asked, and I tried hard to place the voice. The tone and the cadence sounded a lot like Brady and him being the killer wouldn't be totally out of the blue, but I wouldn't have pinned it on him, no matter how much he had wanted the land.

"Since you have a gun or something that feels like a gun shoved into my back, I was keeping my mouth shut so you don't feel the need to use it."

"See? I knew you were smart, no matter how often you seem to try to prove you're not."

Now would not be a good time to scoff. I told myself that as I cleared my throat instead.

"So, here's how we're going to do this. You're going to let Kenneth have his big breakfast, and you're going to keep your mouth shut. You'll talk to him about whatever you cooked up to lie to him about, and then you'll go quietly to your father and tell him that you have no idea who killed Roderick. Burn all notes and forget anything ever happened. This was supposed to be easy. You've made it ridiculously difficult at every freaking turn. No more."

"I was only trying to get justice for someone who was killed in cold blood."

His grip tightened on my arm. "Sure thing, partner."

And his voice and tone and words snapped something in my brain. It was Tobias. The guy who was working nights at Hildy's restaurant, so he would have known Roderick was coming in for dinner. He was also best friends with Kenneth, so he could have weaseled his way into getting some of those lanyards from Hilary.

Not to mention he had also gone to school with Colleen and would have been able to find out where she was working when he took her. And he was Brady's son.

While that all might add up to how he could have done it, I still didn't understand the why.

"How can you expect me to tell my dad that I don't know anything?"

He scoffed and didn't bother to hide it with a cough. "You'll do it because if you don't, I will ruin you. I should have done that to Roderick instead of killing him, but time was tight, and I didn't think it all the way through. I could have just blackmailed him like he'd done to others over the years. When I delivered his specialty lobster that Hildy had ordered for him and his first wife who never showed up, I tried to talk to him about releasing the land. He shut me down and told me I was stupid to try to convince him of something no one had ever been able to get him to do."

"My dad's never going to believe that I didn't figure anything out. Especially after you kidnapped Colleen and tied her up out at the drive-in."

"Fine, then you can tell him you know it's Kenneth right after we get the land. Just keep pretending to look for clues and hold on until we get the deed."

I closed my eyes, waiting to hear the rest while also trying to come up with a plan to get myself out of this.

"I reminded Roderick that he had ruined my family by swindling my mother out of that very drive-in—the one she'd inherited and wanted so badly to bring back to life. How he'd torn my parents' marriage apart by charming my mother into giving everything up for someone who had no intention of doing right by her. He owed us. And it was a chance for me to show my dad that I'm all in."

"All in? How did soaping Delilah's car show you were all in?"

"The same way it helped to tell Dani to spook you at the diner window by yelling. And using the lanyards I stole from the print shop. Distraction—it gave me a laugh. And yes, he's trying to rebuild his business, and with Roderick out of the way, we can actually start making progress. That stupid Hildy won't have anyone to keep us out of her business anymore, and if she knows what's good for her, she'll hand over her restaurant. My dad has big plans for this area and needs this win. I'm going to give it to him with a huge ribbon on it."

There were so many issues with his reasoning. I opened my mouth to rebut and then closed it because there was nothing I could do or say to make this change in Tobias's mind.

"I'm very capable of being ruthless if I need to, and once I tell my dad what I did and how it made everything work for him, he'll give me a stake in what he's doing."

"Somehow I doubt that," I said. I'd been trying to come up with a way to get out of this, but with the gun in my back and my forehead pressed up against the door, I had no room to move.

Tobias whipped me around and slammed me back against the door. A split second later, he shot into the panel next to my head. I took the opportunity to slam my hands really hard against the wood, enough to shake the shoddy door frame that needed desperately to be replaced.

And as the door gave way, I brought up my knee hard. Really hard.

"Discounted milkshakes all around," I said an hour later. I couldn't make them free, but I could maybe save the day from seeming to be horrendous. The diner was full, as in way too full. If the fire department came in right now, we would probably be fined for exceeding our occupancy limits, but I didn't care.

Once Tobias and I had fallen on the floor, Eliot had moved into cop mode faster than I could process. He had Tobias off me and on his stomach with his arms twisted behind his back faster than I could blink the disintegrated molding out of my eyes.

My dad had arrived seconds later and congratulated Eliot on a job well done then nodded at me as he read Tobias his rights and hustled him out the front door. Knowing my dad, I was going to get yelled at for being reckless and then hugged super tight while he told me he was proud of me and never wanted to let me go. I'd take both when he was ready. If he'd hugged me now, we probably would have both been in tears, and that wouldn't have been a good look for a top-grade cop making an arrest.

And that left Kenneth sitting at his table in his blue suit, looking like his whole world had just crashed down around him. And he wasn't wrong. Eliot took him aside and explained about the land, how it wasn't available, and hadn't been Roderick's to give. It was promised to the county to repay debts he'd racked up over the years.

Fortunately, Hilary was able to come in shortly after the hubbub and take him out. I felt for him. I really did. Hopefully, he'd be able to make his dream come true in other ways.

And that left Brady, who must have heard what happened and had walked in two seconds after my dad had left with Tobias.

I pointed him back out the door as soon as he walked in and told him to leave. Just that one word. *Leave.*

And now we were having milkshakes because that was what I needed to make this crappy day better.

"Well, at least it's over," Dani said, pouring milk into the six metal tumblers as we started the assembly line.

"Yeah, my back is killing me though."

"Well, I guess we're going to have to get that door fixed now that it's been shot. And since you broke it, I don't think it's something we can claim with the insurance like the front window."

My stomach cramped. I hadn't even thought of that when I was doing everything I could not to get taken out by Tobias. "Well, crap."

"It's not that bad," Dani said. "I'm sure it'll just be a couple hundred dollars to at least get it fixed until we're ready to do the real thing and get it prepped to rent out."

Except I didn't have a couple hundred dollars…

"Yeah, about that."

"Jax, can I see you for a second?" Eliot stood at the end of the counter, not coming behind it but just on the other side.

"Better go see what the big man wants. Let me know if you need to leave early for a picnic or something." Dani laughed, and I groaned.

"I don't want to go into the avocado room just yet. Can we go in the back?" he asked.

"Sure thing." I did not add *partner* to that when I realized what I had said.

We passed through the door and stood near the lockers. Servers came in and out as I'd asked anyone who could come in to help to do so. We had a steady stream of people who wanted to chat about what had happened, how I had almost gotten killed, and various other issues, like land and men who had thought their wives were cheating. But actually, it was just that they were handing all their money over to Roderick for nothing, even though he'd promised them the world. Part of the dining area in the back was stuffed with men having an impromptu therapy-type session about not feeling so alone by not being the only one who got swindled.

And in the midst of all that, Eliot wanted to talk with me, but I didn't know about what.

"So, what's up?" I asked, knowing I was going to have to tell Dani about my money issues now that we had more repairs to do and nothing to do them with.

"This Smitty guy, was he an accountant at your bank?"

Well, that came out of nowhere. "Yes and no. It was more that he was a loan officer. He helped us finance all the beauty you see around you." I gestured to the lockers and the floors that might need new surfacing and the sinks that probably needed a plumber to make sure they didn't back up.

"You have a refund in process then. Turns out the bank had to seize his account because he'd been embezzling for years. But your account was the one that flagged them to his scheming, and they were able to track him and the money down. You should see a very big deposit sometime tomorrow. Just wanted to let you know before they did."

As if to prove his point, my phone pinged with a new email. I took it out of my pocket and read the message that pretty much stated the exact same thing and invited me to come in to discuss options for how I'd like to be compensated for my anguish.

I could feel my jaw drop, and my hands started shaking. I was having a hard time breathing. So maybe that was why I leaned into Eliot to have him help me catch my breath by sharing his.

That or I just really wanted to kiss him, which I did. For a few minutes until someone shoved the door open and smacked me in my rear end.

"I did not sell this place to you so you could ruin it, young lady. Now where's that key?" Jeb stood with his arms crossed and his feet planted. "I have been looking for it for years. I need to know what Granny Fellows hid and never wanted me to see. And with your apparent deductive skills, you're going to help me find out what it goes to."

The key. The woman who'd called herself Karen had alluded to the key being part of solving the mystery of Roderick's death, but it didn't seem to have anything to do with him from what Jeb was saying. So, what was its significance, and what else would it lead us to? Another mystery? I might just be up for it.

ABOUT THE AUTHOR

Misty Simon always wanted to be a storyteller…preferably behind a Muppet. Animal was number one on her list, followed closely by Sherlock Hemlock. Since that dream didn't come true, she began writing stories to share her world with readers, one laugh at a time.

Touching people's hearts and funny bones are two of her favorite things, and she hopes everyone at least snickers in the right places when reading her books. She lives with her husband in Central Pennsylvania where she is hard at work on her next novel or three. She loves to hear from readers so drop her a line at misty@mistysimon.com.

Check out Misty Simon's books, including the Sunny Side Up Mysteries, here:
www.gemmahallidaypublishing.com/misty-simon

Printed in Great Britain
by Amazon

47542567R00118